F
C

WARS AND WINTERS

BY

ALFRED COPPEL

DONALD I. FINE, INC.

NEW YORK

Still again, for Liz.

Stopping the diary
Was a stun to memory,
Was a blank starting

One no longer cicatriced
By such words, such actions
As bleakened waking.

I wanted them over,
Hurried to burial
And looked back on

Like the wars and winters
Missing behind the windows
Of an opaque childhood.

And the empty pages?
Should they ever be filled
Let it be with observed

Celestial recurrences
The day the flowers come,
And when the birds go.

—PHILIP LARKIN
Forget What Did

PROLOGUE

I awoke on my knees, bound to the bed and spattered with blood from the IV tubes I had pulled free. Two women stood by my bed, trying to force me down, and heparin-thinned blood pumped from the femoral incision onto the bedclothes and hospital gown.

"Mr. Lockwood, please, you are injuring yourself. Please, Mr. Lockwood—" I could hear them speaking to me, but I understood them imperfectly. The triazolam in my bloodstream was distorting my perceptions into nightmares.

One of the nurses gripped my flailing arms and thrust a hypodermic needle into the plastic catheter. I could see it happening as though to someone else. Another jolt of triazolam hit me like a hammer, and I fell back onto the bed with a sickening sense of disorientation. I was terrified.

I was certain I could feel Fräulein Clef's hands on my shoulders, fingers strong as iron. The air was biting cold, and I lay between the frozen river and the black, leafless trees of the wood. It was like being trapped in a mad spider's web. I was a child, a small shivering child. I could hear the sound of men running, shouting angrily.

The nightmare took familiar shape. Fräulein Clef dragged me through the snow toward the gaunt house. "She is never coming back," Fräulein said. "She is gone because he abandoned her."

Why am I always a child on this frozen ground? I wondered. I knew

1

that Fräulein disliked me. She had never said so, but her feelings were palpable, dislike evident in the cruel strength of her grip on my narrow shoulder, in her manner of speech. The language was German, always German. Yet the family would speak only English in America. Someone had told me that long ago. But Fräulein didn't like to speak English. It was an enemy tongue, she said. His language. "He says he will send for you both, child, but men always lie. Forget him. He broke his promise to her, he will break his promise to you—"

I ran somehow free, as I often did, searching. Here between the frozen river and the black willows was where I always searched for her, sometimes in the dark water, sometimes deep in the brambled lanes between the trees. I never found her. And as I ran, the nightmare deepened, and I remembered, as I always did, a last day, when the snow was deep and she carried me against her breast.

She loved to walk beside the river, and as long as she was there with me, I was safe and I loved it too. Usually one heard only the wind and the sound of ice breaking in the river.

But the day of the nightmare was very different.

I heard dogs barking in the distance and the sound of soldiers.

She listened. I could feel the pounding of her heart beneath her breasts. Then she began to run, struggling through the calf-deep snow toward the willows. The web consumed us, arched overhead. But the barking of the dogs and now the sound of voices drew near. She held me so tightly that I could not breathe, and I fought to be free.

"Be still, be very still." As she ran, the breath exploded in steamy puffs from her nose and mouth. Her long blond hair fell loose and brushed my face. I loved the way it smelled. I held on to her with all my strength. Thin child's arms around her neck.

The soldiers and the dogs were among the willows now. I could tell by the odd way the sounds they made echoed among the black trees. She stopped, breathless.

She tore my arms from around her neck. She put me down in the snow, in a clump of the black willows, a place surrounded by wet brambles.

"Listen to me, Liebchen. Hear me. You must stay right here until dark. You must not move. You must not make a sound. Fräulein will find you and bring you home."

Suddenly terrified, I protested.

She struck me across the face. I was stunned. She had never struck me. Never.

She caught me up in a passion of remorse and kissed my face and eyes. She was weeping. I had seen her in tears only once before, over a letter from him.

"Remember," she said. "Remember. Until dark. Fräulein will come."

There were Russian voices. I knew Russian voices. Every frightened German child did.

Then she was gone, running away from the dogs and the voices and away from me. I sat shivering in the snow, and my own tears froze on my cheeks.

I heard shouts and commands to stop. Then gunfire. I buried my face in the snow. Fräulein would never come. Not into the dark forest. Not for me.

But she did come. Just before dark.

I remembered that part of the nightmare still again while the drugs tumbled my thoughts in a hospital room forty years and six thousand miles from that frozen river and clump of black willows.

ONE

---

20 November
to
25 November
1991

1

An unwanted gift.

I<small>T WAS SEVEN WEEKS</small> after I left the hospital, and two days before I was scheduled to leave for Düsseldorf, that the parcel arrived. It came in the same mail as Dieter Langan's letter. I carried the mail into the workroom and opened the flashy *Die Zeit* envelope first, putting aside the parcel from New York.

Dieter Langan's letter was disappointing. His offer of work was still good, but he had changed his mind about taking on as U.S. correspondent, a heart case sight unseen. Instead he offered me world accreditation as a *Die Zeit* reporter on a small retainer (Dieter was never adventurous where money was concerned) and assurances that my material would always get a sympathetic reading.

He was apologetic. Dieter was a sensitive man. But he was also a cautious man. He wanted to see me face-to-face. Then, the letter suggested, we would see. He asked that I come to Düsseldorf as planned, adding that of course, *Die Zeit* was still good for expenses. A rather tentative job offer for someone who had been an editor in chief for eight years, even if it had been only a West Coast magazine. The doctors at the med center said I was as good as new, but Dieter clearly needed to be convinced.

Beyond the rain-streaked windows I could see a stretch of

beach, deserted now but soon to be overrun by tourists and day trippers once the season began. November and December were dark and wet in Carmel by the Sea; January usually brought a change in the weather, brisk ocean breezes and a world-famous golf tournament at nearby Pebble Beach.

But as of this moment there was only the dreary rain, the empty beach and the restless Pacific. Not blue but steely gray in this cold light. I sat down with a tepid cup of coffee and longed for a cigarette.

The Colonel had died three years ago in Mexico City, Janice a year later. I had inherited the Carmel cottage, *de jure,* at last, though I had used the place for years, *de facto,* whenever I needed a place to write.

The year 1991 had been as bad for me as it had been for the Soviet Union. (Political journalists tend to think of specific years in this way, as though there really were some connection between great events and the self-important people who write about them.)

Reeder, my wife of twenty-two years, left me in May. Over the past year and a half she had begun telling me, for my own good naturally, that I was probably some kind of anal retentive type, incapable of relaxing or letting myself go. By fall she had started using her own surname, which was Rutledge. All this should have told me something loudly and clearly, but didn't, and then in May she informed me that, with all the goodwill in the world, she was terminating our marriage "to find herself." To my credit I made no bitter jokes about not knowing she'd got lost. It would have merely proved her point. Our children, Elissa and Brian, were adults, or as near as made no difference. They had shares of the Lockwood inheritance and lives of their own. I couldn't use them as excuses to hold together a marriage that clearly had failed.

Then in June Stan Diskant, my boss and the publisher of the magazine I edited, *Pacific Currents,* told me that he was selling the magazine to an Australian publishing combine owned by a perennial America's Cup contender. Stan moved in those exalted financial circles. He had started *Pacific Currents* just to have something to do while Sparkman and Stephens built his new ninety-foot sloop. In a way it was surprising that he'd held on to the magazine as long as he had. He broke the news over drinks at the Bohemian Club. "I'm sorry about this, Brian," he said, "but he made me an offer I couldn't refuse."

I thought about horse heads in a bloody bed and accepted my severance pay with stoicism. There was Dieter Langan, I thought then. Dieter had been after me for years.

But the year kept sliding downhill. In September Reeder Rutledge, the new feminist who had shared my bed and home for two decades and change, informed me that she had found what she had been seeking. She was going to marry her psychiatrist, a man named Buchanan, a therapist of the peacock feather school of treatment. Reeder even invited me to the New Age marriage ceremony on the Marin headlands. I went, kissed the new bride and headed south to Carmel. I got as far as Palo Alto before I began to feel as though I had swallowed a flashlight. The CHP got me to the emergency room at Stanford Medical Center. I stayed a week in the cardiac unit, was subjected to various medical indignities and survived.

An accomplishment of sorts, but nothing to make November Mondays any brighter.

I put aside Dieter's letter and took up the parcel. I knew no one in New York who might be sending me packages, and I handled it carefully. After eight years as editor of a magazine of news, politics and opinion, one develops a certain caution.

My concern was not fantasy. A few years back I had written a series of articles exposing the rather widespread industrial espionage in Northern California's Silicon Valley. My first tip from an informant was about the French, who were buzzing around the manufacturing firms, especially the chipmakers. As it turned out, the most active spies were connected to the East German intelligence service. When the articles were published, Stan Diskant and I were the targets of blatant attempts at intimidation. In fact, it was about that time that Stan began to lose his enthusiasm for publishing. We got anonymous phone calls in the night, nasty letters threatening lawsuits, veiled physical threats. Stan hired bodyguards for us both for several months. The memory was still green.

So I unwrapped the parcel with some care. It came from a Brooklyn freight forwarder called Tetrac. I smiled at my own caution, thinking it would be a dramatic end to my winter of discontent to be blown up by some angry Stasi's mail bomb. What I found in the parcel was something very different and in its way as explosive.

Between the wrappings and the hardwood box was a sealed envelope. On the envelope was written my name, Brian Lockwood. The Colonel had named me after himself when he adopted me.

The handwriting was strong, angular, angry.

I opened the box first. Inside, protected by a sash of blue silk edged in silver, lay a ceremonial Nazi dagger.

The sheath was of silver-trimmed blue enamel decorated with the eagle and swastika insignia of the Third Reich. The dagger's hilt was of ivory wrapped with silver wire, and the guard was shaped like the wings of a raptor. An eagle, of course. The Nazis were fascinated by eagles. The pommel repeated the eagle motif: a golden eagle's head, beak open and holding a cabochon sapphire.

What I had before me was *ein Adler Dolch*, an Eagle Dagger, one of a very few that had been awarded to men who had served the Third Reich above and beyond the ordinary call of soldier's duty.

And I had seen this one before. Many years ago.

The Colonel and his brother, Dean, had never gotten on well. Dean had managed to avoid military service during the war, while Brian, the elder, was a professional soldier who had commanded a company at Omaha Beach and a battalion by the time of the Nazi surrender.

After the war Dean had spent most of his time in Europe. I think at the Colonel's expense, though I have no hard evidence of it. Dean was a man who operated very close to the line of the law, and sometimes he crossed it. From time to time he would appear at the San Francisco house and there would be closed-door meetings between the brothers, along with raised, angry voices.

The fact was that when Dean was last in his brother's house, he had left carrying a number of valuable articles, one of which had been this very Eagle Dagger.

I had that information from Claire, who must have had it from the Colonel himself. I hadn't seen the dagger for years before Uncle Dean departed so precipitously.

Caught up in memory, I lifted the weapon from the box. I drew the blade from the scabbard. It was polished steel engraved with a pattern of vines, leaves and flowers—an almost Dionysian display, the engraved markings filled with fine gold. And there was that name I remembered: *Sieg Stossen.*

I felt a chill. I once had taken this very dagger from the Colonel's collection of war souvenirs. I don't know what could have possessed me to do such a thing. It was the only time I ever remember the Colonel raising his voice to me. I could not have been more than ten or eleven, and he had frightened me so badly I had dropped the dagger so that it clattered on the tiled floor of the foyer of the San Francisco house.

He retrieved it and apologized to me with a strange contrition that frightened me even more. Then he put the dagger away, and I never saw it again. Until now.

I held the envelope as though it were hot to the touch. I am not a man who loves mysteries. My own shadowy provenance had always been more than enough mystery for me. I looked at the superscription on the envelope. The handwriting had to be Dean Lockwood's. Uncle Dean was the sort of man who sold things—all things. Maybe he wanted money. What little I had heard of him over these last years was that he was making a living of sorts as a dealer in "objects of art." Perhaps he was returning the dagger and expected some recompense.

I opened the envelope with a plastic letter opener and withdrew a single sheet of heavy notepaper. On it were four sentences: "This was always for you, little Kraut Adolf. Go see Clef. She will tell you. Follow the name and learn about Brian Lockwood."

I felt that chill again. Yes, it had to be from Dean. It had his nastiness, his malicious turn of phrase. And which Brian Lockwood did he mean, his older brother or me? In any case, there was malice enough for us both. He had hated me from the moment I stepped off the train at the Oakland terminal, and my appearance simply added to the long list of grievances for which he blamed his brother.

And "Follow the name." Stossen. Who was Sieg Stossen, and what could he have to do with either the Colonel or me? There were many possibilities, none of which was pleasant, none of which I could ignore. Dean Lockwood would know that, of course. My obsession with the woman in my dream had surfaced almost immediately, so the whole family knew about it. Janice had brought it up often enough as an example of my possible mental instability, another reason I should never have been adopted, until the Colonel had warned her off. Fortunately at that time my understanding of English still left much to be desired.

And lastly, there was the reference to Fräulein Clef, the woman who had taken care of me when I was a child in Nuremberg. She had been a cold woman, who showed me little affection. I remembered her sharp slaps, the pinches, the ear pulls, the welts from the willow switch she used on my bare legs. They were all constant reminders that I was a bad child without possibility of redemption. Why else would my beautiful, loving lady have disappeared from my life?

But how in hell could Dean Lockwood have known that I was planning a trip to Germany within days? The back of my neck prickled, just as it had during the time I was researching and writing about the technological espionage by the East German secret police, the Stasi. When I was being followed off and on, and my office files and my house had been searched by an unknown intruder.

But the thought of Dean Lockwood somehow involved with the Stasi seemed ludicrous. I pictured Dean as I remembered him over all those years, an extreme Anglophile. An ascot around his neck, an old necktie worn like a belt (the Colonel used to rag him about thinking he was Fred Astaire), his mustache waxed at the tips as if he had been in the RAF. And his face twisted in an expression of contempt when he saw me peering at him from behind the door.

I rubbed my thumb across the gold-filled letters. Stossen. What are you to me, Sieg Stossen? *Who* are you to me? All the fears I'd suppressed over the years came flooding back. How I had envied my American friends their certitude in this world, their assured places in the natural order of things. On the few occasions I nerved myself to ask the Colonel why he had adopted me, the words froze on my tongue when I was with him face-to-face.

Dean Lockwood had known exactly the right question to raise. The right button to push. I hated him for it, but now I had to face my past.

2

There is anger that even the grave can't contain.

HOLDING THE DAGGER, I sat down on the old workroom couch to consider. I don't much believe in coincidence, though, of course, coincidences do happen, even if rarely. But only last week I had received a call from Stein Davis, the Lockwood family attorney. Stein told me that he had, according to the terms of the Colonel's will, reclaimed from storage a crate of personal documents and letters intended for me and that it was on its way to Carmel.

I wasn't yet willing to dig through so much ancient history. I knew it had to be done; I owed it to the Colonel. But I guessed that there would be papers and letters dating back to the Colonel's stay in Nuremberg when his battalion was part of the guard force for the War Crimes Tribunals, and I had always hated having anything to do with that time, which I barely remembered except in nightmares.

What I had done was call my sister, Claire, and tell her that I would be on the way to Germany when the Colonel's things arrived, and would she come down to the Carmel cottage to receive them? It was one hell of an imposition, but Claire was the only person on earth I could ask to do such a thing. Anything to do with her father was a labor of love for Claire.

There is no one perfect this side of paradise, but if someone were, it would be my adoptive sister, Claire Lockwood Warner —she who gave me a welcome and a life among the Lockwoods when I arrived from Germany, foreign, skinny, bare-kneed and frightened.

The Colonel had been unable to get leave for the occasion, and Dean Lockwood had either elected himself to take charge or been delegated the task by the Colonel's lady, whose name, I was told before leaving Nuremberg, was Janice *Clayton* Lockwood.

I remember as if it were yesterday. I stepped down from the train at the Oakland terminal, dressed in short pants, a thin coat with a paper tag pinned to it, my lank hair blowing in the westerly off the bay. And Dean said: "Christ, he's adopted a little blond Adolf. What next, a pickaninny?"

I understood enough English to know what he meant. I looked up at him. He loomed over me, tall and forbidding. His dark hair was slicked back on a high, pale forehead, heavy dark brows drawn together in a frown over cold gray eyes. His waxed mustache was the one frivolous aspect of his appearance. I'd never seen one quite like it before, and my eyes were drawn irresistibly to the carefully curled tips flanking his sizable nose as they trembled gently in the wind. I had lost my memories, if I had ever had them, of the Colonel. I was among strangers and wished I were dead.

Then Claire, who was barely thirteen, said solemnly, "Please don't talk like that to my new brother, Uncle Dean. I want him to be happy here."

Later she took a dressing down from her mother for speaking disrespectfully to her uncle. But in that one moment Claire won my devotion for life. Whenever she was around, the fact that the Colonel's lady and his brother despised me on sight became bearable.

It didn't take me long to understand that Janice Lockwood was a troubled woman—what used to be called high-strung. She was consumed with a pathological jealousy of anything or anyone connected with Colonel Brian Lockwood. I qualified immediately, and so did her own daughter, Claire. So did the United States Army, an organization for which she reserved an angry dislike. She was from Connecticut banking stock (she herself put it just that way), and she had apparently imagined that once they were married Brian Lockwood would resign his commission and join the Clayton bank. It never happened, of course. The Colonel was a professional soldier, and he loved the Army with a passion I doubt he ever felt for Janice.

I learned quickly that Janice was a fragile woman. There were absences. Claire and I knew that Janice was gone somewhere for a mysterious "rest." We tried to understand and, trying to comfort each other, became even closer.

Claire and I lived for the times the Colonel would be home on leave. Those were our holidays, riding the trails of the Presidio, walking the northern beaches, sailing the Colonel's six-meter on the bay.

It was during this period I met Sergeant Major Allan Cobb, who had served for fifteen years with the Colonel. When Allan retired, he came to live in San Francisco and became, in effect, our surrogate father. I didn't realize it then, but the Colonel had arranged it.

Claire once said to me, "Janice took the Second World War as a personal affront. She thought that's what kept Father from being president of some Clayton bank." Claire always called the Colonel "Father" but her mother was never anything but "Janice." After Janice died, Claire said, "Maybe she's found some peace, Bri. She had very little when she was alive. She always found a way to make her own life hell."

Janice had always wanted to bear another child. Not because she liked children but because she was convinced the Colonel wanted a son. She had the mistaken notion that Brian Lockwood blamed her. I don't think he did. He treated her with respect and consideration always, even long after he stopped loving her. The Colonel was a great one for fulfilling his obligations, no matter how ill considered. He was that sort of man.

Claire had an old photograph taken when Brian Lockwood was a newly commissioned second lieutenant. He sat astride a hunter in the foregrounds of the old Clayton manor house in Connecticut, with young Janice by his side, sidesaddle on a beautiful thoroughbred. She looked elegant and quite beautiful in her element. She had reached across to put a hand possessively on Brian Lockwood's arm. The photograph spoke volumes about possessive love. Poor Janice. To attempt to possess a man like Brian Lockwood must have been a daunting task. I think her failure broke her. I occasionally wondered if there had ever been anything between Janice and Dean. It would have been in character for Dean to attempt to seduce his brother Brian's wife. But I don't think Janice would ever have done anything so crass and untidy.

Colonel Lockwood was an eighteenth-century man. Honor was a very real concept to him. It must have made tolerating a man like his brother Dean, very difficult. I was at Menlo School when Dean disappeared for the last time. Before the "art dealer" stories surfaced, there were other whispers. Stein Davis, the family lawyer, disliked Dean with an unlawyerly passion. He was of the opinion that Dean stole not out of need but out of sheer bloody-mindedness. The comment arose when the Colonel began paying his brother a stipend. It was the first time I had heard the expression "remittance man."

The Colonel was still paying when he was killed by a hit-and-run driver in Mexico City, where he had gone to ease the restlessness that consumed him after he retired from the Army.

Sergeant Major Cobb and I went to Mexico City to claim his body for burial in Golden Gate National Cemetery. We were angry at the carelessness of the investigation surrounding the death. We even hired a private detective to do what the Mexico City police could not: find the driver responsible. But it was useless. The Mexican capital is a municipal basket case, its officials consumed with more immediate problems than finding out the circumstances surrounding the death of a gringo.

The Colonel was killed in 1987. I was still married to Reeder then and developing my own set of marital problems. We had met years before at Stanford, where we both were studying mass communications—the craft that used to be known as journalism.

Reeder Rutledge was the only daughter of a *Time* magazine senior editor. When we met at Zot's, she had just been through a hard fall. She had been—as the saying went—dumped on by one of the flashier men on campus and was ready to be comforted. I did my best.

I was tremendously impressed by Reeder, who was raven-

haired, athletic and sexual, and, I felt, vulnerable and undemanding. She never once asked me about my ancestry or my
past, and I never alluded to it. We married before graduation. It
was the one thing I had ever done that seemed to have Janice
Lockwood's approval.

But the truth was that Reeder was neither vulnerable nor
undemanding. She had a role model for me. It was her father,
and it very soon became apparent that my advancement was not
nearly swift enough to please.

Reeder, to her credit, was a good mother. Or at least, and
measured against the standards of the baby boomer generation,
she did nothing to derail seriously the development of our two
children. Brian and Elissa were good young people, but sadly
for me, I didn't know them well. When they expressed their
concern about my heart attack, I didn't really know how to
respond to them. I had expected them to take their mother's part
in our marital breakup.

They'd had the good sense to be mildly embarrassed by
Reeder's flower child ceremony on the Marin headlands, aware,
as I was, that the New Age fete was legally meaningless since
Reeder's and my divorce had not been final.

Through it all, I had been slowly approaching a point in my
life that would permit me to look ahead to whatever remained,
rather than to dwell on the past.

And here was the *Adler Dolch* and its singular, chilling, mysterious message to "little Kraut Adolf": "Follow the name and
learn about Brian Lockwood."

Why had Dean sent me the dagger, now, after all these years?
All questions seemed to devolve into that one. Was it, as Stein
Davis suggested, sheer bloody-mindedness? A shot at his dead
brother? "Learn about Brian Lockwood," he'd said. Could it be
that the Colonel's Army career had been destroyed because of
some connection with the recipient of Hermann Goering's blessing? Dean had known that I worshiped the Colonel. Any
shadow he could throw on his brother's memory would surely
please him, knowing full well that it would devastate me. Was

Dean still that spiteful? There are animosities that outlast lifetimes; there is anger that even the grave cannot contain.

And was it Dean's work alone? If the Colonel had enemies his
death would not silence, could Dean have made an alliance with
them? But if so, why wait until now? Surely they would have
been better served by exposing the Colonel while he was still
alive. Soon there would be no one left alive to know or to care
what had happened in that long-ago time and place.

I knew very little about my adoptive father's life before I
arrived on the scene. But of one thing I was certain: My father
neither had done nor would have done anything dishonorable.
So that brought it all back to me.

I went into the living room to pour myself a pony of Chivas.
Hard liquor was on the proscribed list for convalescing heart
patients, but the arrival of the dagger made me into a risk taker.

I called Claire's house in Woodside and got her answering
machine. She was a woman with much to keep her busy. I left
my name and told her that I would see her before I left for
Germany and that I had a favor to ask.

Then I dialed Ben Macdonald's office. Ben was Claire's friend
—in the parlance of the day, her "significant other"—the bald-
ing, golfing architect who had designed Claire and Daniel
Warner's house and who now waited with less than philosophi-
cal calm for Claire to put aside her widowhood and marry
again. It was likely to happen one day. Claire was too good a
woman to stay single indefinitely, and significant otherhood
was not really her style. But she was in no rush. She had Janice
Lockwood's aristocratic good looks, but somehow softer and
warmer. Perhaps it was because she had the Colonel's coloring.
Auburn hair and brown eyes, quite unlike the Clayton black and
blue. She had her mother's self-assurance mingled with a wry
sense of humor inherited from somewhere under the bark of the
Lockwood family tree.

Ben Macdonald was a man given to vast enthusiasms. When
he joined the Sierra Club, he acquired the habit (chronic among
Sierra Clubbers and infuriating to the mountain people who
actually live in the Sierra Nevada) of erecting cairns along every
trail he hiked. The local people disliked city folk playing at
pathfinder, and they devoted much of every day, while Ben and

his friends were striding about the wilderness areas in their Eddie Bauer ensembles, to following them and kicking over the offending trail blazes. Ben, chronically afflicted with good nature, never noticed.

Ben's present enthusiasm was Claire. She was fifty-five, and Ben was impatient for her to accept his offer of marriage. "Which would," Claire said wryly, "let him get on with the business of reordering my life."

But Ben had a lot to learn about Claire. It might have enlightened him to have been present the day I arrived from Germany.

Ben Macdonald was just leaving for a late lunch with a client when I called. "Is there something wrong, Brian? You sound terrible."

To Ben, anyone without a positive lilt in his voice sounded terrible, but he was not a man with whom one discussed mysteries. I said, "I am going to ask Claire to stay down here for a few days while I'm in Germany. Can you join her?"

"Love to," he said with enthusiasm. "If she has no objection. Sometimes she prefers the beach in solitude."

I was uneasy about asking Claire to stay at the cottage alone, and I am a man who follows his instincts. "I'll talk to her," I said.

"Wonderful. When are you leaving?"

"Day after tomorrow. Wednesday." I had intended taking the Tuesday Lufthansa from San Francisco but suddenly decided to put off my departure for a day and my departure for Germany for a bit longer than that. My investigative reporter persona was beginning to function.

"You all right to travel, Brian?"

"I'm mended. Stop worrying. I just need a conference with Claire before I leave for Germany. Family stuff. If you see her, tell her I will drive up to Woodside tomorrow."

"You sure?"

"Yes."

"Well, be careful. Don't overdo, hear me?" Ben, prince of overdoers, said good-bye and hung up.

I called Lufthansa and postponed my flight until later in the week, departing from New York. Then I dialed General Bolton in Colorado Springs. Jack Bolton was a retired blue suiter friend of the Colonel's who had good connections with the records people at the Air Force Academy.

Bolton said he would open doors there if I needed help. I accepted an invitation for dinner at the academy officers' club and hung up.

I didn't get much information from Tetrac, the freight forwarders who had sent the dagger. By the time I was off the phone, I knew only that the box and the order had come from Germany, payment by cashier's check from the Bank of Bonn. The sender was listed as Hans Schmidt. That's like John Doe in English, the next thing to anonymous.

I sat for a time staring out at the gray Pacific. The ocean in late November has majesty along the California coast. Dwarfed by the sea beyond him, a red-faced jogger lurched by on the beach. Past the breakers I could see otters diving and feeding in the offshore kelp.

It was tempting to stay where I was and do nothing, to balk Dean Lockwood by inaction. But I couldn't do that. The fact was that the Colonel had taken me out of chaos and, worse, given me a good life. Now I was nearly driven to know why, to know more about the waif that had been myself.

The dagger and the name Sieg Stossen stirred up deep questions. The dagger was such a peculiarly *Nazi* artifact. I had lived too many years with people who knew my background looking at me askance when the Third Reich was mentioned. I had the feeling that the dagger was pointing me in the direction of forced self-knowledge. Perhaps it was past time for me to lay the ghosts that had haunted me since I was a child.

It was nearly two in the morning in Düsseldorf now. If I waited an hour or two, I might catch Dieter Langan in the office at this time. Dieter had strange working hours.

I thought about Allan Cobb, who had been with the Colonel in Nuremberg. I didn't see him as often as I should. He lived in Hollister—not too many miles from where I was now. The sergeant major must know many things. I began to feel like a journalist again, starting to research a story. And the *Adler Dolch*, barbaric and enigmatic, lay on the table in my workroom, urging me on.

3

A man on the berm.

AS I WAS GROWING UP, Sergeant Major Cobb was an important part of my life. He willingly substituted for the Colonel more times than I want to remember. I understood that my adoptive father was a soldier and that he had to be away from his family for long stretches of time. There were times when Claire and I visited him—at places like Fort Ord, Fort Sill, even once at Schofield Barracks in Hawaii. Janice never accompanied us on those trips, but Allan Cobb did.

While I was at Menlo and Claire was still at Dominican, Allan was stationed at the San Francisco Presidio. He used to buy season tickets to the pro football games, and on autumn Sundays we would go to Kezar Stadium to watch the 49ers. This was long before anyone took the team seriously, but we did: Claire, the sergeant major and I.

I remember foggy afternoons at the old stadium, Claire and I wrapped in Allan's cold-weather gear, shivering and agonizing as Frankie Albert and Y. A. Tittle were sacked and sacked again by Paul Brown's white-clad villains from Cleveland.

I understood even then that our Sunday outings were financed by the Colonel. Well, so be it. Allan Cobb was my surrogate father.

* * *

I picked up the telephone and dialed his Hollister number. He seemed pleased when I asked him to meet me for dinner in Monterey.

"There are things to talk about, Sergeant Major," I said. I usually called him that because he liked it. He had retired from the Army almost eighteen years ago, but he still identified himself as a soldier, and his memories meant a great deal to him.

"I want to talk about the Colonel in Nuremberg," I said.

I had never asked Allan why the Colonel left me in Fräulein Clef's care for so long before sending for me. The answer, it seemed to me, was Janice. Brian Lockwood had been one of the youngest full colonels in the Army when he was ordered home from Germany. Fräulein Clef, the housekeeper, told me that he had not wanted an adopted war orphan underfoot until he was ready. I remembered that all right. And when I arrived in California at last and met my adoptive mother-to-be, what Fräulein Clef meant became very clear. All Allan ever said to me about it was that "the Colonel's an honorable man, Brian. When he wants you to know more, he will tell you." But before that could happen, he died crossing El Paseo de la Reforma.

My troubles with Reeder began to multiply swiftly. Then came the loss of a job I enjoyed and in which I had become comfortable. Maybe too comfortable.

Suddenly now I wanted questions *answered*. My life needed reordering, and the place to begin was with my days in Nuremberg. It was time to distinguish nightmare from memory. The arrival of the Nazi dagger stirred deep, unsettling emotions—as Dean Lockwood must have known that it would.

"We need to talk, Allan," I said.

"All right." He paused. "Are you okay now?" He sounded upset at not having been kept up to speed on my medical condition. But I hated talking about it. Yet if Allan was my surrogate father, I was his surrogate son. I owed him a great deal. He was entitled to my consideration. He had earned it.

"I'm fine," I said. "It was more of a skirmish than an attack. There was a blocked artery, and they opened it with a catheter and a balloon." Actually I had watched the procedure on the fluoroscope screen with queasy interest. "Where do you want to meet?" I asked.

"Casa Munras." Allan had done his basic training at Fort Ord a long time ago. He loved the Monterey Peninsula, and he had returned to a town as close to it as he could afford on a sergeant major's retirement pay. Casa Munras in Monterey had been a soldiers' favorite for years.

There was talk of closing Fort Ord. It was, the politicians said, made superfluous by the collapse of the Communists in Eastern Europe and by the explosive events in the Soviet Union. The Seventh Light Infantry Division, in which Allan had served for some of his last year, was to be posted to Fort Lewis, Washington. Half the locals were moodily considering a county without its military payroll; the rest were regarding Ord's seaside acres covetously. It really appeared then that Operation Desert Storm might be the last large-scale military engagement of our time.

Allan Cobb had enlisted in the Army in 1939 at the age of nineteen. He served with Colonel Lockwood from 1943 until the Colonel retired. Now Brian Lockwood was dead, lying in a national cemetery on a foggy, windswept hill.

"Casa Munras it is," I said. "Shall I pick you up?" Hollister is not far from Monterey, but there was no convenient public transport. Even Greyhound was trying to cancel its service between Hollister and Monterey now that Ord was slated to close.

"You're the walking wounded, not me," he said. "I'll meet you in the bar there at eighteen hundred."

I put on an anorak and stepped outside into the overgrown garden of ivy, oak and windblown cypress. The street abutted on a berm that separated the dead end from the beach. The rain had almost stopped. It came down in what we Californians insist is only mist. I climbed up and down onto the gray sand. I slogged down to the water's edge, where the footing was hard and wet-packed. Strands of kelp littered the beach from the recent storms. The air smelled of salt and decomposing kelp bulbs. On the rock promontories at the far curve of the beach, sea lions barked, oblivious of the exploding surf. To the north lay the great coastal scoop of Monterey Bay, to the south Monastery Beach. The kelp forests just offshore were populated by otters, seals and wheeling gulls. There would be no sun today until late afternoon, when the sky between clouds and horizon might open and turn a glowing rose for a few moments before dark.

A half mile offshore and fifty feet down was the edge of the Monterey Trench, a place where the smooth, pale sand of the coastal shelf suddenly plunged into the abyss. I learned to use SCUBA over that white shelf. From who else? Allan.

I shoved my fists into my pockets and walked along the almost deserted strand. From another beach house came the faint sound of country and western music. I thought about how Allan Cobb had always fancied Willie Nelson's songs about the heartache of the Wild West. His favorite began: *"Mammas, don't let your babies grow up to be cowboys—"* Only, with the sergeant major and his buddies, it usually got changed around to *"Mammas, don't let your babies grow up to be soldiers/ They'll never stay home and they're always alone/ Even with someone they love."*

Allan appreciated that, and, in a kind of soldier-by-proxy way, so did I.

My thoughts returned to Reeder. I had been giving her much thought of late. I had loved her once. But like the cowboy-soldier in the ballad, I was always alone, even with someone I loved. It was later, in the increasingly empty and discontented years, that I began to understand what an incomplete man I really was. Some people can exist comfortably without a childhood. I could not. Reeder thought she deserved better. And she did, even though we were far apart in our ideas of what that "better" might be.

When we were first married, it had seemed to me that what Reeder wanted was a life that allowed her to do what she pleased when she chose to do it. Her idea of a day well spent then was a morning at Elizabeth Arden, lunch at the latest hot restaurant with a few select friends and an afternoon shopping on the third floor at I. Magnin.

Reeder had never shown any interest in my work, even though it was through her father's connections that I got a job right after graduation with the *Chronicle* as a reporter—actually as a gofer. Then I went on to editorial work at a local radio station. I got a few free-lance articles about local techies working in their garages accepted in a national magazine at just the right time. The new industries in electronics and computers were aborning just south of San Francisco, soon to be dubbed Silicon Valley. That led me to an editorial position at a computer magazine.

Of course, I'd never talked to Reeder about what it was that I wanted to do: set the world on fire as a great political reporter and columnist of my time. I went about "committing experience" over the years, as one of my Stanford professors advised all of us who wanted to write, and when Stan Diskant started to publish *Pacific Currents*, I thought I'd finally found my niche in life. And I thought Reeder was happy with her friends and family and the work she did for all the community organizations she headed.

But apparently I had misjudged her. How else explain her decision to "grow" (her expression) with a soft, whispering man with a handshake like warm milk and a practice made up of women in thousand-dollar gingham dresses and men described as "upwardly mobile"?

I had failed to be like her father, I thought; ergo, our marriage collapsed. But clearly it was not that simple. It had begun to occur to me that not all the failings in our marriage had been hers. And as far as I could tell, Reeder was now quite happy. It made me wonder how well I had fulfilled my responsibilities as a husband.

I turned and started back along the empty beach to the cottage. The mist felt slick on my face and tasted salty on my lips. Far out to sea, almost lost in the mist, a heavily loaded container ship sailed south. Bound where? I wondered. I always had a deep urge to wander. It created a conflict. Ever since my arrival in California all those years ago, I had the unsettling feeling that if I should happen to stray, I might return and find myself unrecognized and unremembered.

I wondered if I had inherited that from my nameless parents, a man and woman I had always imagined dead in the rubble of a lost war.

I looked away from the sea and far up the beach to the berm protecting my street. There was a man standing on the berm among the cypress trees. He was watching me through field-glasses. I thought at first it might be Dr. Ershad, a Dravidian neighbor given to scoping everyone from ambush. But the stranger was too tall. I began to jog in his direction.

Not fast enough. When I reached the cypress grove where the man had stood, there was no one there. I scuffed about in the ice plant. A crumpled empty pack of Gauloise cigarettes had been discarded there. Carmel was too politically correct to have many smokers left in residence, and even fewer would smoke anything as harsh and unfiltered as Gauloise. Allan used to call the fat, short cigarettes the French equivalent of mustard gas.

I stood for a long while in the place where the large man had been. It was a chilling reminder of the time when Stan Diskant and I had had to be protected by hired musclemen, when the East German intelligence service had threatened us because of the exposés we'd been publishing in *Pacific Currents.*

I made a point of getting to Casa Munras early. I don't like tardiness. I often wonder if this is because of my Teutonic genesis or simply my upbringing in a military family. I didn't want to keep Allan Cobb waiting for me after I had kept him waiting weeks for a phone call.

I had only just sat down at the bar when the sergeant major walked in, fifteen minutes early. I stood up and greeted him. He was seventy-one years old, still straight as a bayonet. Military metaphors came naturally when one described Allan Cobb. He was lean and muscular with skin sun-browned to the color of a Sam Browne belt. In his mid-forties he had been good enough at martial arts to teach me what I needed to know to earn a brown belt in tae kwon do. That was back in 1967, while I was at Ord, expecting that each day I would be on the next Starlifter for Da Nang. And later, when I was convalescing from the meningitis that took me off the shipping list, he came every day to exercise me and convince me that I would make it all the way back.

"It's good to see you, boy." He gripped my biceps, his not-so-subtle way of checking my muscle tone.

Allan's hair was white and cut as short as the nap on a piece of felt. He patronized an ex-soldier's barbershop, where he said you could still get a basic-training cut for a dollar.

Cobb wore a made-in-Hong-Kong suit that closely resembled one the Colonel once owned. The sergeant major had used the Colonel as a role model for most of his professional life. Class wasn't a factor in the sergeant major's value system, but rank and loyalty were. He would have given his life for Brian Lockwood. And on the Omaha Beach at Normandy he almost had.

We went to the table I had reserved. The sergeant major ordered a Guinness—a taste he had developed among the Rhine Army Brits who served with him in occupied Germany. He had a professional soldier's measured opinion about the Germans. Until the Colonel's battalion overran Sachsenhausen concentration camp. From that time on Allan Cobb's war became personal. It wasn't until many years later that the Colonel told me that the sergeant major had been raised by Jewish foster parents. Their Judaism hadn't taken, but their sense of family had. What the sergeant major saw at Sachsenhausen made him an enemy of the Germans for the rest of his life. Yet he never took it out on me. Years after the war, when I was a grown man, he said to me, "You were only a child, Brian. It was never your fault."

I remember wishing that certain core members of the Lockwood family could have been as tolerant.

My health was the first subject of conversation, and Allan got right to it.

"How bad an attack was it, Brian?"

"I told you. Just a skirmish. I was lucky. There were some dicey moments when they couldn't stop me leaking out of the hole they made for the catheter. And I found out I am not at my best when I've taken triazolam."

"What in hell is triazolam?"

"It's what the medics call a minor tranquilizer. But there are people who hallucinate when they take the stuff. I discovered I'm one of them. I guess I gave the nursing staff a hard time. Or so they tell me. But the rest of it was routine. They cleared an artery, and I'm fit for duty."

"Claire scared hell out of me," Allan said.

"I'm sorry. She shouldn't have done that."

"When would you have gotten around to telling me?"

"Now."

"Shit. I could have been useful," he said.

"You can be useful now." I told him that the Colonel's crates had been taken out of bonded storage by Stein Davis and were to be delivered early next week. "I am going to ask Claire to come down while I am in Germany. I'd like you to look in on her."

He took a long drink of his Guinness before replying. "Davis sent me a packet from the Colonel," he said.

"I knew he had something for you. I didn't know what."

Allan Cobb's eyes had always been pale, but they were an almost colorless gray now.

"Does it still bother you, Brian? The way the Colonel died? Sometimes I wonder about that."

"We did what we could, Allan."

"Remember the witness? The old man who said it looked like the car was driven straight at him?"

"Damn it, of course I do. You were there. We tried to make sense of it. What more could we have done?"

"Something, Brian. Some damn thing or other. I'll never really leave it alone until I know."

Nor would I. But what was the point of discussing it now? "What did he send you?" I asked.

"A battalion history he wrote. Old maps and orders. Five thousand bucks in cash. So I could pickle my guts in Guinness, he said. His DSC from Normandy with a note telling me I should have had it instead of him but that they gave it to him because he was a colonel and I was an ugly buck sergeant. It was vintage Lockwood." The sergeant major looked at me sidelong with half a smile. "He was right, you know. They gave me a Silver Star, but I saw the citation he wrote. It was for a Congressional Medal of Honor. He put the packet together just before he took off for Mexico City."

"What else did he will you?"

"Old soldier stuff. A personal letter. He told me that eventually you were going to ask a lot of questions. Are you?"

"Yes."

"I don't know everything. The Colonel was a private man."

"Let me show you," I said. I reached into my coat pocket and took out the dagger. I placed it on the white cloth on the table. It seemed to radiate malevolence in the candlelight. "That was in the Colonel's collection once, wasn't it?"

He picked it up and turned it over in his hands. "Yes," he said. "It was stolen." He looked at me. "How did you get it?"

"Can't you guess?"

"Shit, Brian, don't try to con me. Your uncle Dean stole this Nazi pigsticker years ago. Why is it here?"

"Because he sent it back to me. With a note."

"Let me see the note."

I put the message on the table next to the dagger.

Allan Cobb studied it for a long time. "That son of a bitch," he said.

"Who is Sieg Stossen?"

"I don't know."

"Damn it—"

"I mean it, Brian. I really don't know. I do know the Colonel hated the name. But he brought this thing back from Nuremberg, and it was important to him. I don't know what to make of it. I never did."

Cobb drew the blade from the scabbard and looked at it.

"I remember this. There aren't many around. They were given to very special Germans for doing very special things."

"You disappoint me, Allan. I thought you were to answer my questions."

"There are some things I can't answer, Brian. I told you, the Colonel was a very private sort of man." He turned the weapon over in his hands. "When did this arrive?"

"It came with this morning's mail. From a forwarder in Brooklyn," I said. "I called, and they said it came to them from Germany. I'm leaving for Germany this week. Coincidence? It doesn't seem likely."

"No, it doesn't, does it?" Cobb drank some Guinness and sat for a long while just looking into space, remembering *what*? After a while he pushed the dagger and the note across to me. "Are you going hunting, Brian?"

"I think so, Sergeant Major. I think I have to."

"I'd go with you if I could."

I think he felt the dead hand of the Colonel. Pushing him.

"No, Allan, it's for me to do. Dean has done me a favor."

"Dean Lockwood never did anyone a favor, Brian. Remember that."

"Will you look in on Claire while I am gone?"

He nodded.

"There was a man snooping around the cottage. It may have been nothing at all. But it brought back some unpleasant memories."

"I'll watch out for Claire," Cobb said.

We ate dinner in near silence. After coffee and a brandy I said, "Claire has always believed the Colonel got into political trouble in Nuremberg. With the Russians."

"I don't know anything about that," Allan said. "But I do know he hated the Russians almost as much as he hated the Nazis. He would never say why. I only asked once. You learn in the Army not to mess with officers' private problems."

I didn't believe him. Allan and my adoptive father had always had a close relationship. One serving the other, maybe, but they were confident of each other. If anyone knew about the days in Nuremberg, Allan Cobb did. Claire contended the Colonel had been shipped home from Nuremberg under some sort of cloud. If he had been, Allan Cobb would know, although he would never say why.

One thing was certain. Colonel Lockwood's postings after that time were not what one would have expected for a Regular Army officer of his quality.

Allan asked, "You've been back to Germany, haven't you?"

"Twice."

"Are you going to look up Marianna Clef?"

"Yes." My memories of Marianna Clef were not warm ones. But Dean had made her part of the chain. I had no choice and said so.

"She took care of you—"

"She was a terror," I said. Marianna Clef would be in her seventies now. Her daughter, Ursula, would be in her mid-fifties, with a life behind her. Local gossip in Nuremberg had it that Fräulein Clef had been one of the *Lebensborn* women. Others said she was raped by the Russians. No one believed the story she told about a soldier husband killed on the eastern front.

The sergeant major said, "The old girl might like to see you."

"I doubt it," I said.

"Well, when you get back, come see me. We'll talk then." Cobb wasn't subtle, guile was not part of his MOS. But he believed that to be worthy of trust was the highest calling. He didn't want to choose between his affection for me and his loyalty to the Colonel. Not yet, in any case.

That was the point. If it had simply been a question of knowing where I came from, I might have long ago done some investigating. But I could never bring myself to believe that the Colonel had simply scooped up a German war orphan to take home as a souvenir of Nazi Germany. One thing I knew well about my adoptive father: He never in his life had done anything quixotic. He was not a foolish man.

Cobb said, "What else about the snooper?"

"He carries binoculars and smokes Gauloise."

"That's all you can tell me?"

"He was good at disappearing." I began to think I was making too much of a nonincident. After all, a man could carry binoculars to the beach without my permission. "I thought it might be Dr. Ershad," I said. "But Ershad is five feet three."

"Ershad?"

"Edmund Ershad. House up the street. A Bangladeshi. Professor of Dravidian studies at Cal Santa Cruz. He's on sabbatical and hasn't enough to keep him busy."

Allan's pale gray eyes were steady. "Be careful in Germany. The place is overrun with out-of-work Stasi hoods at loose ends."

"Why should the Stasi have any interest in me?"

"They did once."

"Ancient history."

Allan and I parted at about ten. The rain had begun again as I drove back to Carmel. The rhythmic slap of the windshield wipers was like a mechanical heartbeat. Or a clock ticking. It was now many years since Colonel Brian Lockwood—indulging God knows what altruistic impulse inherited from his Yankee forebears—rescued a boy from the bombed-out ruins of Nuremberg and turned him into the example of American probity—I flatter myself—who now made his way home through the rainy dark.

Few knew why the Colonel did it, but I thought Sergeant Major Cobb did. He had obviously been surprised by the reappearance of the *Adler Dolch*.

It wasn't easy to live in the shadow still cast by Colonel Brian Lockwood. The man's secrets should have died when he died. But they lived on. The weight of the dagger in my pocket made me think of old phantoms. Dean's words echoed in my mind: "learn about Brian Lockwood." I shivered, and not from the damp cold. It was not difficult to manufacture such phantoms on nights when the fog rolled in from the Pacific. I turned seaward on Ocean Avenue.

At this time, in this weather, downtown Carmel was all but deserted. The native folk had been concerned some years before that having movie star Clint Eastwood as mayor would destroy what they called "the ambience." But Eastwood came and went and did no harm at all. Carmel remained basically unchanged from what it had been when I was a boy. A bit bigger. More crowded in tourist season (but it had always been "more crowded"). Essentially Carmel by the Sea was a California version of a Northeast Coast village in Maine or Massachusetts. Carmel was unlikely to change.

It was also an improbable place for anything like dangerous intrigue. Still, I looked carefully through the dark cottage and, feeling rather foolish, tried to remember where I had stored my Army Colt automatic, before remembering it was in my bank safe-deposit box in San Francisco. Fat lot of good it would do me there. But whom was I going to shoot? Poor Professor Ershad, who already thought Americans were the most violent people on earth?

Tired and unarmed, I turned in and slept restlessly until dawn.

4

"I waited too long to ask him."

I AM A CHILD being carried by a slender blond woman, no more than a girl. She walks under a silver gray sky by a frozen river. Frightened that she might leave me, I cling to her. There are black willows along the riverbanks. Farther back, there are leafless birch trees. Someone calls, but the woman doesn't seem to hear. Suddenly she puts me on the ground and is gone. And the dream collapses into chaos and darkness.

I woke up sweating in spite of the cold. The dream was not so vivid and well developed as the drug-driven hallucination I had had in the hospital, but it was terribly familiar. I had dreamed of the woman and the frozen river ever since I was a child.

I sat up, listening to a persistent tapping noise. A pallid morning light illuminated my room. The windows of the Carmel cottage faced west, toward the berm and the beach. The sound of the surf soughing onto the strand was never absent. It was one of the most appealing things about the place.

Dr. Edmund Ershad's dark face was close to the glass, eyes bright as polished obsidian. He was rapping on the pane with the end of a plastic pen. When he saw me, he called out, "Mr. Lockwood. Open the door, if you please?"

I looked at my watch on the nightstand. It was just after six.

34

Early for casual visiting, but the shank of the morning for Dr. Ershad, who was a fanatically early riser. "My religion requires it, Mr. Lockwood. I assume Christianity does not," he had often said, anxious for a discussion of comparative religions I was not competent to engage in.

Ershad had been unable to promote enough grant money to return to Bangladesh for his sabbatical, not enough even to travel abroad, as most of his UC Santa Cruz colleagues were doing. Grants for Dravidian Studies were in short supply. Apparently there was a limit even to California's militant multiculturalism.

I got myself out of bed, put on a robe and went to the side door. I opened it to the cold, damp morning and Professor Ershad, who stood on the step dressed in a running suit with the University of California at Santa Cruz crest on it. Across his chest was stamped the legend "UCSC LACROSSE." The suit hung on him like the skin on a starving cat.

"Mr. Lockwood, sir, oh, my goodness. Isn't it cold, though? May I come inside? When, if you please, will summer arrive?" The month was November, and technically winter had not yet begun. Summer fogs dominated the weather of the Monterey Peninsula from June through July and, as sometimes was the case, into August. Late August brought some glorious weather and tourist hordes. Then came the November rains and chill winds. In January there would be some bright, clear days and skies of an achingly lovely blue. But for now it was deep winter in all but name.

Ershad was not carrying binoculars, although he often did, purportedly to watch the seals and otters playing offshore but actually to examine the neighbors, walkers, joggers and passersby on the beach.

His narrow, fine-featured face was solemn, alert as a bird's. He examined the inside of the cottage with avian interest.

"Let me offer you some coffee, Professor," I said. I was not waiting for some explanation for this visit because there would be none. Dr. Ershad was lonely, and he was also, like Mr. Chatterjee in Graham Greene's *The Confidential Agent*, "a mass observer." Or, in the American vernacular, a snoop.

"My, yes, indeed, that would be most kind, Mr. Lockwood. I am quite chilled to the bone."

He followed me into the kitchen, an old-fashioned room with dark wood cupboards and a gas stove made of enameled spigots and black iron pipes as old as the cottage. Nothing ever completely collapsed into uselessness in the cottage the Colonel built. The stove was ancient but robust. The refrigerator, a Frigidaire as old as I, was a triumph of longevity from the days when American appliances were the best in the world. It had a cylindrical stack of cooling disks on top, and it whirred like an iron dragonfly when it ran. Now it was cold enough in the house for the box to be silent, vigilant for any minute rise in temperature. This was unlikely, since the Colonel had never installed central heating.

I put a kettle on the stove and brought out the freeze-dried coffee. I hate the stuff, but it was what I drank each morning, part of my campaign to simplify my life.

"Sit down, Professor," I said. "The kettle will boil in a few minutes."

"Most kind, most kind, Mr. Lockwood." Ershad perched on a kitchen chair, looking around my kitchen like a sparrow parsing his surroundings.

"Mr. Lockwood," he said, "something most strange has been happening. I wonder if you have noticed."

The kettle began its whistle, an importunate, shrill, unpleasant sound that invariably prods me into motion. I spooned instant coffee into earthenware mugs (part of a going-away gift set from Mildred Boon, my onetime editorial assistant on *Currents*) and filled them with boiling water. I handed Ershad his and sat down across the old redwood table from him while he greedily sugared the mixture. "Strange, Professor?" I prodded. With Professor Ershad, it could be anything. Or nothing.

"A rather large and, my goodness, I must say it, quite menacing fellow has been lurking about the street." The bright black eyes glittered alertly. "For several days now. Surely you have noticed?"

I thought at once of the man on the berm. But I had no desire to set Ershad off on some mass observer's fantasy. There were always odd people about Carmel. It was that sort of artistic bohemian town.

Dr. Ershad sipped noisily at his syrupy coffee. Like many Asians, the professor thought it impolite to eat or drink silently. It implied a lack of appreciation.

I said, "Several days, Professor Ershad? Yesterday, too?"

"Actually I was not about the neighborhood yesterday, Mr. Lockwood. Dear me, no. I took the Greyhound omnibus to Santa Cruz for tea with Professor M'bata, the dean of Ethnic Studies." The mobile dark face showed a deep sadness. "I had heard that there was a fifty-thousand-dollar open grant available for minority cultural research. But such a pity, I was too late in enquiring. The grant has been given to the Black Studies department." He sighed. "It is difficult to convince financial committees of the importance of Dravidian Studies, Mr. Lockwood. I find that surprising, don't you?"

"I do, Professor Ershad. But you were saying?"

"The neighborhood interloper. Yes, dear me. I saw him on Thursday, and on Monday, and before that on the previous Friday. You were away then, I believe. In San Francisco, was it?"

Ershad rambled on. "A tall man, Mr. Lockwood. As tall and blond as yourself. But heavier, my goodness. Quite muscular and menacing. With very cold eyes. Deeply set." He drank more coffee. "We seldom get intruders in this neighborhood. Mrs. Gallagher assured me that there would be no interruptions of my work in her house." Mrs. Gallagher was an eccentric old woman who owned half a dozen houses and cottages in Carmel and lived well by renting them. She had sent her agent to inquire if I was interested in selling.

"Have you spoken to the police, Professor?" I asked.

"Oh, dear me, my goodness, no, no. One should first observe most carefully, and only upon the reaching of very strong and detailed conclusions take action."

The kitchen clock moved toward seven. I said, "I must get dressed, Professor. I have an appointment."

"With whom, may I ask, Mr. Lockwood?"

His innocent interest in everything took the edge from the intrusiveness.

"With my sister, Professor Ershad."

Ershad was on his feet. "Oh, Mrs. Warner. Yes. Yes. Such an elegant and cultured lady, sir. I have seen her here on several occasions since the beginning of summer."

"You may see more of her, Professor. I plan to ask her to stay here while I'm in Germany."

"Dear me, you are planning a trip abroad? When, may I ask?"

"Later this week."

"But Mrs. Warner will use the cottage?"

I tried to contain my impatience. Ershad was a lonely man. "Yes," I said.

"Splendid, Mr. Lockwood. I look forward to seeing her here. Yes, quite. Oh, my, yes." This was followed by one of Ershad's characteristic swerves of conversation. "Ah, Germany. I have never been to Germany, Mr. Lockwood. It is my understanding that it is one of the most beautiful nations in Europe, and enjoying a remarkable renaissance of democratic values. My, my, yes. May I enquire, is it business that takes you abroad?"

"It is," I said shortly. "And I need to be on my way this morning."

"Then I shall be on mine, dear Mr. Lockwood. I thank you most kindly for the coffee. Americans make the best-tasting coffee in the world, my goodness . . ."

I saw him out, wondering how anyone who had just finished a cup of hot water flavored with freeze-dried coffee crystals and sugar could believe such a fantasy. It made one question his other observations.

I called Claire and told her I was coming. "Fine, Bri. Meet me at the Woodside Pub. You can buy me lunch." Claire had only intermittent help, hated to cook and loved the menu at the Pub. She was also the only person who called me 'Bri,' which, I pointed out to her, was close to being called by the name of a French cheese.

By seven-thirty I had packed for a long trip, called the airlines again to rearrange my schedule and telephoned General Bolton's friend, a Colonel Sam Regis, at the Air Force Records Center in Colorado Springs, for an appointment. At eight-fifteen I went outside to look at the beach and the cypress groves on the berm. I watched for almost an hour, but no menacing figure appeared. I began to think we, the professor and I, were victims of the imagination a solitary life encourages.

By nine-fifteen I was driving north.

Claire was my one firm connection to the Lockwood family. When I was a child and Claire hardly more, she became my advocate and I fell in love with her. Claire has always been the woman against whom I measure all women. She has a large capacity to love and understand without conducting inquisitions. She was middle-aged now, a widow who understood that she had years of living left to do. She was an independent thinker and a joy to be with.

Small—almost like a miniature of her mother—but with the Colonel's coloring—Claire's features are softer than her mother Janice's, which had always seemed carved from marble. Claire's nose is shorter and her mouth more generous. Her eyes are brown. The word that comes to mind is "velvet." Perhaps Claire isn't a classic beauty in the Janice Clayton Lockwood manner, but there has never been a man I know of who didn't snap to attention when she walked into a room.

She had loved Warner and given him the sort of marriage few men knew about, warm and fulfilled. When he died of a heart attack suddenly and unexpectedly, she grieved privately but not for long. There's too much life in Claire for mourning.

I waited at the window table at the Pub, and presently I saw her Bronco pull into a parking space. She came striding into the restaurant fresh from shopping at Roberts, saddle bag swinging from a strap, auburn hair glistening. When she kissed me, I inhaled a scent of Joy.

I may as well admit that I'm one of those people affected by scent. Perfume chemists must love men like me. I suspect I would never have married Reeder if she had not worn Antilope, which was what Miriam had worn. I know I haven't mentioned Miriam Halprin, but I will later. Too many digressions can spoil the narrative flow.

Claire greeted me with "I heard from Ben. You invited him to take care of me. Are you sure you want us living in sin in your cottage?"

"I'm a tolerant man," I said while she slid into the booth.

"I'm sure, little brother." She studied me critically. "How are you? You look healthy. Are you?"

"I feel fine," I said.

"Should you be driving around? What about Germany?"

"We'll talk about that. Order first."

A young waitress appeared as though by magic. Somehow waitresses always do when Claire is on hand.

"I'll have a glass of Mondavi Cabernet Sauvignon," she said. "Then a grilled lamb chop and a spinach salad." She knew the Pub's menu by heart. She and Ben ate there often.

"The same for me," I said. "Except make mine a martini. Up, with a twist of lemon."

Claire reached across the table and squeezed my hand. "You look—I don't know—alert?"

"Thanks, I think."

"Is that black Audi Quattro yours? Ben said last week you were thinking of buying one."

I suppressed a smile. Ever since Reeder's Marin headlands ceremony, Claire had been telling me: "Write a book. Buy a toy. Have an affair."

"I took part of your advice anyway," I said.

While I was married, I drove practical and inexpensive cars. But the Audi gran turismo I had bought on impulse was neither practical nor inexpensive. It was all black lacquer, alloy wheels and air dams. It was, the salesman in Monterey had assured me, capable of 150 miles an hour. Where one was supposed to drive that fast in California, where the speed limit was fixed at fifty-five, was a mystery. But I did enjoy the Audi with an almost childish pleasure that Claire at once recognized.

"Good for you, Bri," Claire said. "I love it."

"It's yours until I get back from Germany."

"If I go down to the cottage, the menagerie goes along."

She meant her aged cat and dog.

"Understood."

Our drinks arrived. I said, "I have one of these a week."

We touched glasses and drank.

"Now tell me," Claire said.

"It's been two years since Janice died," I said. "Remember the Colonel's will?"

"The funny business about keeping his personal papers in bonded storage until two years after Janice."

"Stein has been the good soldier and brought the stuff out of storage. It will be delivered to the cottage next week. And I can't be there. I have to see Dieter Langan. His offer of an American bureau has suddenly got soft. We have to talk. He has to *see* me."

"Do you need that job, Bri? I always hoped you'd settle down and just write."

"Write what? Most of what I know, other people have already written. And fiction? Who would try to make a living doing that?"

The entrée arrived, and we settled in to eat. Claire ate like an athlete, never gaining an ounce.

After a while she said, "All right, you have to see Dieter and you want me to accept the Colonel's things. Anything else?"

"Look at them, that's all."

Her eyebrows arched. "All right. Leave it that way for now."

"Something else happened yesterday," I said. "Do you remember that elegant Nazi dagger the Colonel had in his collection?"

"I don't think so, Bri."

"Of course you do. I sneaked it out of his library when we were living in Pacific Heights. I showed it to you. Got a rocket from the Colonel for it."

"That was *years* ago."

"Then you do remember."

"Uncle Dean stole it."

I nodded. "That's what Allan said, remember that?"

"Yes, Father was very angry."

"I have the dagger. It's in my luggage."

"*You* have it? How come?"

"Dean sent it to me. With this." I took the note from my pocket and handed it to her.

She read it, then looked at me.

"He knew just what to write," I said. "He even mentioned Fräulein Clef."

"What a terrible man he is, Bri."

"Did you ever hear the Colonel talk about Sieg Stossen?"

"The name on the dagger blade." Claire frowned, sensing where I was leading.

"The Colonel, anyone?"

"Never."

"I saw Allan last night. He says the same."

"You don't believe him?"

"I'm not sure." The waitress cleared our table and brought small cups of dark Italian coffee.

When she had gone, Claire said, "The sergeant major wouldn't lie to you, Bri."

"He would if the Colonel wanted him to."

"What are you going to do?"

"Find out what I can about Stossen. Go to Nuremberg. I have to do that now, Claire."

She folded the note and handed it back to me. "I wish you'd just tear it up, Bri. Fräulein Clef was never very kind to you, was she?"

"She did her duty. German."

Claire ignored the self-deprecating comment. "The name," she said. "*Sieg* means 'victory,' doesn't it?"

"Yes."

"And Stossen?"

"*Stoss* means 'a blow.' *Stossen* is the plural."

"My, that does sound very—ah—National Socialist."

"I'm sure that occurred to Dean."

"Bri," she said, "you've always had a vivid imagination—"

"Still," I said, and put the note in my wallet, "it makes me try to remember."

"Bri, Janice is gone. I'm sorry for the way she treated you, but that's over. Uncle Dean has been away for years and isn't ever coming back. Miriam has been married twice and has four kids, and you aren't a knobby-kneed war orphan any longer. Has it ever occurred to you that there is nothing sinister for you *to* remember?"

I looked about me at the sparse early-lunch crowd at the Pub. Everyone seemed prosperous, comfortable, well fed. "Speaking of remembering, I don't remember ever being hungry, but I must have been or I must have been with people who were. I can never eat well without feeling slightly guilty."

"You looked small and half starved when you got off the train in Oakland," Claire said. "I always thought maybe Fräulein Clef cheated on your keep."

"Last night Allan and I talked about Mexico City and what happened to the Colonel."

"We *know* what happened to the Colonel," Claire said. "He got into a fight with the Russians in Nuremberg and the politicians hung him out to dry for it. I don't think he was very careful when he stepped into that street in Mexico." Her eyes seemed to glitter with an old anger. We never discussed the Colonel's postwar career without a bitterness for the blunt, stolid Communist ideologues of the old Red Army and the politicians who had been afraid to confront them. The Colonel despised them all, and so had we. But it was all so long ago, so buried under so much politics and so much history that we had stopped asking questions. Years and years ago.

"You and Allan still think someone deliberately killed the Colonel," Claire said. "I think he was already dead, Bri. Whatever happened in Germany ruined his career. He was never the same after that. You didn't know him before. He was a happy man, Bri; he was like a kid."

"The war, Claire."

"No. Something happened in Nuremberg. But that's all over now, years ago. I don't want you going off on some crazy hunt just because Dean Lockwood still hates his dead brother."

"Not only his brother, Claire."

"No, of course not. I do understand, Bri. I truly do. I probably never mentioned to you that I ran into Uncle Dean in New York once, about ten years ago. It was at that antiques show where the superprestigious dealers come from London and Paris and Vienna to give the New York dealers fits. I saw him only long enough to say hello. He was dressed to the nines, as usual, but he'd gotten stout and red-faced and he was as rude as ever. He was with Countess Somebody-or-other, and he was scared to death I'd stick around and embarrass him."

"Did he still have that silly mustache?"

"Yes, but no waxed tips now. It's brushier, more on the J. P. Morgan style."

What Claire said about the Colonel may well have been true. My only real memories of him were from my early times in the United States, and I recalled a silent, melancholy, stern man with a strangely demanding sense of duty toward me.

There was always a distance between us that didn't match the fact of his having brought me to the United States to live in his care. It was an emptiness, a chasm we couldn't bridge. As a child I spent most of my time in boarding school, and as a man I saw my adoptive father only a few times each year. Not my choice. His. But you don't come off the streets of a bombed-out city without being a survivor. And in that I had Claire's great help.

Midday pleasantly drifted into early afternoon as it often did when Claire and I were together.

There seems to be something hopelessly square about a man feeling real affection for his adoptive sibling; I suppose a good Jungian shrink could find something quasi-incestuous about Claire and me. I sometimes wondered if one could *be* incestuous with a sister unrelated by blood. It was, I often thought, one of the burdens of our time that every emotion, every instinctive response to another human being, had to be pruriently vivisected in the head doctor's consulting room.

The Victorian truth was that neither Claire nor I had ever been driven to experiment with each other's anatomy, not even when we were children. And still we managed to keep our glands functioning conventionally when exposed to attractive people of the opposite sex. The simple truth was that Claire and I shared a lot of values, and foremost among them was a deep consideration for each other that was lifelong.

This never prevented Claire from playing the matchmaker with me. She had livened my adolescence and young manhood with a continuing parade of nubile women. But she had not selected Reeder, and she had the grace not to remind me of that. Now that I was single again, the parade was slower and more sedate, as befitted my age, I guess, but attractive as ever. Some were widows like herself. Others were surprisingly young. "You may not be Cary Grant, Bri," she said, "but you are big and blond and a great deal sexier than most of the men we widows meet."

The Pub's lunch crowd emptied out until it was quiet and dim in the intimate dining rooms. We left the restaurant about two-thirty, and I followed her Bronco into the hills and oak forests up to the end of Patrol Road, where the Warners had built the house Ben Macdonald designed for them many years before.

I put my carry-on baggage in "my" room, a smallish wooden den, but with a deck and a window overlooking the steeply falling hillside and its stands of scrub oak and chaparral, so typical of this part of California. Claire was pleased that I was leaving her in charge of my house and my car. But in reality who else would I leave to watch over what was mine? My children were too busy, and my friends not really available.

Jefferson, Claire's aged springer spaniel, gave me a wet-nosed hello, and her large Himalayan cat, Stack (so called because according to Claire he resembled a haystack), ambled into the room, climbed onto the bed and settled in my open luggage.

I met Claire out on the side deck, from where one could look through the trees and see the rising bulk of the Coast Range. These were the mountains, I thought sentimentally, of which the Stanford Hymn sings. As a student I took a secret pride in the fact that my alma mater's motto was written in my native language: *Die Luft der Freiheit weht.* The winds of freedom blow. Another personal quirk only Claire knew about.

Claire served coffee, brewed strong in the Italian style. Neither of us was much for coolers, although the weather had become less unsettled, and it was too early for cocktails.

I sat and drank my coffee and looked around at the redwood siding the color of driftwood, the flat, unfashionable roof with the broad California overhangs, the fallen leaves on the deck underfoot and the forest reflected in the sliding doors and windows. The house suited the couple who had lived there until Dan Warner died, and it suited the woman who lived there now with a housekeeper coming in each day to tidy up and care for the animals while Claire was away.

"Are you going to marry Ben, Claire?" I asked.

"I think so."

"Good."

She smiled at me. "You looked like the Colonel just then." And then switched to: "Bri, you aren't letting this knife business get out of hand, are you?"

The truth was that I didn't know the total answer to that. I only knew that Sieg Stossen's Nazi bauble had the makings of an obsession.

"Speaking frankly, sis, I'm at loose ends. I accepted *Die Zeit*'s and Dieter Langan's offer of airfare, so I'm committed for Germany, at least to talk. It's natural to have my reporter's curiosity aroused by this peculiar arrival."

"That's all it is? Journalistic curiosity?"

"There may be a story in it." I forced a laugh. "Maybe a book."

"Will you really go to Nuremberg?"

"Yes. Fräulein won't be pleased to see me, it's been so many years. I hardly even remember what she looked like. But I'll go there. I don't really have a choice, do I?"

Claire's answer was a question. "Have you seen Reeder?" Her brown eyes looked burnished in the westerly light. "Are you getting over that?"

"I don't think much about Reeder any longer."

"Not more than once a day."

"Reeder's gone. I look ahead and see a long blank space here . . ."

Claire regarded me calmly. "For forty years you've been Brian Lockwood. A week in Germany isn't going to change that."

Stack wandered out of the house, jumped to the top rail of the deck and settled down to watch us. Jefferson was already lying at his mistress's feet, thumping the floor with his tail.

She stroked the old dog's head. "They like the beach."

"My house is their house. And yours. But watch out for Professor Ershad. He thinks spaniels are attack dogs."

"That odd little man. Is he always underfoot?"

"About six days a week. He devotes one day to chasing down grants. Without much success, it seems. As he points out, Dravidian Studies are not politically correct at Cal Santa Cruz. No Western oppressors. Anyway, you can do your part by listening to him while I'm away. But remember, *he's* an early riser. He woke me up at six this morning. Jogging, for God's sake, in his lacrosse suit."

I stood, and Jefferson did, too. I'm one of those people who somehow *know* that domestic animals can read our intentions. How else would they put up with us? Stack, too, knew I planned to take a walk along Patrol Road. He considered it, discarded the idea as impractical and went back to sleep.

"Don't overdo it, Bri," Claire said.

"The quack tells me it's good for me."

Jefferson followed me down the deck stairs, out the gravel drive and along the quiet road to the crest of the ridge. There was no bay view there, only the clouds high above the treetops and the flanks of the Coast Range in a slanting, wintry sunlight. The air was cool and still and smelled of fallen leaves. For nearly an hour I sat on an oak log and threw branches for Jefferson to retrieve, then walked slowly back to Claire's house.

When I climbed the stairs, she was reading a book, something of the Colonel's about ceremonial weapons.

"Anything?" I asked.

She closed the book and shrugged. "Nothing."

"I didn't think it would be that simple."

"Go slow, Bri. We'll find out what we need to know."

I smiled. "Calm Claire," I said. "I always used to think of you like that. Calm and steady. Even when we were kids."

"Someone had to be, in this family of overachievers. You have no idea how sorry I felt for you the day you arrived. You were skinny as a stray cat. You looked hungry and only half as tall as you should have been. You've improved."

"I had a sister," I said.

"You still do. . . . Was it bad, Bri? The hospital? When I visited, I had the feeling you were ready to make a break for it."

"The idea occurred to me every time they served a meal or put a catheter into me. But eventually you settle down to being A Patient. You decide it's this or die. Once you decide to live, the rest isn't so bad. I even developed a morbid interest in the procedures. Mostly routine for a heart case. But it's never so simple as you want it to be. I had a bad reaction to one of the tranquilizers. The dream—you know my dream, the one about the woman

and the frozen river . . ." I hesitated, almost unwilling to re-
visit those memories—if that's what they were. "It's as though
the drugs enhanced memory. There was more this time. Much
more."

I sat on the sofa and told her about the dream or hallucination, whatever it was, in detail. "You know what I think of
dream readers, channeling, holistic shrinkery and all that Shir-
ley MacLaine Esalen New Age bullshit. But that dream is not
just a nightmare, Claire. It *happened*. It's *real*."

She put a hand on my arm. "Bri, there was no woman on the
riverbank. You were living in the *streets* when Father found
you."

"When, Claire? The *date*? How old was I?"

"I don't know, does it matter?"

"It matters a great deal. The dream matters. It happened. It
happened to me."

"Is that the real reason you're going to Germany?"

"Who am I, Claire? The Colonel might have told me. But I
waited too long to ask him. Now I have to ask Clef and some
shadow named Stossen."

"You are my brother, Brian Lockwood," Claire said firmly.
Claire is like that. For her there was no other answer. "I'm sorry
you and Father could never talk to each other. Janice might have
had something to do with that, but we'll never know now. I am
sure of one thing, although it may be hard for you to believe:
Father loved you, Bri. Very much. No matter what, you must
remember that."

Was it possible she knew more than she was willing to tell me
then? More than was good for me to know?

5

"Things were tangled in Germany then."

THE 737 DESCENDED steeply through the high mountain air. To the east the snow-clad Rockies gradually gave way to rolling hills and then to grasslands. Directly below lay Colorado Springs, and to the north I could see the steel and glass constructs of the Air Force Academy. A late-morning sun glittered on the hard, reflective surfaces of the aggressively contemporary architecture and on the snow that lay in patches on the ground. There is a great difference between this academy of glass and stainless steel and the gray *gravitas* of West Point and Annapolis. Once, when she was talking about architecture, Janice said that everything she despised seemed to come from Germany. She had been criticizing the glass boxyness of the Bauhaus style, but I took it that she included me. It was not a question of oversensitivity. Her dislike of me was simply a fact I lived with.

Last night over a nightcap Claire and I had reminisced—if that was the word—about Janice.

"Janice never really felt safe until Father died," Claire said. For a moment I had thought that a pretty harsh judgment, but thinking about it, I decided Claire was right. Janice may have been the elegant, self-assured debutante in the 1930s when she met and married young Lieutenant Lockwood, but the Janice I

knew was a frightened, resentful and jealous woman whose
grip on reality (I came to realize) was none too secure. The
Colonel, though, would never have left her. His sense of obliga-
tion and duty was too well developed. Janice's condition was
silently accepted by everyone in the Lockwood and Clayton
families. Her "breakdowns" had begun when she was at Mount
Holyoke and continued all her life. Each challenge, each frustra-
tion, each denial endangered her uncertain stability. Clearly, the
shock of my sudden appearance had badly unsettled her.

Janice had a thousand ways of letting me know how she
disliked me. But she was, after all, Claire's mother, and a
woman who produced such a daughter earned some indul-
gence. As I grew older, I wondered if Janice hated *me* as much as
she hated the circumstances of my arrival. Would it have been
different if the Colonel had consulted with her before lifting an
orphan from the litter of war-ravaged Nuremberg? We never
knew.

The tires squealed on the runway at Colorado Springs Airport,
and I gathered my belongings. The Eagle Dagger had given the
security people at SFO some pause when it showed up on the
X-ray screen. But the airport guard-in-charge was a recently
discharged Desert Storm veteran fascinated by what he recognized as a rare war souvenir.

At Colorado Springs the terminal was uncrowded; there were
Air Force blue suits everywhere. I made my way to the taxi rank
and ordered up a ride to the nearby Apollo Park Hotel. I
checked into my room and, even before unpacking, called General Bolton's house. A housekeeper, German or Austrian by her
accent, answered. We are a race of order takers, I thought. *Befehl
ist Befehl.*

"The general is on the golf course, Mr. Lockwood. He says
1900 sharp at the club. Is that satisfactory?"

I heard the echo of the Colonel's manner in the peremptory
command to appear for dinner. "Seven o'clock," I said.

I called the Records Center and arranged to meet Colonel
Regis in the visitors' area at one, then went downstairs to the bar
for a sandwich and a beer.

* * *

Colonel Sam Regis was a short, muscular man about my age. Everything about him said "fighter pilot." He wore command wings and four rows of ribbons, including an Air Force Cross. I wondered what career decision or congressional economy had him sitting at a desk in the Air Force Records Center.

"Jack Bolton says you're researching a book on the Luftwaffe?"

I learned as a journalist and correspondent not to deny bona fides offered you by someone who knows the system and how it works. "I need information on a name, Colonel."

"What name?"

I produced the dagger. "Sieg Stossen."

"We can run it through the computer." Regis was more interested in the weapon than the name. He handled it with great care. "This is an Eagle Dagger, Mr. Lockwood. And in mint condition. There aren't more than a dozen of these things in existence, did you know that? *Ein Adler Dolch.* Do you speak German?

"As it happens, I do."

"I don't. Not very well. But I picked up some of the language when I was stationed at Rhein Main. The *Adler* is a particular sort of ceremonial dagger the Nazis—probably Hermann Goering, because this is a Luftwaffe version of the Eagle Dagger— awarded officers for very special services. This one is probably worth ten thousand on the collector's market. I've only seen one before this, at the Wehrmacht Museum in what used to be East Berlin. Before the Wall came down. An oppo in the East German Air Force was showing me the sights, pushing the Commie version of the economic miracle. But it always came down to bragging about what great soldiers the East Krauts were. This *Adler* is jazzier than anything they had in East Berlin. Stossen must have been a big-deal VIP." He handed the dagger back to me regretfully. "I'm a collector in a small way, but I couldn't afford anything like this."

I took back the dagger without enthusiasm. "I'm more interested in the name than the dagger, Colonel."

Regis stood up. "Showboat that he was, fatso Hermann didn't hand out Eagle Daggers every day of the week. Stossen is probably in our Luftwaffe historical data base. Let's go see."

He led the way down a long corridor lined with color paintings of military aircraft. At the end of the passageway we went through the soundproofed glass door of the computer room.

Inside, behind sound and heat baffles, stood the main central processing unit of the resident IBM mainframe. "We keep trying to get a Cray and the GAO keeps telling the Armed Services Committee the records center can't afford such expensive toys. They say stop asking for B-2 bombers and then we'll see." Regis pulled the dust cover off a work station. A young warrant officer appeared and got into a sotto voce conversation with the colonel.

"We may be able to help," Regis said when the murmured exchange ended. "What search parameters can you give Warrant Officer Hartman? A date, say?"

"Let's start with November 20, 1945, and work backward. That's the day the War Crimes Tribunal opened in Nuremberg."

"Good. We'll try it."

Hartman seated himself at the console and began typing at a terrific pace. Keywords and passwords flashed across the monitor screen. I said, "Rank of major and above."

"No Stossen in the Luftwaffe on the date specified," Hartman said. "At least not that our data base knows. The records only go back to July 1945. Things were tangled in Germany then."

An understatement, I thought. "What's the source of the material in the data base?" I asked.

"Some Luftwaffe records we got from the West Germans. It's been juiced up a bit with material we buy from what's left of the East German intelligence service," Hartman said. "They've been a good source for us. Selling secrets has gotten to be a cottage industry in unified Germany."

"They ask crazy prices," Regis said. "But some of their stuff is good. The Stasi had the poop on just about everything in Germany since the war. And of course, they inherited the Nazi records from the Gestapo and Sicherheitsdienst."

"How much Stasi material have you?" I asked.

"As much as we could afford to buy. Congress hasn't been generous with Air Force intelligence. Most of the people on the Hill figure the Cold War is over."

Obviously Colonel Regis did not agree.

"Congressmen don't much believe in military intelligence. They think it's an oxymoron." The man in uniform's bitter joke. Since the days when the democrats of Athens exiled Miltiades, the man who won for them at Marathon, the coming of peace had turned warriors into pariahs. The colonel had gone through the same bitter sense of being diminished by peace.

"Is the Stasi material available?" I asked.

Regis said, "It sounds as though what you're looking for may still be secret. If it is, you'll have to be cleared."

Hartman, the data-processing specialist caught up in the hunt, said, "A big batch of that stuff has just been declassified, Colonel. Shall I run the name through?"

Regis said, "Ain't *glasnost* grand, Mr. Lockwood? Sure, let's have a look, Mr. Hartman."

Screens flashed across the monitor in rapid succession. Suddenly the display paused. Hartman highlighted a name. "Tallyho, Colonel. Here he is, big as life. '*Sieg Dietrich Eugen von Stossen.* Son of Helmuth and Freya von Stossen. Born in Stettin, Prussia, November 9, 1916. Heidelberg University, 1935. Medical degree, Marburg University Medical Faculty, 1939.' " He whistled. "An M.D. at age twenty-three. He must have been real smart. National Socialist Party Card Number 4243. One of the first five thousand. Joined the Luftwaffe as a commissioned surgeon, 1941. This looks like your man, Mr. Lockwood."

I tried to stay calm. "Anything else?"

"That's all of it, sir."

Colonel Regis said, "We can make an educated guess. Stossen may have been a flight surgeon. More likely he was an aeromedicine researcher. When even the Stasi records are so slim, it probably means that Stossen was tapped for intelligence work early on, probably while he was still in school. The Wehrmacht intelligence services were split a dozen ways, mostly by armed forces branch. They spied on one another, too, so just because Stossen wore a blue suit, it didn't mean he wasn't SS or

Sicherheitsdienst. The SS could recruit anyone anywhere, and I never heard of an ordinary air officer of the line being given an Eagle Dagger. The award usually carried a lot of perks. Villas, dancing girls, whatever. When Sieg Stossen buckled on his dagger, he had clout, Mr. Lockwood. The question is, what did he do to earn it?"

"Can you access files of the judge advocate's department of the Army?" I asked. "The denazification records from the military government branch?"

"Some. It depends."

"Look for Stossen as a wanted war crimes suspect."

"You have what intelligence calls a dirty mind, Mr. Lockwood. That's a compliment."

Hartman accessed a different directory. There was another torrent of key words and encrypted files.

Hartman turned to the colonel. "Look what we have here. There *was* a Colonel Stossen on the wanted list. He was the Luftwaffe doctor in charge of some of the medical experiments conducted at Auschwitz and Sobibor concentration camps. The experiments are described as dealing with 'cold survival' and 'high-altitude tests.'" He looked at Colonel Regis. Perplexed in the face of horror. "High-altitude tests? Cold survival?"

Regis said, "What do they teach you kids in school these days about the war? Luftwaffe doctors froze prisoners in iced water and then tried to revive them by injecting hot liquids. When that just killed them, they froze others and tried warming them with women prisoners. As a sex show it must have been a disappointment. A near-dead man and two or three starving women don't put on much of a display. For high-altitude survival experiments, they just put prisoners into decompression chambers and reduced the pressure to simulate high altitude. When the blood boiled and they died, they wrote down the numbers in their combat manuals. Very methodical. Very correct. Very German."

So Stossen was one of *those* Germans, I thought, and Dean Lockwood had sent *me* his Eagle Dagger.

Hartman went back to his computer. He seemed unaffected by what Regis had just told him. My generation had My Lai to remember, but Hartman's had nothing but easy victories and "good" causes.

I asked, "Is there nothing to tie Stossen specifically to anyone in Nuremberg?"

"Who, for instance?"

"Anyone. Military or civilian."

"No," Regis said, "but these records are sketchy. And it's been years." He examined the display. "The Russians wanted Stossen as early as 1945. According to this, they had special NKVD teams out looking for him. But they never found him. He was killed in the Battle of Berlin. His body was identified by an aide."

Warrant Officer Hartman said, "Look, sir. Stossen's parents were still alive last year."

He searched further and shrugged. "That's all there is. Stossen might have been interesting to the Russians, but not, apparently, to us. The file is marked 'closed.' "

I didn't ask for a printout. I wouldn't have been given one anyway.

Sam Regis straightened up and prepared to usher me out of the computer room.

"I guess," he said, "Colonel Stossen's dagger is yours, Mr. Lockwood. Unless his parents claim it, you're the only one with clear title to it, it seems."

Dean's message was taking shape. A threat? Whatever, a bubble of pain had settled into my chest.

General Bolton was now in his mid-seventies but looked twenty years younger. His conversation was still laced with military academy slang. His skin was burned to the color of tanned leather by the Colorado sun, his eyes were alert and his golf handicap, he told me almost at once, was ten.

We talked over dinner in the chrome-and-blue plush art deco of the senior officers' dining room at the Academy officers' club. As for Sieg Stossen, Bolton's contempt was palpable. It was inconceivable to him that an air force officer could have lent himself to the bestialities of Auschwitz and Sobibor. That the officer was also a physician made his crimes even more revolting.

"I was twenty when the war began," Bolton told me. "Twenty and a first classman at the Point. Mine was the first class of West Point cadets to take flight training before commissioning. I got mine at Cal-Aero Flight Academy in Southern California. Then I got my wings at Luke Field in Class 42K. Never looked back." He sipped at his claret. "It's been a damned fine life. Being a soldier and an airman is something to be proud of. Vermin like Stossen aren't soldiers. What happened to him?"

"He died in the war."

Bolton's blue eyes glittered with displeasure. "The rocket men we snatched—well, I guess you could say they were serving their country and maybe an ideal, although there are people who would give you an argument about that. I sure would have in 1945. I was with a Lightning group in Kent when the buzz bombs started. But men like Dürnberg and Von Braun—you *could* make a case for what they were doing. And it was a good thing they worked for us instead of the Soviets. But *medical* doctors doing live experiments on concentration camp prisoners —*no one* can excuse that. I'm sorry the shit didn't survive so we could have hanged him."

When dinner was finished and the general had ordered a pair of bulbs of Armagnac, he asked about the Colonel. I didn't expect what came next.

"I liked your father, Lockwood. For a gravel pounder he was a fine officer, a golden boy, on the way to the top. He could have been chief of staff of the Army, but he got screwed. I don't have the real poop, but it was rumored that he crossed the goddamned Russians, our *allies,* and got in the deep stuff with the politicians in Washington. We were so damned eager to be friendly. Like a pack of slobbering St. Bernards. I'd say Brian Lockwood got sacrificed to 'Allied cooperation.' That Nuremberg posting was a snake den, and Brian Lockwood got bit. I guess he used up all his luck in Normandy. He bought the farm crossing a street down in Baja, I heard. Is that so?"

"Mexico City," I said.

"Jesus, that's lousy luck. And then that brother of his. Brian didn't deserve that."

"You knew Dean Lockwood, General?"

"Well enough to be happy he wasn't *my* brother."

Over time I guess I'd thought that family skeletons were private matters. Wrong.

"Don't misunderstand me. Dean Lockwood was a bad one, but he could charm a bird off a branch." Bolton breathed in with his long nose in the goblet. "What was I saying?"

"That my uncle Dean was a charmer."

"That's what made it so easy for him to get in trouble and out again. The word is, he stole things when he bugged out." The eyes regarded me intently. "Maybe even that Nazi pigsticker that's troubling you so, boy."

"Possible," I said.

I didn't want to discuss my personal problems with a seventy-five-going-on-sixteen USAF general, so as soon as I decently could, I left him and went back to the Apollo Park. The altitude was bothering me, and there was a pain in my chest. I slipped a nitroglycerin pill under my tongue and waited until my breathing calmed, then telephoned Claire. The first thing she wanted to know was how I had handled the flight. I told her I was fine. "They keep cabin altitude at five thousand feet. Anyone can handle that," I said.

"You sound out of breath."

"I've just jogged around the block."

"I worry about you, Bri."

We talked for a few minutes. Talking to Claire always settled me down.

"Do something for me," I said. "Call Stein Davis tomorrow and see if he has an address for Dean."

"I already have, Bri."

"What did he say?"

"He said he'd call the German police and for me to check with him later this week."

"I'll call Stein myself," I said.

"Don't go looking for Dean, Bri . . . but if you decide you must, please be careful."

"I must and I will. Good night, Claire. We'll talk again soon."

The pain in my chest had gone, but I took another nitro just to make sure. Then I slept badly. The altitude bothered me. My biological clock was beginning to complain. I really feared the return of the dream. But when sleep did finally come, it was heavy and dreamless. I was grateful for that.

6

"What are friends for?"

I AM SOMEONE WHO—until this gloomy late-November day—had never been to Brooklyn.

To me it has always been a place you overfly on the way from California to John F. Kennedy Airport, a city of brick tenements and row houses sentimentalized by Hollywood in the forties and fifties. But this time I looked around me.

The names were familiar from the "Six o'Clock News." Bad things happened in Bensonhurst, Bedford Stuyvesant, Flatbush. In the steadily falling rain the streets looked ordinary rather than threatening. People went about their business, bundled against the weather; scowling, it's true, but they were New Yorkers, after all. I know, I know, spoken like a true out-of-towner. To New Yorkers, just another hick from the hinterlands.

I had taken a room at another new airport hotel, the Meadowmere Hilton. My Lufthansa connection was scheduled to depart JFK at ten-thirty the next morning; that left me the afternoon and evening to investigate Tetrac Freight Forwarders. I chose to stay at the airport for convenience and because I just didn't much like Manhattan. People Claire's age remembered a smart, cosmopolitan city, a Cole Porter kind of place. I had no such memories. As a temporarily displaced Californian, I re-

membered bad-tempered natives and humid days with the mer-
cury at ninety, so that even the plastic seats of buses and taxicabs grew slick with sweat. To those memories I could now add
a wet afternoon, with the temperature near to freezing and daylight as cheerful as that inside an abandoned warehouse. To
make matters gloomier, today was the twenty-eighth anniver-
sary of the day John F. Kennedy was killed.

Tetrac Freight Forwarders turned out to be located in a storefront on a street lined with hunch-shouldered brick buildings
with dirty windows. I opened a glass door covered with smeary
handprints and stepped inside out of the rain. The room was
divided by a wooden counter into an office and a waiting room.
There were boxes stacked on the floor, tagged and ready for
pickup.

It appeared that Tetrac was a functioning business. But at the
moment it was an untended business. At the rear of the room a
half door led to a warehouse area.

On a desk behind the counter was a personal computer gar-
nished with Post-It notes. Beside the PC was a telephone, handset off the hook. On the counter was a hand-lettered sign: ON
DUTY 2 SERVE U: MS. CYNDI GENOVESE. The *i* in "Cyndi" was dotted
with a happy face. A second line read: WHAT R FRIENDS 4?

The floor creaked under me as I went to the half door.
"Hello?" I called out. "Anyone there?"

As though teleported, a teenage girl appeared, carrying a
heavy cardboard box with Italian postal markings stamped all
over it. The girl, perhaps the Ms. Cyndi Genovese of the sign,
had tangled dark hair and wore a polyester blue dress that
reached barely a third of the way down her thighs. On her feet
were blue plastic shoes with spike heels.

"Give me a minute," she said after she lowered the box to the
floor. She picked up a telephone and spoke a colloquial Italian
that developed into an exchange lasting several minutes. *"Si, si.
Prego,* I got it down, okay?" She scribbled on a sheet of notepaper. "You'll get it by messenger first thing, okay?" She ended
the conversation with a cheery "Have a good day" and hung
up.

She said to me, "People are so impatient. Those are old books
in that box and he's waited six weeks for them, but he has to

have them today. Men." She sighed heavily and dialed a number. "I'll be with you in a minute, really."

When her call went through, she said, "This is Cyndi at Tetrac. Where's the messenger I called for two hours ago?" She covered the mouthpiece and smiled conspiratorially at me. "I didn't call that long ago, but you have to prod people or they won't work as hard as they should." On the telephone: "Well, okay, Mr. Cincotta, if you say so. But if he isn't here in ten minutes, I'll have to call someone else, okay? . . . Yes, you, too. Have a *nice* day." She hung up and said, *"Now,* what can I do for you, mister?"

"I called from California two days ago. About a shipment that came through here. My name is Lockwood."

She took down one of the clipboards hanging on the wall above her battered desk. "Lockwood?"

"The shipment from Germany. I may have talked to you."

"You talked to Eileen. I'm Cyndi. Well, actually, my name is Claretta." She indicated the hand-lettered sign. "But I like Cyndi. And I always sign my name that way, with a happy face. It makes people feel good. Oh, here it is." She found what she wanted on one of the sheets of her clipboard. "What do you want to know?"

"The sender's address."

"Oh, that would be on the bill of lading."

"Could I see that?"

"I'm sorry. BOLs are always kept in the safe. I can't open that. Not allowed." She rolled her eyes in a collegial expression of exasperation with higher authority.

"Could you get someone else to open it? I really would like to see whatever you have."

"Mr. Grgich could do it. He's the manager. But he's gone for the day. I'm sorry. Really."

"Could you call Mr. Grgich?"

"This is his night to visit his mother in Canarsie. But I could ask him to make a copy of the BOL for you tomorrow. Would that be okay?"

"I guess so, it'll have to be," I said.

Cyndi Genovese produced a clipboard with a pad of forms.

"This is a request for the duplicate BOL," she said. "I'll make it out for you."

Holding a ball-point pen cramped between her fingers, she filled in a dozen blanks. "The addressee has to sign here," she said, offering the clipboard.

"Thanks," I said. "I've put you to some trouble—"

"You aren't making a claim or anything like that, are you? Your parcel was sent to California by UPS. They used to lose stuff, but they're reliable now, real reliable."

"It arrived safely," I said. "I just want to know who sent it."

"You mean you don't know?"

"Not a clue."

"You're sure this isn't a complaint."

"No. Did I sound as though it were?"

She shrugged and shook her shoulders. Her breasts strained at the open V neck of her dress. "People come here mostly to complain. Particularly when stuff gets shipped uninsured. There's nothing we can do if the shipper doesn't want to pay for insurance."

"I'm not making a claim. I'm not complaining," I said. "I just need some information."

Reassured, she offered the pen, and I took it. "Well, if all you want is to know the sender's address, I don't think anyone will mind that."

"No," I said, "I shouldn't think so." I signed the form. "Send the bill of lading to this address, will you? By air." I wrote Dieter Langan's Düsseldorf address on the form.

The girl looked at the address. "You are going to Europe. To Germany. That's real neat." The smile faded. "Oh, look. I'm sorry, mister. The pen leaked."

I looked; my hand was ink-stained.

"There's stain remover soap in the bathroom. Back there." She indicated the half door. "Way at the back." She opened a gate in the counter.

"Would you phone for a cab for me while I wash up?" I asked.

"Are you going to Manhattan?"

"The Meadowmere Hilton at Kennedy," I said.

"I hear that's expensive but nice. I'll phone. It won't take long."

"Thanks," I said. "You're very kind."

The smile reappeared. "What are friends for?" she asked. She pointed to the sign. "My motto, right?"

I went through the doorway into the back of the store. The storeroom was surprisingly cavernous and dimly lighted. I found the toilet and turned on the light. A bottle of liquid soap stood on a shelf above a grimy basin.

As I washed my hands, I wondered what I really hoped to establish by examining the bill of lading for the Eagle Dagger. Dean Lockwood was unlikely to be waiting for me to track him down at the end of a postal trail. And if I found him, then what? What did I have to say to him after all these years?

But long journeys, the Chinese say, begin with a small step.

As I wiped my hands on a paper towel from the naked stack on the shelf, I heard an odd sound. It was like an automobile's gearbox being badly handled, a grating, ripping noise that froze me because the sound was terribly familiar. I had heard it long ago on a trip for *Pacific Currents* to Israel's Negev. It was the sound of an Uzi being fired on full automatic.

I ran from the bathroom into the warehouse area. There was no more sound from the storefront. At the door I pulled up short. I could see into the storefront. Cyndi Genovese lay on her back, head twisted to one side, her cheek against the baseboard. Red smeared the wall and the doorframe. Under the girl a pool of blood was spreading across the floor. The front of her dress was soaked in blood. Her upper body had been pulped by high-impact bullets.

Acting on instinct, I crashed into the room. A man wearing a ski mask crouched over another, who lay facedown on the floor. The man in the mask had laid the Uzi on the floor beside him. He was searching through the pockets of the second man's shredded raincoat. As I came into the room, I could see the startled eyes seeming to fill the holes in the ski mask. The room smelled of cordite and blood. He grabbed up his weapon, pointed it at me and pulled the trigger. Nothing happened. He cursed and went through the door.

At almost the same instant the storefront's window dissolved into shards and splinters. From a car stopped on the street outside came a spray of gunfire. The walls of the room exploded into shreds and pieces of wallboard, wood splinters and dust.

I threw myself onto the floor. Through the now-empty window frame I could see people running. The car door opened and slammed. Tires squealed on the wet pavement. The car sideswiped a light standard and sent it crashing to the ground. Then it was gone.

I looked around me. The storefront was an abattoir. The man on the floor—who must have been the messenger Cyndi had called for—lay unmoving. It was like a bad dream. My breathing was deep and regular, unreal in its steadiness. Cyndi Genovese's dress was bunched around her waist. Her stomach was streaked with blood. I knelt beside her, took off my raincoat and covered her with it. Ms. Cyndi Genovese. With the i in "Cyndi" dotted with a happy face. Goddamn. I looked around me, at the dead messenger, at the slaughtered girl. As people began to crowd into the wrecked storefront, I stood up and stared at the sign that rested, untouched, on the bullet-shattered counter. ON DUTY 2 SERVE U. Somehow I knew that all this had been meant for me. Oh, Christ, I thought. WHAT R FRIENDS 4?

7

"In hell, if there's any justice."

AT CONSIDERABLE COST to Dieter Langan and *Die Zeit*, I sat in the
first-class section of the Lufthansa 747 and stared, unseeing, at
the top of a high overcast extending all the way from the Cana-
dian Maritime Provinces across the top of the world to northern
Europe. I was red-eyed, angry at the Brooklyn police and even
angrier at myself for having brought disaster to that poor Brooklyn storefront. The stink of blood and cordite was still in my
nostrils. I couldn't get the Genovese girl out of my mind.

I could not explain exactly *how* I was responsible for what had
happened, but I knew that I was. The man killed at Tetrac was
identified by the police as the messenger Cyndi Genovese had
called for. The gunman in the ski mask had taken him for me. I
couldn't prove it, but my gut told me it was so.

The policeman who questioned me, Detective Delancey,
thought I was some sort of head case. "How could anyone possibly have known you were going to be in that place at that time,
Mr. Lockwood? And what would they have been looking for?"
When I mentioned the Eagle Dagger, I really lost my credibility.
"I realize you've been through a bad experience, Mr. Lockwood,
but you shouldn't take it all on yourself. These things happen,
too often, around here."

I asked him how he could be so damned calm about it when he had two homicides on his hands, and one of them a young girl.

"Look, Lockwood," he snapped, "don't tell me my business. Just be thankful you weren't in the front when the place was hit. They were after the messenger's load. He was a known mule. The girl was in the wrong place at the wrong time. It happens. You go on about your business. I had sixty gang killings on my desk. Now I got sixty-two. Count your blessings, Mr. Lockwood, and get the fuck out of here." Delancey was convinced that the crime was drug-related.

"Then what happened to his load? All the shooter carried away was his weapon."

"You can't be sure what you saw, Lockwood. You got rattled."

I offered to postpone my flight to Germany, but he said, "You don't have anything useful for us. You're not even an eyewitness; you didn't even see the messenger or the girl go down, did you? Can you identify the man in the ski mask?"

Of course, the answer to that was no. Delancey had seen my press credentials and made it clear that "journalist" was not the most popular occupation with the Brooklyn police.

They returned my raincoat. It still had a patch of Cyndi Genovese's blood on it. Then they escorted me out of the station house and into the squad car. I was back at the hotel by 2:00 A.M. —with the routine request in such circumstances to "get in touch" when I returned from Germany.

As I sat now in the airplane, still in a state of near shock, I tried to make some sense of it all. I had a feeling that all the events of the last few days were connected, but how?

Dean's note with the dagger—the more I thought about it, the more I believed that I was the means rather than the ends of whatever Dean Lockwood had in mind. Was it possible Dean didn't know the Colonel had died three years ago? That seemed unlikely. But I really didn't know my adoptive uncle all that well. Maybe it was his style—an assault on a dead man. His brother he envied.

But the pattern still lay fractured in my mind. Stein Davis had once warned Claire and me that Dean's reported success as a dealer in art objects had to be fraudulent. "Dean knows nothing about art of any sort," Stein said. "If he is making money, he's almost certain to be doing it illegally. Who knows who he is mixed up with in Europe?"

I thought immediately of the East Bloc intelligence services. Dean was the sort of man who would deal with them for money. Yet there was still something not right about that picture. The action in Brooklyn had been meant to kill, and it had. Brutally. That didn't jibe with my notions about Uncle Dean. The one certainty was that Dean *had* sent me the dagger. He had always been aware that my secret fear was that I was a *Lebensborn* child or something equally hateful.

I got up, walked to the toilet, let myself in and washed my face with cold water. I stared into the mirror. An ordinary man stared back. But blond, blue-eyed. One could easily imagine that man in a black uniform, wearing a cap with a death's-head device.

I returned to my seat, no nearer to making any sense of what had happened than before. Dean Lockwood's use of the Eagle Dagger was in character. He was such a sly, malicious man. He wanted to drive me, herd me along. But kill me? Yet the attack on Tetrac had been savagely violent and helter-skelter. The contrast was jarring—unless Dean had joined forces with someone. Someone who wasn't willing to wait patiently until I followed Dean's tortuous trail. Someone who wanted the dagger so badly that he—or they—would commit murder to retrieve it. Or perhaps they didn't want me to start digging into my past. The possibilities were too damn many.

The bar steward stopped at my seat and asked me if I wanted a drink. It was the wrong time of day, but I had one anyway. There was a leaden weight just under my ribs.

The odd thing was that there was no fear, no *feeling* of any kind. After my session in Colorado Springs, I had returned to my hotel gasping for breath and riddled with imagined pains and terrors. Twenty-four hours ago I would have lied to myself and claimed that I hadn't been afraid and that if I suffered another heart attack, I only wished it to be swift and conclusive.

That was bullshit, and for some reason I could admit it now. Seeing the dead girl and the messenger at Tetrac had impressed on me that there were no guarantees, none. Anyone can die at any time. My personal fear of extinction was gone. In its place was anger. Unfocused but very real.

I finished my drink, lay back in the seat and closed my eyes. I needed many things: information, good luck and persistence. But most of all I needed sleep. I closed my eyes, and amazingly, sleep came.

I woke up in afternoon twilight. The five-hundred-plus knots of the 747's eastward flight had truncated the day. Far below lay the misty green northern European countryside, a broad and fertile checkerboard of plowed earth and crop-bearing fields. I could see a smog-wreathed city far to the east but had no idea what it might be. I had no idea, in fact, of how long I had slept. I rang for a flight attendant.

A girl, as dark as Ershad and a lot prettier, appeared. She wore a caste mark on her forehead. Since reunification I had been reading stories about a rebirth of German fascism and racial prejudice. The media reported hate crimes on the rise, with skinhead neo-Nazis assaulting blacks and Middle Eastern-ers. But skinheads and neo-Nazis were not in charge of Luft-hansa. A black-skinned Indian flight attendant might be only a token, but she was a pretty one.

The girl said in a singsong voice like Dr. Ershad's, "We tried to wake you for dinner, Herr Lockwood. But you must have been very tired. May I bring you a sandwich and something to drink? We will be landing in Düsseldorf in less than an hour."

"Please. And a bottle of beer."

When the food came, it was some sort of delicious sausage on dark rye bread. The beer was the color of the flight attendant's eyes.

When Arminius slaughtered Quintilius Varus' three legions in a German forest almost two thousand years ago, he inadver-tently set in motion a train of events leading to, among other, weightier things, the frosty stein standing on my Lufthansa tray. So *something* good came of it all, I thought. It was what Claire liked to call the Law of Unintended Consequences.

There were fewer than a dozen passengers in first class. I

leaned over the empty window seat beside me and looked down at Germany. I was struck, as always, by the physical difference from the United States. Hectare for acre, Germany is overwhelmed by the mass and splendor of America. But Germany is a land that has husbanded its natural comeliness to an extent far exceeding any other European country, even France, with its lush Valley of the Rhône and lovely southern coast.

To mature in a land with so many magical scenes might well create a race of people imbued with a sense of their own superiority, I thought. Forests of pine and great oaks, mountains of stark and powerful presence, rivers as broad and swift as running oceans. All that, coupled with the achievements of German musicians, German scientists, German writers, poets, painters. It was as though the Almighty had created the Germans to provide the people of the earth with an example of the hubris, the arrogance and eventually the *Schrecklichkeit* to which mankind is heir.

Then, looking at the Indian stewardess so gracefully representing a German airline, I wondered if the Germans had not *finally* learned their bitter lesson. It was hard to know. The evidence was equivocal. Very.

The hotel American Express had booked me into was a new one. In fact, each time I've visited Düsseldorf I've stayed at a new hotel. They seem to pop up like mushrooms. My first, many years ago, was a place called the Park, which even then offered remarkable amenities. Later there had been Hiltons and Holiday Inns which had made me feel as though the city beyond the sealed windows were probably Dallas or Los Angeles. W. Olaf Stapledon, the Brit futurist, had predicted in the 1930s that the planet would eventually become totally Americanized. Even then he had seen world leadership slipping away from Britain to the transatlantic cousins, and he had hated it. But he had been an accurate prophet. Sixty years later the politically correct wisdom agreed with Stapledon. But I did not. True, my adopted country is remaking the world in its own image. But there are far worse models.

My hotel was the Schlossturmerhof, built on the eastern bank of the Rhine with windows overlooking the Schlossturm—the thirteenth-century remnant of an ancient castle that had survived the Allied bombings that had reduced most of Düsseldorf to rubble.

The hotel faced the Hofgarten, and there were other beautiful views of the Rhine as it curved and meandered through the heart of the city. It was a handsome building in the postmodern fashion, without the harshness of the Bauhaus style that Janice had despised, yet unmistakably German.

The offices of *Die Zeit* were on the west bank of the river, on Düsseldorfer Strasse near the docks, where much of the city's heavy industry was located. It was a ten-minute taxi ride from where I stood on the balcony of my room, but I didn't feel ready to face Dieter Langan and his questions.

As I stood in the darkening dusk, looking down at the barges on the river and the lights coming on across the city, I realized I had forgotten to call Stein Davis to ask about Dean Lockwood, as I had told Claire I would. A thing one learns immediately after a brush with mortality is that a missed telephone call or a failed appointment alarms people.

I picked up the telephone and dialed Stein Davis's office number. Stein answered.

"Stein, it's Brian."

"Brian, my God, where the hell are you? Are you all right?"

"I'm fine, Stein. I'm in Düsseldorf. I slept most of the way. Did Claire ask you about Uncle Dean?"

"She asked, but I have no information on Dean. The German police have lost track of him. Why do you care about that son of a bitch?"

"He returned a war souvenir he stole from the Colonel some years ago."

"That's out of character. He'd be more likely to sell it to you."

"No idea at all where he might be?"

"In hell, if there's any justice. But no, I'm sorry, Brian. I can't even guess."

"All right, thanks."

"Call Claire in Carmel, Brian. Elissa is with her for the weekend, and she's worried about you."

That surprised me. My daughter, Elissa, was a sweet young

woman, but she had never been any sort of daddy's girl. "I'll call," I said. "Take care, Stein. Remember me to Leah."

I hung up and thought about Stein's wife, Leah. She was a large, warm and expressive woman. Except for Miriam, she was the only truly Orthodox Jewish woman I had ever known. . . .

I guess I should go ahead here and tell about Miriam Halprin. Okay. I met her at Stanford when we were freshmen. I fell in love with her. It wasn't hard. She was sweet-tempered, pliant and sexy as hell. We made love in backseats. We talked about marriage. After graduation, of course. But when I told Miriam I was a German war orphan and not a blood Lockwood, she told her parents. And their reaction was swift. The Halprins had lost relatives in the Holocaust. They were good people, but the idea of their beautiful Miriam marrying a blond, blue-eyed *German*, conceived by God-knew-who in Nazi Germany, was more than they could handle.

Miriam was sent away to Israel to study at the Hebrew University, and the next time I saw her, two years later, she was Mrs. Gershon Agron and pregnant with her second child. I didn't meet another girl I cared about until my senior year. That girl was Reeder.

I went back inside and called Dieter Langan at his office. He answered with a brusque *"Langan hier."* Answering his own phone was Dieter's concession to *die Demokratie*.

"Dieter, it's Brian Lockwood."

"Lieber Gott, you finally called. Your sister has been trying to reach you since this morning."

"What is it? Is something wrong with Claire? Or Elissa?" After what had happened in Brooklyn, I was damned skittish.

"No, no. Frau Warner is all right. Actually it's your neighbor. You have an Indian neighbor in Carmel?"

"Professor Ershad?"

"That is the name. He has been injured. Listen. If there is anything I can do, please feel free to call on me. If I come to your hotel, are you free for supper?"

"Yes, sure."

"Where are you staying?"

"The Schlossturmerhof."

"I will be there in thirty minutes. You will want to call California now."

The moment I broke the connection, the telephone rang again. It was Claire. Using her uncommon common sense, she had figured I would have had my local Amexco office arrange my hotel reservations.

She sounded upset, and why not? She had driven with Elissa down to the cottage in Carmel, spent the night, and in the morning—both women hating to cook—they had driven to Carmel Valley for breakfast.

"When we came back, we found Professor Ershad in the garden. We thought he was dead, Bri, that's how bad he looked. We called the paramedics and had him taken to the emergency room at Carmel Valley Hospital. Bri, the cottage has been broken into and things scattered all over. It was awful—"

"Sis, are you and Elissa all right?"

"We're fine. I went to the hospital to see Professor Ershad, and he was awake enough to tell me he stopped by the cottage and looked in the window. There was a man inside, where he had no business to be, searching your things. He saw Professor Ershad looking in at him, and he went out and beat him."

"Why don't you go home, Claire?"

"I'm not going to be run off by some damned thief. Don't you worry. The police are driving by the house every half hour. They're upset, Bri. Things like this aren't supposed to happen in Carmel."

"Claire. *Go home.* Take Elissa with you."

"No. Ben is here now." There were words in the background; my daughter's voice. "Elissa wants to talk to you."

She came on the line sounding breathless. "Daddy? Are you all right? You didn't call me or Little Bri before you left. He's been worried, too." My son hated being called "Little Bri." Always had. It surprised me to hear Elissa reverting to the language of childhood. And I guess it surprised me some that my children were so worried about me. Reeder and I had raised Brian and Elissa to be independent, but Elissa's anxious voice made me wonder if we had not done them—and ourselves—an injustice.

"I'm fine, Lissa," I said, using her childhood nickname automatically. "I'm sorry I worried you. It was thoughtless of me."

"Yes, it was," she said firmly. "When I saw Mother, she said that you had 'a little episode.' Bri and I had to talk to Dr. Fry to get any real information. He says you're going to be fine but that it was no little episode. It was a real heart attack. We want you to take care of yourself. When are you coming home?"

"Lissa, I just got here."

"I know that. But how long are you going to stay?"

"A week. Maybe two."

"Do you have to?"

"Yes, I do."

"Well, *be careful.* I love you, Daddy." Abrupt and positive as her mother, but much warmer. "Aunt Claire wants to talk to you."

"I love you too, Lissa," I said. "Very much."

"Good-bye, Daddy. Here's Aunt Claire."

"Pay attention to your daughter," Claire said. "I have half a notion to send Ben after you and bring you home."

I closed my eyes and took a long breath. I was not even tempted to tell Claire about what happened in Brooklyn. Knowing her, she would hear of it soon enough. I asked, "Is anything missing?"

"Not from the house, Bri. There's never been anything worth stealing here. But the Colonel's things arrived this afternoon. Could someone have been looking for something of his?"

"Claire, call the sergeant major and have him put the things back in storage until I get back."

"No such thing, Bri. I've started unpacking the crate already. Don't worry about us. The police are watching."

I sat back on the bed and stared at the night beyond the windows. It was near noon in Carmel, not the time for nightmares. I wondered if Ershad would agree with me?

"Claire," I said, "please tell Edmund how sorry I am and that we'll do everything possible to make it right."

It seemed the professor's "observations" had finally earned him a beating. Was it from a man on the berm? Again, the act was so brutal and stupid that one had to wonder what sort of personality we were dealing with here. Ershad was a wisp of a man. He might have been killed.

Two attacks now. One brutal. One murderous.

I looked across the room at my open carry-on bag. Wrapped in its silk sash, in the bottom of the bag, lay the Eagle Dagger. Was that the cause of all this?

"Claire, I'd feel better if you and Lissa went back to Woodside."

"Bri, we don't get run off so easy. Elissa is going back to Santa Barbara tomorrow. But Ben and I are staying here."

And that was it with Claire.

I had no sooner hung up than the desk called to tell me that Herr Langan had arrived and was waiting for me in the bar.

8

A man for our time.

I FIRST ENCOUNTERED Dieter Langan while doing a series on the West German Green Party in 1982. Stan Diskant, flush with the fat advertising revenues of the early Reagan years, had sent me to Germany as a special correspondent. It was Stan's single attempt to develop a genuine international section for *Pacific Currents*. It failed to become a regular part of the magazine because our readers preferred to read about the wicked doings of Big Oil off our own California coast. The tantrums of European Greens left them indifferent, and Stan was fearful that the advertisers would abandon us. There was little chance of that. American industry's advertising departments seem to take a strange delight in being the hand that gets bitten. But the magazine money was Stan's, and he made the decisions.

Dieter, though, remained a distant friend. He had been a charter member of the Greens, but by the time the eighties rolled around, he had had enough. He had come into his inheritance and was considering purchasing *Die Zeit*. The Greens' agenda no longer appealed to him. Actually he was very like our typical *Pacific Currents* reader. He was a precursor and had an unerring instinct for being politically correct. Like his father, Klaus Langan (an Austrian Catholic industrialist with a very shadowy history), Dieter was a flexible man. Over several bottles of wine, he had once paraphrased George Bernard Shaw: "There is nothing so bad or so good that you will not find a New German doing it, but he does everything on principle. I am a New German, Brian." Shaw had been speaking of Englishmen. Dieter had appropriated the axiom without attribution. On principle, of course. He had been, in turn, a student radical, a Red Army Faction sympathizer, a Marxist, a Green and, now, an affirming Roman Catholic. A half-dozen years after the death of his father, Dieter Langan had returned to the faith of his family. "I gave up Marxism when I came back to the church," he wrote me at the time. "Papa's will insisted on it." He had just returned from a visit to Managua and added wistfully, "Nicaraguans can be both, but a German can't be a Marxist and a Roman Catholic. It outrages our Hegelian principles." It would certainly have outraged old Klaus Langan.

Dieter was unusually outspoken with me. He relished impressing Americans, and I was the sort of American he most liked to impress. I spoke his language; I accepted his political shifts without being—that Woodstock of a word—*judgmental*.

Dieter had been genuinely distressed, I think, by what had happened to me at *Pacific Currents* and his offer of a job had been sincere. But I had badly upset matters by having a heart attack. Dieter hated sickness. His father had become an invalid in the last years of his life and had used his illness to badger Dieter. Dieter had cause enough to dislike him. Klaus Langan was a tyrant, with connections to the underworld and to the Nazi old guard.

Dieter's principles transmogrified his filial animosity into a phobia of illness. He shied away from anyone who became unwell, and my five days in Stanford Hospital withered whatever enthusiasm he had for hiring me. At least he had the grace to feel guilty about it.

Klaus Langan had been suspected of being a Nazi enthusiast—hardly surprising, since there were nearly eighty million Nazi enthusiasts in Germany in 1939. The Langan case, pushed hard by the Soviet occupiers and the German Communists, never reached the denazification courts. The story was that old Klaus had friends in Washington and London.

Dieter's forays into leftist causes were calculated to allay the suspicions of his countrymen. His affinity for radical politics gave him the aura of what passed for liberalism in the sixties and seventies. He intended that it should. By the time he left the Green Party, he had acquired useful credentials with the left-wing establishment of West Germany. And don't think for a moment that there was no establishment among the West German leftist intellectuals. After the Wall came down and Germany reunified, they temporarily stopped making excuses for the Baader-Meinhof terrorists or the Red Army Faction. But given a resurgence of the murder gangs that had terrorized Germany (in the name of the North Vietnamese, the poor, the Palestinians and the Shia Muslims among others), German intellectuals would quickly fall back into line. It was a source of many near-acrimonious discussions between Dieter and me. Of course, Dieter could argue either side with equal conviction.

The end of the East German state and the Soviet Union had interrupted the collegial relations between the Baader-Meinhof and Red Army Faction terrorists and the Stasi and, through the Stasi, the KGB. But the interruption was only temporary. I never doubted that a German failure to digest East Germany or a successful coup in the Commonwealth of Independent States would cause the old love affair with Marxist-Leninism to reach a flashpoint and reconsummate.

At the moment, reunified Germany had a spate of *right*-wingers to deal with. Neo-Nazis and yobbos of every description were attacking tourists and the foreign workers West Germany had imported by the thousands during the years of the Economic Miracle. Was there, I wondered, a gene for political violence in the German genotype?

As I walked into the Schlossturmerhof dining room, I noted that Dieter now dressed like a trendy seminarian. His hair was long and well styled, and since I had last seen him, he had grown a handsome beard. It gave his dark and deep-set eyes and narrow face a Dominican look. He wore tight black American jeans and an expensive black linen jacket with the sleeves pushed up to display wrist chains and a gold Rolex. There were more gold chains around his neck, nesting in his chest hair above an open black silk shirt. Known and deferred to everywhere in his home city, Dieter already had a bottle of Rhenish chilling in a polished pewter bucket, and caviar and enhancements waiting on a mound of shaved ice on top of a crystal platter. His appetites were not those of a Dominican seminarian. They never had been.

He got up from the table and came across the room to greet me with such warmth I felt ashamed of what I had been thinking about him.

"Brian, dear fellow," he said. He spoke English learned at Cambridge long before his Green Party days. "Did you reach Frau Warner? Is she all right?"

"She is," I said. "But Edmund Ershad is in the hospital."

"Your Indian academic friend? But wait, let's have some wine first. Sit, please. Then you can tell me what happened." He poured me a glass of wine that looked like liquid amber.

He drank from his glass and looked to me for approval of the wine. I was not in the mood for niceties.

"Welcome to Germany, old comrade," he said. "Now, tell me. Frau Warner said there had been an incident at your cottage. What happened?"

"Professor Ershad happened to come by and discovered someone in my house. The man came out and attacked him, put him in the hospital."

"But that's terrible. Why, Brian?"

I took the Eagle Dagger from my pocket and put it on the table. "Maybe for this." It didn't fit, but it was the only excuse I could think of.

Dieter's eyes glittered. He loved pretty things. *"Ein Adler Dolch,"* he said. He lifted it reverently. "A beautiful one. To whom does it belong?"

"To me, I think. Two people may be dead because I'm chasing an *Adler* ghost," I said.

"I don't understand. I thought your neighbor was only injured."

I drank some of the wine and drew in a deep breath. "Edmund Ershad was only assaulted," I said. And I told him about the Tetrac affair.

"The man in the ski mask was searching the messenger," I said at the end. "I think he mistook the messenger for me."

"*Lieber Gott*, Brian. And you just out of the hospital. What are the authorities doing about it?"

"I have been out of the hospital for seven weeks, Dieter," I said irritably. The way everyone focused on my illness was natural enough, but it was beginning to grate. I had been on the move ever since leaving California, and I felt as though I were coming down with flu. I hadn't the time to be sick. My momentary weakness in Colorado Springs was the last concession to bad health I intended to make.

"But what is this about an eagle ghost?"

I unsheathed the dagger and showed him the name engraved on the blade. "My uncle Dean sent me this in the mail. He suggests I follow that name. Does it mean anything to you?"

"No. But we can try to find out."

Suddenly I felt very tired.

"What am I thinking about?" Dieter said. "You've had no supper. Let's eat and then talk. At the office." His tone changed. "You really look quite well, Brian, considering that terrible business in Brooklyn."

"Did I say Brooklyn?"

"It was on an international news broadcast, Brian. I didn't want to upset you by mentioning it."

"Don't patronize me, Dieter. A young girl and an innocent man were killed yesterday, and I don't know why. Now Ershad. And before I left home, there was some damned man watching my house. Probably one of the East German goons marooned in California after the reunification. I saw enough of them when they were following me every place I went. They aren't hard to spot. The Stasi favors Aryan prototypes."

"Are you sure the man you saw was Stasi?" He seemed genuinely worried.

"Jesus Christ. Of course I'm not sure. It just seems right. Up to the day the Wall came down, the East Germans were operating out of the KGB's pocket from the Soviet Consulate in San Francisco. Then, when the August coup self-destructed and everything unraveled for the USSR, the Stasi hoods were all on their own. You must remember the trouble they gave Stan Diskant and me after we published those articles about their industrial espionage. I know that Stan told you about it, the bodyguards and the rest of it. There are at least fifty of them for hire in Northern California. I know because I interviewed some of them for a follow-up piece that never got written. They're there, all right, looking for work. Their kind of work."

Dieter toyed with a fork. "Who do you think might have hired Stasi? Your uncle?"

"What do you know about my uncle, Dieter? And have you heard of Stossen? Sieg von Stossen, who seems to have been a genuine Nazi war criminal."

Dieter said quietly, "Not here, Brian. After dinner."

He glanced around the almost empty dining room. "This is not such a good place to discuss such things."

"I'm not hungry," I told him. Until a moment before, I had been, but I'd lost my appetite thinking about Cyndi Genovese and the messenger. I had never known his name, but I would never forget his blood-spattered face.

I looked across the chrome and teakwood room at the rank of waiters and busboys lined up like Potsdamer guardsmen near the maître d'hôtel. They gave me a twinge of apprehension. A few short lifetimes ago, did someone sit over wine and caviar in a place like this one and see almost exactly what I was seeing, while the first National Socialist chants, hysterical with hate, were heard in Turmstrasse?

Stop it, I told myself. There had been no place like this in the Düsseldorf of the 1930s. And German waiters and wine stewards had been lining up like guardsmen since Bismarck's day. I said to Dieter, "The Brooklyn police think I'm imagining things. They want ordinary explanations. Familiar ones. Is that what you expect?"

Dieter looked at me. "Well, Brian, I would certainly prefer it. You make me feel damn uneasy, my friend."

After our meal we drove back across the river in Dieter's brand-new BMW 730i. The car still had the showroom smell of new leather seats and fresh lacquer. It seemed to whisper its way across the Achenerbrücke. The night had grown dark and starless, and only a few city lights reflected from the swiftly moving Rhine.

"*Der Stern* sent a Jewish reporter here last May to investigate some Stasi people who had set up an enterprise on the river docks," Dieter said, guiding the BMW across the old steel cantilever spanning the river and the dock area. "He was found washed ashore twenty kilometers downriver at Duisburg. I don't want you to have any illusion about the kind of people you may have to deal with if you insist on bothering the Stasi. They had their fingers into everything in the East until reunification. And on this side of the Wall what they couldn't steal, they bought. Now the USSR is the CIS and pure in heart. The Stasi are desperate. Instead of buying, they sell. But if you bother them, well, they can hurt you."

I changed the subject. "Tell me what you know about Dean Lockwood. You investigated him—didn't you?—when you thought I might come to work for you."

"Let's wait until we get to the office, Brian."

"What the hell happened here, Dieter?"

"There have been . . . inquiries about you."

"How could anyone know I was coming here?"

"How, indeed? Well, if you think about it, there are many ways."

"Who inquired?"

"I am still trying to find out. I have my sources, Brian, but they take time and they're not neat."

I looked at him. I knew about the Greens, the Communists and the terrorist connections. Probably some underworld connections dating back to his father's time.

"You should be very careful, Brian."

I looked through the raked windshield at the deserted street. *Die Zeit*'s plant and offices were in Düsseldorferstrasse, an area only recently being (as Californians say) *gentrified*. To the right lay the river, dark and powerful. "Don't dramatize, Dieter," I said.

"This is not California, Brian. And it is not the Germany you remember from a few years ago. Without the Cold War, everything is different."

Dieter stopped the car in front of a dark, flashily remodeled building. "The fellow from *Der Stern* didn't believe what I told him. He believed the Stasi were running weapons to the PLO, and he was determined to expose them. But *Stern* never got enough of a story to print. They didn't get their reporter back either."

"And were they smuggling arms?"

"Why ask me, Brian? Gun smuggling is illegal." Dieter opened the car door. "I just want to discourage you. If you are on some sort of personal mission, you will have to go east. And the eastern part of Germany is—how do you Americans say it? —Indian country. Fort Apache."

"You don't sound very happy at getting half your country back."

Dieter shook his head. "We took on far more than we knew when we greeted the breaking of the Wall with such hosannas."

He walked around the car, and I followed him to the dimly lighted entrance. A watchman came to peer through the inch-thick glass door and bob his head at Dieter.

The old man unlocked and swung the door open. "Good evening, Grau," Dieter said. "Has everyone gone home?"

"Everyone but me, Herr Langan."

Dieter smiled at the watchman with a kind of distant camaraderie. The feudal system is alive and well in Germany. With the steady departure of American troops, the imposed egalitarianism was disappearing. With the threat from the east gone, many Germans could not be rid of the American military presence fast enough. Soon a half century of American occupation, garrisoning and cohabitation would be forgotten.

"We will make some calls," Dieter said. "We shall see." We left the steel, glass and marble foyer by way of a private elevator operated by Dieter's personal key.

The upstairs hallway of the executive suite was deeply carpeted. There were paintings on the walls, good ones. Dieter spent old Klaus's money wisely. I wondered if *Die Zeit* was a money-maker. If not, it would be. Dieter Langan had his faults, but a lack of money sense wasn't one of them.

There was a night-light on in Dieter's office, which was a huge room on the top story. A long window curved around a corner of the building to overlook the riverine dock area, where barges were waiting to be unloaded. "Look down there, Brian," Dieter said.

There was no activity whatsoever on the quays. A watchman stood slackly by the gate.

"At what, Dieter?"

"At what is wrong with Germany. The stevedore crews are supposed to be unloading those barges. We have a shipment of paper aboard. What do you see?"

"Nothing," I said.

"Precisely. Behold the new Weimar. The Russians have infected us with the Slavic virus. How do they like to put it? 'The state pretends to pay us, and we pretend to work.' Maybe the Stasi are right. Performance for pay. Real pay. They are the only true capitalists east of Berlin. Are you ready for that?"

Without waiting for a reply, he went to a built-in bar and found schnapps and glasses, poured and handed me a drink. Then he settled behind his large empty desk and motioned for me to take a deep leather chair across from him. "May I see the dagger again?" he asked.

I put down my glass and slid the Eagle Dagger across the desk. He drew the weapon from the scabbard and ran a fingertip over the decorations etched into the steel.

I told him what I had learned at the Air Force Records Center about Stossen.

He resheathed the weapon and pushed it back across the table. "Maybe I can help."

He unlocked a drawer to withdraw a telephone. "This may take some time. My friends in the East are not always immediately available." He dialed a number, pressed the speakerphone button and laid the handset in its cradle.

"Von Stossen is an East Prussian surname," he said. "The area on the Polish border is full of similar ones. *Stoss, Stossen, Halm. Speer, Lanze, Schild.* Stroke, thrust, blade, spear, lance, shield. There is usually a 'von' but not always. In the Nazi time it didn't always pay to announce yourself an aristocrat." He drained his glass and poured another. In this light his eyes looked black, hooded. "There is a data base in Leipzig and another in Stettin. The Stettin facility is the best. Leipzig is in the hands of people who would prefer to forget the past." He regarded me curiously. "You don't want the Leipzig information; it has been corrupted to bury old Nazi records. But the Stettin data is probably for sale. Have you any money?"

"Some."

"Stettin pretends to be Polish, but in actual fact, it is Prussian. At heart it always has been. The records there were gathered by the Stasi, of course, with Soviet help. West German intelligence is after it, and they'll get it, too, when the price is agreed on. But we might tap into it before that happens. When Germans negotiate with one another, matters always go slowly. Forgive me, but I still think in terms of East and West. It will take some time for that to change. Before Polish liberation, Stettin was a joint venture of the Stasi and the KGB. No Poles involved, or allowed."

"How is that possible?"

"Simple. A reader of history like yourself should remember that in the early days of the Cold War the chief of the Polish general staff was a Russian marshal. His name was Rokossovsky. He said he was Polish, he wore Polish uniforms and everyone behaved as though he were, in fact, Polish. But that did not make him any less Russian. The Soviets inherited the Great Russian tradition of the Potemkin Village. Nothing has really changed. They are masters of *maskirovka*. Stettin Center is supposed to be Polish, property of a democratic state. But the armpit stink of the KGB is all over it."

"If the Russians still run it, they'll remember Stossen."

"The First Chief Directorate researchers have always been as keen for keeping records as we Germans. It's their old Communist sense of inevitability. They have never stopped believing that the dialectic of history will prove that they were right all along. Communists collect dossiers. They can't help themselves. It's a compulsion. At Stettin Center the staff is still Communist and Russian, no matter how often they call themselves democrats and Poles. Of course, they are Polish enough to do business. It's what's called converting to a market economy. If Stossen was important, his records will be there, and Stettin Center will sell them."

"Stossen died nearly fifty years ago," I said.

Dieter refilled our glasses. "The way the Nazis were about Jews, the Communists are about Nazis. They never throw records away. Well, why not? Stalin trusted Hitler, and see what it got him. Whatever there is to know, they know. And they store it all away to be used some rainy day. I would guess that if you wanted to know about the strange sexual habits of the Dalai Lama, the East Germans would have a dossier. Are you determined to follow this search to the end?"

"Yes," I told him firmly.

"Then let *Die Zeit* unlock some doors for you. It's the least we can do." When a masculine voice came from the speakerphone, Dieter picked up the handset, pressed the privacy button and began to speak softly into the telephone in Polish.

After a time he stopped speaking, listened, spoke again. He cupped a hand over the mouthpiece and said, "We had no idea how bad things were in the GDR. *Lieber Gott,* it's a cesspool. The land reeks. What a fine irony. Bonn was years trying to climb into bed with the East, and when it finally happened, it is near to bankrupting us. But we go ahead, even bribing the Russians to leave. We are paying, but who is the whore?"

"I thought reunification was something Germans longed for."

Dieter muttered something Polish into the telephone, then looked at me. "We longed for it, yes. But didn't some clever English homosexual once say, 'When the gods wish to punish us, they answer our prayers'?"

He loosed a torrent of suddenly angry Polish into the telephone, changed to German and said sharply, "Find out, then, you idiot. Do it now. I will wait." Aside, he muttered, "Damn Poles." He frowned. "Why did Dean Lockwood send you the dagger?"

"I'm not sure. That's part of what I'm after."

"I understand."

"Do you?"

"You think he may have discovered something about your . . . origins."

I nodded. Not quite knowing what to say.

"This Dean Lockwood, he made your adoptive father's life hell, I believe?"

"The next thing to it."

"Unprincipled," Dieter said. "A perfect man for our time."

The telephone in his hand came to life, and a rapid conversation began that went on for several minutes before shifting again to German. Dieter once more covered the mouthpiece and said in a whisper, "How much can you pay?"

"For what? Spell it out."

Into the telephone he said, in German so that I would understand, "The client wants to know what you are offering."

After a pause Dieter said, "A dossier on the von Stossen family. And their location."

"Which Stossens?" I asked, my heart beating harder.

Presently, he again covered the mouthpiece and said: "Helmuth and Freya von Stossen. You'll be given the dossier and instructions on how to find them. Do you *want* to find them?"

"What's the price?"

"Make an offer. These are new capitalists."

My mouth felt very dry, the way it used to feel when Fräulein Clef was intent on dousing me with her bitter remedies. Now, how in hell did I remember that? I wondered. I was a child, a squalling, diapered child—

"Five hundred," I said.

"Not enough. Try a thousand. And they want dollars."

"All right. If the information is good."

Dieter transmitted my acceptance and began writing on a notepad. He hung up, ripped the top sheet from the pad and handed it to me, then tore off four more sheets and burned them in a spotless bronze ashtray.

"I almost envy you your uncle, Dean Lockwood, Brian," Dieter said, replacing the telephone in its locked desk drawer. His eyes were bright. "The man has set you to searching for your German roots." Dieter always seemed to know more about a subject than one expected.

He leaned back in his fancy chair, his manicured fingers steepled before pursed lips, Dieter playing Dominican Inquisitor.

"My German roots, as you put it, Dieter, have never been anything but a pain in the ass to me," I said.

"Yes, well, ah, your circumstances are unique . . . being that it was an American colonel who adopted you."

Our conversation languished. I had received much of the information I required, and I had learned whom to approach for more. I didn't want to discuss Marianna Clef with Dieter. She had to be an old woman now, and I didn't want her being troubled with interviews about bits and pieces of the Cold War.

As Dieter drove me back to the Schlossturmerhof, he said, "We never talked about your position with *Die Zeit.*"

"We don't have to, Dieter. I got the message before I came here."

"We have to tailor my offer to your capabilities," he said.

"You've been a great help, and I appreciate it. But I'll decide what my capabilities are. Let's leave it there for now."

"Brian, this is my country. I'll help if I can. I've shown you that. But this is all wrong for you. It's dangerous, believe me."

What he said was probably true, but I was in the grip of an obsession. We drove in silence to the Schlossturmerhof. Dieter stopped the car at the entrance. "Politeness aside," he said, "you look *scheissig.* At least take a day or two to rest. The Stossens have been around since the Paleolithic. They can wait a few days more."

I hadn't told him I intended to go east by way of Nuremberg, stopping to question Marianna Clef. There was no reason to tell him. I didn't need to add to his store of fungible information. I got out of the BMW. "Thanks for everything, Dieter. I'll be in touch."

As the BMW pulled away into the late-night traffic, it began to rain and I shivered with sudden cold.

9

"A no one's child."

IT IS ONLY a short flight from Düsseldorf to Nuremberg, thirty
minutes at most. But it is also like stepping backward in time.
Nuremberg bears a heavy burden of history. It is a city of bloody
memories.

In the thirteenth century the most skilled armorers in the
world worked in Nuremberg, creating for the nobility magnifi-
cent knightly weapons; for commoners they constructed such
machines as the Maiden with her impaling spikes, the Boot and
the Wedge, the Testicle Crusher.

Witches and warlocks did black magic in the Lorenzer Wald,
and no town in old Germany responded with more fervor to the
Protestant Reformation, exploding time and again in joyous
anti-Semitism and bloody pogrom.

It was in Nuremberg that Adolf Hitler chose to build the
stadium where the party rallies were staged, Nuremberg where
the Nazis shed their porcine Munich beer hall persona and
joined the dark current of German history.

Where else could the victorious Allies more appropriately
have staged the tribunals to punish the Third Reich? I remembered my leaving this place when Fräulein Clef put a shivering,
frightened child aboard an Air Transport Command plane

loaded with American military dependents headed for New York. Between then and now Nuremberg had become for me a bad dream. The silent woods, the white meadow and the icy river of my nightmare were here, in this strangely alien city.

I taxied in from the airport on the Erlanger autobahn to the city center and registered at still another hotel that smelled of paint and newness, the Lorenzerhof on Regensburgerstrasse. From my room I could see stands of young trees growing in the *Wald*. At the end of the war Nuremberg had been a shattered mound of wreckage, more tel than city. The Nazis had turned the *Wald* into a labyrinth of trenches and bunkers to be garrisoned by the old men and children of the Volkssturm. The suicidal defense demanded by Hitler never took place. When defeat finally came, Nuremberg went supine, husbanding what resources remained on the banks of the wreckage-choked Rhine-Main-Danube Canal.

Now the Lorenzer Wald was a beautiful forest of pine and aspen and birch. There had been a light snowfall earlier in the day, and the winter-nude deciduous trees made dark, spidery patterns against the snowy ground, accenting the heavy green of the pines.

It was noon when I arrived in Nuremberg. I had the address Allan Cobb had given me as Fräulein Clef's last address; it was in Sandruth Allee just off Kohlenhofstrasse, a district where the city map I found in the wardrobe showed more railroad lines than streets.

I ordered some coffee and considered my options. Would Marianna Clef remember me? Uncle Dean seemed to think she would.

I drank my coffee, stared out the window at the city. A cold front had moved in over the Franconian plain. The temperature, the concierge told me, had dropped nearly ten degrees since the morning. "I hope you have brought warm clothing, sir. It gets quite cold in Nuremberg."

It was already cold in Nuremberg. The television news reader warned about ice on the roads by evening. And there would be ice on the Rhine-Main-Danube Canal. I was reluctant to wear my raincoat, which was still stained with Cyndi Genovese's blood. I packed it away and went downstairs to a new arcade where I found a clothing store and bought a gray loden cloth duffle coat. The clerk informed me that the Germans make the best loden cloth in the world and dared me to disagree.

A churning diesel Mercedes taxi deposited me in the cobbled street before 14 Sandruth Allee and trundled away in the direction of Kohlenhofstrasse. I stood on the street in snow turning to muddy wetness.

I hunched in my new coat. Loden is very German, nearly impervious to rain and snow. It is like thick felt, a sturdy barrier between wind and wearer, but it's an unfriendly cloth. It adamantly refuses to shape itself to the person it clothes. So far and no farther, it seems to say. I will keep you warm but I make no concession beyond that. I will not make you comfortable.

I wondered what was getting into me, arguing with the coat on my back.

I looked up and down the narrow street, which was closed in by walls and facades that shut off the thin sunlight trying to break through the overcast. The building the taxi had left me in front of appeared to have been part of a larger structure at one time. In this district of Nuremberg there were warehouses that had partially survived the saturation bombings of a generation ago and had been converted to private dwellings. Everything standing bore some scars of the war.

In this place, when one spoke of the War, it had only one meaning. Even years after the last bombs had spilled out of the Forts and Liberators and Lancasters, the Nurembergers remembered.

At Number 14 there was a narrow-shouldered door of heavy wood, very old and thick with numberless coats of black paint and varnish. Everything around me bore the marks of age or destruction.

Down the street a pair of dark-skinned children stood watching me. They looked part of another landscape, another place, as I suppose they were. This part of Nuremberg was open to guest workers and their families. Their un-German families. The children watched me.

I went up the steps to the door of Number 14 and worked the bellpull. I could hear it ringing inside, but there was no immediate response.

The children had sidled closer. I asked them, "Is this where Fräulein Clef lives?" They turned and ran off without looking back. The wind blew litter along the narrow street. The sky had lost any semblance of blue as the cold closed in. A stray snowflake fell onto my cheek and melted there.

I heard the door open behind me. I turned, prepared to see an aged Marianna Clef. Instead, I saw a young girl with a short straight nose, a smudge on her cheek, uncombed auburn hair and curious green eyes. *"Ja? Was gibt?"*

"Your pardon," I said in German. "Is Fräulein Clef home?"
"Was?"

"Marianna Clef. Have I come to the wrong place?"

The curling, icy wind pressed the blouse she wore against her. There was nothing under it. Her nipples showed dark and erect under the thin cloth.

"Come in," she said abruptly. "Come. It's freezing out here."

I followed her into a dark hallway. The flat was cold, musty, with that smell of antiquity existing only in rooms where old people have lived for a long time, their personalities somehow rubbing off on the walls year after year. You rarely encounter such places in the United States, and never in California. There were lights in the rear. "You did say Fräulein Clef?" the girl asked.

"Yes. Does she still live here?"

The girl looked at me. "Who are you, please?"

"My name is Brian Lockwood."

She studied me, her hips tilted, one sandaled foot extended, resting on a heel. I don't know why, except that I was lonely and had been for a good long while, but I found her appealing. Very. *"Lieber Gott,"* she breathed, "I have heard about the Lockwoods ever since I was a child. Come into the back, Herr Lockwood. There is a fire in the kitchen stove."

I followed her down the unlighted hall, past a narrow stairway, through an empty room and into a kitchen. The floor was cluttered with packing boxes, but everything was neat and clean. I imagined I smelled the astringent odor of the cleaning soap Fräulein Marianna used all those years ago.

"Do you live here, Fräulein?"

"Only temporarily," she said. She looked at me curiously. "You are still quite young."

I didn't know what to say to that, so I asked again after Marianna Clef.

"I'm sorry," she said. "You must think I am very stupid. I should have said right away. Fräulein Clef died in September. She was my grandmother. I am here collecting my things."

Anticlimax, I thought. Did Dean know Marianna Clef was dead? If so, what had he hoped to prove by guiding me here?

"Mutti always said you would come visit her one day," the girl said.

"I'm sorry to be too late."

"Don't trouble yourself, Herr Lockwood. Mutti lived comfortably. Thanks to your family. Your father provided for her. I know this place does not look grand, but it would have given a better impression if you had arrived before I sent all the furniture into storage." She had shifted easily into English.

"You are—" I racked my brain for the name of Marianna Clef's rarely seen child.

"Ursula's daughter. My name is Annaliese Rykova." She eyed me as though her opinion of me would be determined by my reaction to her Russian surname. "Rykova was not my mother's married name. She had none." She tilted her head with a touch of defiance. "Not that it makes a difference now, but I was married to a Russian soldier."

"Well, you speak English very well," I said.

"Yes, also Russian and Polish. I have a big talent for languages."

That may well have been true, but it was so ingenuous, so childishly boastful that I had to smile.

She smiled back, and it transformed her face. "I really can speak Russian and Polish. Some Czech and Turkish, too."

She indicated one of the chairs at the kitchen table. "I forget my manners. I have been among Russians too long. Please, sit down. I have no coffee, but there is schnapps. Americans like schnapps."

"Do they?"

"The ones I know do."

I sat and, warmed now by the fire in the hearth, loosened my coat.

Annaliese Rykova was reaching into a high cabinet for the liquor, a movement that defined the muscles in her calves and the backs of her thighs and made me feel distinctly uneasy. She couldn't be much older than my daughter, yet the backs of her thighs and the indentations behind her knees were very erotic to me. When she collected the bottle and turned, a knowing expression flickered across her face. Or was I imagining it?

I hadn't said I wanted schnapps, but I accepted the glass she poured for me. "Ursula," I said. "What's become of her?"

"Dead." Annaliese sipped at her glass. "Years ago. Mutti Clef was all I had." It was a statement that under different circumstances could have been mistaken as a pitch for some pity. Clearly, though, it was nothing of the sort. Annaliese Rykova had pretty obviously lived a lot in a short time.

She looked at me intently. "Are you rich, Herr Lockwood? Mutti always said the Lockwoods were rich. May I call you Brian?"

The quick switch from intrusive to ingenuous reminded me how young she really was. "Not all Lockwoods are rich," I said. "And yes, you certainly may call me Brian." Suddenly it seemed very natural and easy. Reeder had always said I was a pushover for pretty young girls.

"Brian. I like that name." Once again that smile. "I am sorry you are not rich, though."

"So am I, Annaliese," I said solemnly.

I looked around the room. There was nothing young here. It was an old woman's kitchen. I could imagine Marianna Clef living here, but not Annaliese Rykova. "Where is your home?" I asked her.

"In Riesa. On the Elbe. There used to be a Russian garrison there. My husband was a tank commander."

"I lived," "used to be," "my husband was . . ." All past

tense. What had happened to her life while the USSR came apart?

"Where is your husband now?" I asked.

"In Russia, I suppose. Or dead. Who cares? I was away on a visit to the West when the garrison went east. He left me nothing. Not even a note. He was not a good man." She shrugged and sipped the last of the schnapps in her glass. "I shouldn't blame him. He was afraid. At the end they all were." Again she smiled, but this time it seemed brittle. "You should have seen the base after they ran away. It was as though pigs had lived there. It all happened so quickly. They were not that way in the beginning."

"I'm sorry—"

"Why? It doesn't matter. For years we *Ossis* knew it would end like this. It's the *Wessis* who got a shock when the Wall came down. More schnapps?"

I let her fill my glass. "Did Fräulein Clef leave you anything?"

She shook her head. "Only the furniture. No money. What she had, she willed away to a second cousin in Hanover. She was very angry with me when I married a Russian. She hated them. She said they were pigs, rapists and murderers. Was it like that in the old war? In school in the Democratic Republic we were never taught anything bad about the Russians."

"Yes," I said. "It was like that."

"Poor Mutti. She was not a nice person," Annaliese said. "Perhaps that is why. Was she good to you?"

I shook my head, remembering. "No."

"She said the Russians killed a woman she loved. She would not say who it was or why they killed her. But she never forgave them for it." She sighed theatrically. "It was all very long ago."

"Yes," I said. "Very long ago."

"Why are you in Germany, Brian?"

"I'm doing research for a news story." It seemed enough of an explanation for now.

"You are a journalist? I have never known one. It is a grand profession." She sat with her knees lifted, showing me the inner side of her thighs.

"No," I said. "It really isn't."

"But it *is* a profession of importance. Where are you going to do this research?"

"In the East. Around Stettin, I think. I'll have to see how it goes." A headache was growing behind my eyes. My back felt clammy.

"You don't speak Polish, do you?" The green eyes were alert and anxious. The eyes of a girl with no place to go and few prospects. I could almost hear my sister, Claire, telling me: *"Slowly, Bri. Go slowly."*

"No," I said. "I don't speak Polish."

"You should if you are going east." She stood up. "I am hungry. Are you? I would give you something here, but the cupboard is empty."

I remembered a couplet of Rainer Maria Rilke's:

> *Ein Niemandskind, danz arm und bar*
> *und ich kann dir nicht sagen wie.*

The lines translate this way: *"A no one's child—I cannot say how or why—but alone in poverty."*

It also made me think of Cyndi Genovese at Tetrac. Such children grow clever. Or if they are unlucky, they die.

10

A clump of black willows.

WE SAT AT A sidewalk café, shielded from the cold wind by banks of electric heating elements in the overhanging canopy. Annaliese had eaten well, *Nürnberger rostbratwurst* with sauerkraut washed down with draft beer. A German meal for a German girl. I had little appetite. I was tired and felt feverish but strangely alert. As bad as I felt, I was enjoying Annaliese Rykova. It had been a long time since I'd shared a meal, or anything else, with anyone so young and attractive.

In a perverse sort of way she reminded me of Miriam Halprin. I say perverse because I wondered how Annaliese would like to be told that she reminded me of my lost nineteen-year-old Jewish love. What I knew about the new Germany made me question how much like the old Germany it still was. Still, Annaliese was a New German, a member of a generation presumably taught to be ashamed of the Nazi past.

We were on the St. Sebaldus side of the Pegnitz River in a part of the old town redolent of a history far older than any memory of the National Socialists and the war that turned this city into rubble. The burghers of Nuremberg were prosperous. There were Mercedeses and BMWs on the streets, and the shops were filled with merchandise. The staggering debt West Germany had accepted to become whole was not readily apparent here. I wondered if the former Easterners were living half as well. I'd find out soon enough.

I quickly discovered that I had the evidence in front of me. Annaliese Rykova may have been a West German by birth (though I wasn't even sure of that), but she was effectively an East German—probably with all the ideological baggage one would expect. By this time I was convinced that her marriage to the tank commander was a rather touching fantasy. And her regard for the West was proportional to her hunger for the surfeit of consumer goods that surrounded us. Her state of mind even had a name; she called it *Osthunger*.

"To the people I lived with in Riesa," she said, "heaven would be a free day in an American mall. I have seen such *pictures*, Brian." Then, with a disarming smile: "Is that what is meant by the failure of communism? Just listen to me. I was taught in good East German schools. How ashamed of me my teachers would be."

Annaliese had changed into what was probably her most fashionable outfit—a shiny black imitation leather skirt and jacket over a green silk blouse that made her eyes bright as emeralds. She wore black plastic boots with high heels. But even in heels she was not very tall. The effect was a little like a child dressing up in her mother's clothes. She wore no overcoat but seemed unaware of the cold.

With cognac after the meal I swallowed the pills I'd been ordered to take with my midday meal, Procardia and Mevacor. She watched me with what I read as concern.

She had scrubbed her face, put on lipstick and combed her hair. On the table beside the few leavings of her meal was a guidebook. Plainly she intended using it to lead me through a tour of old Nuremberg's heavy medieval charms. I would rather have gone back to the hotel and slept. After all, there seemed little else I could do, having struck a dead end at 14 Sandruth Allee.

But Annaliese Rykova was determined to make herself indispensable to me, and I confess I didn't mind. "I want to show you the very place where Mutti once kept house for Oberst Lockwood and you."

She looked at me. "What was it like, a little boy living along with Mutti and the *Oberst?* Were you lonely, Brian?"

"It wasn't like that," I told her. "Colonel Lockwood was ordered back to the States, and I stayed here with your grandmother. I don't remember him in Nuremberg. Just your grandmother."

"How old were you when you went to America?"

"Five." I could have added that I *thought* that I was born in 1945 but had no way of knowing for sure. My records were the wartime fabrications of a man determined to shelter a German war orphan. For a while I had imagined that Fräulein Clef might have been my mother, but Allan Cobb had laughed at that idea. I might have said any of these things, but I didn't. They weren't things a grown man said to a very young, very eager girl looking to make herself indispensable.

It was meaningful, I thought, that Annaliese persisted in calling her grandmother "Mutti," German slang for "mother."

Her real mother must have been a neglectful parent. Still, Marianna Clef couldn't have been much better. There was a kind of universality in the alienation Annaliese felt toward her relatives. Perhaps it drew me to her since I felt some of the same thing.

I wondered how Fräulein Clef had taken to the idea of her granddaughter living with the Russian enemy. Not too well, I would bet. One of my clear childhood memories was of Fräulein calling the Soviets "brutes and rapists."

"The house was on the St. Lorenz bank," Annaliese said.

"I'm sorry, what did you say?"

"The house. Yours and Mutti's," she said, "it was on the Ostendstrasse side of the river. Near the Ost Bahnhof. With a fine view of the Wohrder See. It is torn down now, but Mutti showed me the place years ago when I was a little girl. Don't you remember it at all?"

"No." I said it more abruptly than I intended. "I didn't come to Nuremberg to reminisce."

"I know you came to visit Mutti. But let me do what she would have done for you."

"Maybe I gave you the wrong impression, Annaliese. Your grandmother and I were not close."

She seemed upset. "But you came to see her. All the way from the United States."

"I came for a lot of reasons. Only one of them was to look up Marianna Clef." I suddenly felt angry. I was in no condition to be answering a silly girl's intrusive questions about, of all things, my childhood, who I was, where I came from. . . .

"I only want to be useful," she said quietly.

We hired a taxi from the rack outside the restaurant and began making our way through the heart of the city. Between the buildings one could see the medieval walls of the Old Town. In a way it would have been more fitting to be on muleback or astride a war-horse in this place.

Annaliese sat on the worn leather car seat, alert as a bird. She cautioned the driver, a dark-skinned Pakistani, to be sure he was taking the shortest route to Ostendstrasse, warning him that she knew the way and that he was not to think he could cheat the American tourist.

We passed by a group of leather-jacketed young men with shaved heads. They wore their jackets like uniforms, and they shouted an obscenity at our taxi driver.

"Fascists," Annaliese said. "They were never allowed in the East, but now things are different. They attack foreigners if there are no police around. The government says they have the right to assemble. What does that mean? Assemble. Is it like that in the United States?"

"Sometimes," I said.

"I hear things are terrible in the Soviet Union now. No food in the stores, people in the streets. They can call themselves Commonwealth of Independent States, but what is independence when people are hungry?"

Where else but in Germany would I be having this discussion? And with an adolescent girl?

"It's the Middle Easterners the fascists object to," Annaliese was saying. "And the—you know"—she gestured to the back of the driver's head and lowered her voice—"the Paks. Mutti used to say we had been sold to the Third World. I didn't believe it but now I wonder. Some of my friends say the *Wessis* don't want

to work, and *Ossis* don't know how." Again, she used the popular—and pejorative—term for West and East Germans. She shivered. The taxi was unheated.

"Are you cold?" I asked.

She said, "My feet are," and she giggled. "I have no stockings
on under these boots."

Her comment touched me, but I didn't want to show it. Instead I asked her about the so-called guest workers who suddenly seemed so unwelcome in the new unified Germany.

Once again she sounded old for her age.

"You Americans are so touchy about race. But wouldn't it be
better for Germany if the *Wessis* hadn't refused to dirty their
hands? By working, I mean. At the jobs no one wanted." She
looked at her own hands. They were small, with long nails covered with chipped lacquer, red from the cold. She had short,
delicate fingers.

Annaliese Rykova was no Sieglinde. Perhaps, I thought, a half
century after our own version of *Götterdämmerung* we had finally taken our place among the mortal folk of the world.

And suddenly I was shocked to realize I was thinking of
myself as German. *Our Götterdämmerung? We? Our* place in the
world? It was this damned medieval town and the gray, time-
less winter sky. And maybe this small, appealing German girl
with a lousy past and no future. She made me think of what I
might have been like if the Colonel hadn't taken me out of the
postwar rubble. I'd have been living by my wits, just as she was,
living on the edge, clutching at any opportunity to pull myself
out of the pit.

At that moment she put a hand on my thigh. She looked at
me. "You don't mind my doing that? Touching you?"

"I have children as old as you," I told her.

"But you don't mind?"

"No," I said honestly. "I don't mind."

She settled against me. "Good. That's all right then."

The wind became stronger as the afternoon faded into early
evening. Annaliese Rykova seemed fixed on showing me the
grounds of the old mansion where I had spent my earliest years
with her "Mutti." The taxi took us by underpass beneath the

railroad tracks of the eastern railroad station, the Ost Bahnhof. Beyond a plaza and a narrow road I could see what remained of an old park. With the rebuilding of Nuremberg, what had once been an elegant residential district had become an industrial area with ugly factory buildings lining the railroad.

But the Pegnitz riverbank was still open and wooded, banded by small meadows of the sort so often unexpectedly found in European cities. The taxi slowed, crossed the tracks once again, and the Pak driver looked back to Annaliese for instructions.

"There," she said. "To the right. Follow the riverbank."

The taxi left the expressway and went down to the riverfront road near where the Pegnitz widened to flow into the Wohrder See. "Here," Annaliese told him. "Park here and wait for us."

Outside the car it was very icy and getting dark. I took off my coat and put it on Annaliese Rykova's slender shoulders. She took hold of my hand, apparently excited to be in a place familiar to me.

The air was like an embrace of ice. I followed where she led, along the river, through a meadow whose brown river grasses extruded from the thin blanket of snow that crackled underfoot. I could smell the Pegnitz, brownish water, swiftly flowing. It had a scent of river bottom mud, somehow familiar.

We crossed a pedestrian bridge. It was brutally new, made of stressed concrete and narrow steel supports. We walked across it to the opposite bank and stood in a meadow dotted with birch, laurel and willows.

Through the trees I could see the colorless surface of the Wohrder See. Black mud hens swam there, unaware of their ugliness and as confident as swans.

Annaliese stopped and looked at me. "The house was across the river."

I looked around at the woods, cold and forbidding. The wind cut through my clothing. It was all familiar.

My God, I thought suddenly. She's right. This is the place. I felt dizzy and weak in the knees.

A child is carried in the arms of a slender blond woman, no more than a girl. The woman hears the sound of pursuit from the river. She puts the child down in a clump of black willows, strikes him and, in a

*voice he has never heard before, commands him to be absolutely silent
or he will surely die.*

*Hiding, breath clotted with terror, he watched armed men follow the
woman into the woods. There are shots. I can't speak . . . I can't
breathe. . . .*

"What's the matter? Are you ill?" Annaliese's voice came
from a great distance.

I was shivering, with shock and cold. My hands were shaking,
and I jammed them into my pockets.

Annaliese put her hands over mine inside my pockets. "You
are icy. Here, take back your coat. Hurry."

"No. Let's just get out of here, away from this place. . . ."

I have always scoffed at the psychobabble people use to describe
the terrible effects of childhood terrors. But the shock I felt by
the river was real. It was as if I were a spectator at a street
accident, devastated and helpless.

I had told Claire that my nightmare and my hallucinations in
the hospital were real and that they had happened to me. If I
had needed proof, I had it now.

Annaliese guided me back to the Lorenzerhof, to my room,
ordered a bottle and a meal. Then she as much as forced me into
a hot shower. When I finished, I found a supper was laid out,
and Annaliese handed me a glass of schnapps with orders to
drink it. It was a remarkable performance. And under the circumstances I was truly grateful.

We ate in silence, she in that silly faux leather outfit and I in
my equally silly wrinkled traveling robe. She watched me
closely as I ate.

I broke the silence with a "Thank you. I wouldn't have got
back here without you."

"What happened, Brian?"

"I knew that place by the river. I was there a long time ago. I
think—I think my mother left me there."

"How terrible." It was as though someone had written it
down for her to say. No, that was unfair, wasn't it? Then: "You
are feverish. You need to rest a day or so."

"I'm going east tomorrow."

"So soon?"

"Yes." Dieter Langan thought I was obsessed, and he was right.

"Then take me with you. *Please.*"

I only stared at her, but somehow I had been expecting this. She was alone, with no prospects. I needed someone who spoke the Eastern languages. Suddenly it seemed inevitable. And for more reasons than I realized at the time.

"We'll talk about it in the morning," she said. Across the city, church bells were tolling nine o'clock. Time had slipped away. Beyond the window the snow had given way to a light freezing rain that fell into the street below and reflected the lights of Nuremberg as though from a city beneath a lake.

Annaliese stood up, rolled the table to the door and left it in the hall, then crossed the room to the switch and turned off the overhead lights. Now the room was lit by a single small lamp that cast a yellow pool of light on the large bed.

I started to speak; she came over to me and put her fingertips on my lips. "Don't," she said. "Don't say anything."

She pulled off her boots, shed the jacket and the blouse under it. She was naked under the thin cloth. Poverty or design . . . what the hell did it matter? She slipped the miniskirt down over her hips and stood for a moment in black bikini briefs.

She remained still and let me watch her. In that instant she established our relationship, although it took me some time to realize it.

No, that's dishonest. I *needed* her. And that need established what we were to become to each other.

She was so slender her ribs showed, but her breasts were full with large aureolas and erect nipples. Her belly was flat with a deeply indented navel, and when she pushed the briefs down over her thighs, she exposed a pubic bush darker than her head.

She came to me. I put my arms around her hips and kissed her belly while I ran my hands down her buttocks and thighs. I stood up and kissed her mouth. Her tongue came to mine. I could not remember a time in my life when sex was like this, bitter and yet sweet as honey.

She opened my robe. "You are like fire, Brian, and now I am really cold. Warm me."

I threw back the counterpane and put her on her back. She raised her hips, spread her thighs and lifted her knees. For the first time, but not the last, we made love.

TWO

26 November
to
29 November
1991

11

"Can you smell the burning?"

AFTER OUR FIRST TIME I shivered with sweaty exhaustion. Yet I found it fulfilling to drive myself. I was surprised by my adolescent sexuality. I had not been with a woman for months, and now, suddenly, I was making love to a girl who was hardly more than a child.

Was I ashamed of what I was doing? I was not. Perhaps this is the story of all men of a certain age when they unexpectedly find themselves making love to a lubricious stranger. The experience on the riverbank had left me shaken; then Annaliese's sexuality urged me to excesses I had not even attempted since college days with Miriam Halprin. Finally, around dawn, I came down to earth and fell asleep.

I was in a rubbled camp in a red screaming night. I ran to a bunker and opened an oven. Inside, a woman was burning. She was naked. Her skin crinkled and flaked away, turning her into a horror. Blood and bones steamed and bubbled. A man in a black uniform and Stahlhelm *smiled at me and said in a voice like the roar of the flames:* "Well done, Jugend. This is what we do. Can you smell the burning? . . ."

I slept, although the dream seemed endless.

*   *   *

I woke up at eight, alone. The bed was damp and smelled of sex. I was still feverish. I picked up the telephone, ordered my bill prepared and told the concierge to arrange for a rental car, which I would use to drive east.

I realized it was a long trip to the border, but I had made up my mind to follow the trail Dean had laid out for me. He had challenged me to find the Stossens, and I meant to do it, no matter how. My better judgment was to take Dieter's warning seriously and go straight to the airport and return to California. That was the very reason I had no intention of going anywhere but east.

I opened the window and looked down at the street. It was slick with rain. Patches of snow lay in the gutters and against the trunks of the leafless trees in the *Wald.*

I looked from the *Wald* to the hotel grounds and saw three men standing next to a gray late-model BMW. One of them, in a black chesterfield coat and homburg, was looking directly at me. An old man but heavily built with sloping, muscular shoulders, a brushy mustache and a clipped gray beard. It was a shock. It had, after all, been years since I had seen Dean Lockwood, but the man below certainly looked like him. The same heavy brows that I remembered, the same cold, deep-set eyes and the same broad, thin mouth. But he seemed too robust, too obviously moneyed in his chesterfield and homburg to be my errant uncle. Still, the man came close to fitting Claire's description of Dean ten years ago. I had long since convinced myself that, considering Dean Lockwood's behavior toward the family, he could not possibly have done well. That was nonsense, and I knew it, of course. If only the virtuous prospered, it would be a very different world. I stood in the window, staring back at the man. No, it was not Dean Lockwood. In the last few days I had hardly thought of anyone but Dean; that must have been why I thought I recognized him.

The others were younger, bulky men in imitation leather coats slick with rain. The older man had stopped speaking. All of them raised their eyes to my window, but the older man's face seemed to show an astonishing hatred.

It's imagination, I told myself, the product of too many nightmares. . . .

All this was in a matter of seconds. I grabbed at my clothes, ready to rush downstairs and confront the old man. But he now had looked away and climbed into the rear seat of the BMW. One of the men joined him. The other walked into the lee of the building and disappeared. The car rolled down the hotel's drive, joined the traffic moving along Regensburgerstrasse and was gone.

I stood there, holding my trousers and staring after the vanished car for several minutes before the cold made me close the window with unsteady hands. *Had* I actually seen my errant uncle? The image was hard to retain. Had I imagined the hatred in the man's face? Was I becoming paranoid? All were possible.

I finished dressing, packed my bag and went downstairs. The first thing I did was step outside to look at the parking lot. Nothing. I turned back and went into the lobby. Off again, on again. Yes, it had been Dean Lockwood; no, of course it had only been a bad-tempered stranger. . . .

Annaliese, in blue jeans and an anorak, was standing by the concierge's desk speaking to a tall, long-haired young man also in tight denim. He had a guitar slung over his shoulder. Annaliese spotted me and said something sharply to the young man. He looked my way, then turned and walked swiftly out of the lobby. Annaliese came over, carrying a backpack.

She slipped a hand into mine and said, "You haven't changed your mind, have you?"

"Who was that?"

"*Niemand.* He is taking some of my things back to Riesa. I am ready to go, Brian. May I still call you Brian?"

I considered the absurdity of this conversation after the night we had spent together. "Would you like to invite *Niemand* to have breakfast with us?"

"No." No explanations. Just *no.*

"Then let's pick up the car. I want to get moving."

"You're in such a hurry. You weren't last night," she said slyly.

I didn't want to stand in the lobby of the Lorenzerhof and

discuss my sexual athletics of the night before. "Let's just *go*," I said.

I drove the rented Mercedes faster than my usual pace. I was upset by dreams and by sexual thoughts. Last night I had had more and better sex than I had enjoyed in years. This led to thoughts about my petulant reaction to the guitar-toting young man in the hotel lobby. Good God, I thought. I'm *jealous*. Absurd. I had no claim on Annaliese Rykova. She hadn't suddenly and miraculously become my chattel.

We got all the way to Leipzig by evening. The East German roads were lightly traveled, and what traffic there was, consisted of trucks from the West and shoals of drably dressed people on bicycles. The fields lay fallow. When the farming collectives broke up, the people scattered. Now the large agribusiness firms of Western Europe were buying up the land, although they had not yet made it productive. Forests that had once lined the route between Nuremberg and Leipzig were gone, clear-cut, leaving the land naked. When I wondered why the Communist state had allowed such a thing, Annaliese said, "For the fuel. The winters are very cold here. East German coal was for making steel or shipping to the Soviet Union." What a Marxist triumph, I thought. Timber rape in a country with some of the largest coal deposits in Europe.

Westerners were still discovering just how badly the governments of the former East Bloc had treated the environment. But by now we were aware that the German economy was staggering from the shock of realizing what reunification was going to cost.

Annaliese looked at me, once more with a wisdom beyond her years. "Bad, isn't it, Brian? It takes time to know how bad. I'll make an *Ossi* of you yet."

In Leipzig we registered at the Hotel Deutschland in what used to be called Karl-Marx-Platz and was now called Freiheitplatz. The inhabitants of the city told visiting Westerners that the name change was expected of them. Annaliese described them as *schroff,* abrupt. The first excitement of reunification was over now, and the people were beginning to realize that all would not be a golden tomorrow. They were *schroff* because they could see ahead to the long, hard slog to capitalism. The prospect of spending the next few decades learning how to live without a tyrannical and paternalistic state controlling every aspect of life cast a spell of apprehension over the East. West Germans were having second thoughts, too.

The hotel was once a perquisite of the GDR's nomenklatura. In the "glory" days of Erich Honecker, East German bureaucrats, members of the satellite nomenklatura, had lived very well here. But the Hotel Deutschland was now the Grand Hotel Deutschland and the domain of tourists, Western businessmen and visiting *Wessi* bureaucrats.

"We've been conquered all over again," Annaliese said as we registered. "By Visa, MasterCard and American Express." She was absolutely right. The decals on the glass doors said it all. But her disapproving tone surprised me. I'd thought that East Germans of Annaliese's generation loved plastic money.

Poor old Marx, I thought. He had been so certain the workers of Germany would lead the way to world socialism. Whether he was presently sitting on a cloud or roasting in a bonfire, he had to be disappointed in his Germans. When the first movement came, they had opted to totalitarianism, to be sure, but Brown rather than Red. They had had to be conquered from the East to accept communism. And now they had abandoned his dream.

The lights were on in the Deutschland's lobby because the afternoon was dark, overcast, cold and grim. The concierge announced stoically that there were repeated power outages because the new government was concerned about the condition of eastern Germany's aging Soviet-designed nuclear power plants and had taken them off-line. And the elevator was out of order because parts were no longer available in Minsk, where the elevator had been built some forty years ago.

But the telephone console built into the backrest of the bed in our room was Japanese, looking like part of the space shuttle and in good order. I promptly put it to work to telephone Claire.

It was 8:40 A.M. in California, and Claire was, typically, up and doing. The cottage would have an otherworldly sparkle when I returned. It would take weeks to dull it down to where it resembled a place where a single man lived.

An errant thought stuck me. Claire had no children. She'd never said why, and I'd never asked. Perhaps by choice, or by chance—or perhaps because she'd been pushed into premature parenthood when I came on the scene? Certainly Janice Lockwood was not about to be my surrogate mother, and the Colonel was absent a good deal of the time.

When my children began growing up, Reeder had decided that she preferred being "friends" with Little Bri and Lissa to being a parent. So if they needed mothering instead of "friendly" advice, they naturally went to Claire. Strange that I'd never even considered this before. I must be a navel contemplative as well as an anal retentive. Perhaps the carapace I'd built over myself was cracking. Perhaps this dangerous voyage of discovery would not be all bad. . . .

Claire sounded as though she were in the lobby. "Brian," she said reproachfully, "where have you been? We've been out of our minds with worry. Gloria Wilson telephoned me. She read your name in the *Times*. Wasn't Tetrac the name of the company that sent you the Colonel's Nazi dagger?"

Claire had busybody friends everywhere. And leave it to Claire to make all the connections. "Yes," I said. "It was. Just a coincidence, sis."

"But you were there. You were a witness."

"Let's not talk about it now. I'm not alone."

Annaliese's face was framed in the steaming, partially open door of the bathroom. Watching me.

In California Claire said, "Oh?" Claire was a woman who could speak volumes with a single word. "All right, Bri. But I expect an explanation when you get home. Allan Cobb is coming for dinner tonight. Is there a message for him?"

"Yes," I said. "Tell him Marianna Clef died two months ago. I met her granddaughter. She's traveling with me."

There was a long silence. "Traveling with you?"

"Don't lecture me, sis."

Annaliese smiled a secret smile and closed the door.

I said into the telephone, "I'll have some stories to tell you when I get back."

"I've no doubt of that," Claire said dryly. "When will that be?"

"A week, maybe two."

"What are you doing in the East?"

"Driving to Poland. Dieter has located the Stossen family for me. Just across the frontier. I want to talk to them."

"I don't think I like that, Bri."

"Don't worry," I said. I listened to the girl moving about in the bathroom and said, "I may be in danger of making a fool of myself, but nothing more."

"What more is there?"

I ignored the question. "I haven't had a chance to call Stein again. Ask him if there's any possibility that Dean might be in Germany."

"Good Lord, Bri."

"Well, this morning I saw a man I thought *looked* like him."

"Bri, how would you know how Dean Lockwood looks now? You were at Menlo when you last saw him. That was years ago."

"You're right, of course. Just a thought. How's Ershad?"

"Indignant, but I think he's having the time of his life being a hero with the nurses."

"I'll call again in a few days."

"From where?"

"From wherever I happen to be." I hung up, lay back on the pillows and closed my eyes, wondering if I still had a fever. My other symptoms seemed to be on hold.

Annaliese reappeared, wrapped in a towel. Her hair was damp and tousled. "Your wife?"

The question surprised me. I suppose I thought my man-alone image was obvious. Apparently not. "There's no incumbent Mrs. Lockwood," I said.

"You said you had children," she said, walking barefoot across the creaking hardwood floor.

"Two."

She sat down on the bed beside me. Her eyes were almost moss green in this light. "I have friends in Leipzig. May I call them?"

"Go ahead." I wanted to make up for my churlishness about Mr. No One.

"Later," she said, and shed the towel.

Perhaps this is a moment for me to make some sage remarks about how difficult it is for a man of a middle age to maintain his dignity when overwhelmed by the sexual appeal of a young girl. But I am no sage, and I have no words of wisdom to offer. I met Annaliese Rykova, and in a matter of hours I was young again. It's a story too familiar to need commentary from me.

Annaliese Rykova was a member of a generation I knew only from a distance. My children had never shared much of what they thought and believed, how they lived, what mattered to them. It was my fault, I knew that. As I was growing up, the Colonel gave me every material advantage, but he didn't share emotions with me. Over time I came to understand—perhaps *sense* would be a better word—that he was one of the war's walking wounded and that somehow I was involved in his personal grief. But because he was as he was, and I was as I was, I went from childhood to manhood without ever learning how to touch or be touched by another human being.

Claire was the exception. I could tell her things I could tell no one else. We shared intuitions about each other. We had since we were children. But our intuitions were limited. For example, neither of us had ever discovered what it was that had frozen the heart of our austere male parent. We both believed it had to do with his rebuff from the country and service he loved.

But surely, I thought, there had to be more. Something to do, perhaps, with the blond young woman I so often dreamed of seeing in a forest on the banks of a frozen river. But to my great regret, I had no way to reach the Colonel.

Annaliese lay in my arms, her breasts flattened against my chest. She said, "I have a confession to make."

I waited. How bad could it be?

"I opened your luggage. I spied on you while you were in the bath. Are you angry?"

I was, a little. "Why?"

"It's the way we have always lived in the East." I could hear the capitalized letter.

"What did you think I was? CIA?"

"I don't know," she said very quietly. "Nothing is certain, no one is ever what he seems to be."

I pushed myself to a sitting position against the headboard. I was soaked with sweat. My fever had broken.

"Don't be angry."

"I'm not." Disappointed, maybe, but what did I expect?

She sat up, cross-legged. Her breasts were soft and marked with a tracery of tiny blue veins just beneath the fair skin. She looked very vulnerable.

"Don't send me away," she said.

"I won't do that."

She smiled bleakly.

"So what did you find in my luggage?"

"A Nazi dagger."

"I should have told you," I said. "It's no secret. The dagger belonged to a German Air Force doctor named Stossen. He was killed in the war. I'm trying to find out about him."

"Why? Why should you care? You are an American."

"I am also a German," I said.

She sat there like a small Buddha, legs crossed, eyes hooded in thought.

"Remember I told you I have friends in Leipzig?"

"Do you want to see them?" The idea did not appeal to me. I had a flashback to the guitar-toting fellow in Nuremberg. The trouble with a man of a certain age sleeping with a young girl is that a simple remark can transform the generation gap into an abyss.

Instead of answering me, she asked, "Will you tell me why you are here? What you plan to do?"

I told her about the dagger and about the stranger on the berm in Carmel, about Professor Ershad, about most of what General Bolton's people in Colorado Springs had discovered about Stossen. I did not mention Dean Lockwood or the killings at Tetrac. This didn't seem the time.

For a while she sat still, perhaps thinking about how she

might find an advantage to herself in all this. By now I understood that an edge—of any sort—was what she was always seeking. I could understand it. She had, after all, been born into a world of ideological certitudes. She had also seen her world come apart. Her Russian tank commander had vanished back into the mystery of Russia. Her mother and grandmother were dead. Except for a few worn-out household goods, she owned nothing. And now she sat naked in bed with a foreigner who might desert her tomorrow. If there was advantage in that situation, I thought, she was entitled to try to find it.

"Why did you bring me with you, Brian?" she asked. "Besides the fucking."

Fair question. If a bit *schroff*.

"You said it. I need a guide, a helper who knows the border. You speak Polish."

"All right. Yes, I see that. Better now than before." She pursed her lips. It made her look like a little girl. "The people you should see are the ones who used to be Stasi. You understand that?"

"A friend explained it. In detail," I said dryly.

"If he told you they will do anything for money—which he must have done—he is *almost* right."

"Almost?"

She nodded, got up from the bed, walked to the door and double-locked it, walked to the window and looked down into Freiheitplatz (giving any passersby a fine view of her nakedness), then closed the shutters. She came back to the bed, picked up the telephone handset, removed the cover of the mouthpiece, inspected the innards and replaced it, reassembled, in its cradle.

"Some Stasi are still political," she said.

"Diehard Communists?" I swung my feet to the floor, wishing for a cigarette. (I had not smoked for six years, but every now and then I craved tobacco.)

"Some are. Some are rightists. Some have cut off their hair and act like Englishmen. Some kill Turks and Arabs. Jews, if they can find any. Germany is like that, Brian. Get used to it." She seemed much older and wiser than she had moments before.

"Do you really intend to search out the Stossen family?" she asked.

"Yes."

"If there are any Stossens left, they must be very old."

"I'm prepared for that."

"My friends might help."

"Why do you think I need help?"

"In this part of Germany you can't have too many friends. The people I know would be glad to help an American."

"For a price?"

"Things being as they are, a small price."

I looked around the cold room. The floor was made of thin lathes of hardwood woven like lattice. It creaked when one walked on it, like the Nightingale Floors of Japanese castles. The ceiling was high and shadowy, the lights dim because of the power shortage. Shutters over the narrow windows sealed us off from the fall of night over the square and the city.

"It would be a good idea to have someone looking out for us, Brian. Mr. No One was once a Vopo." She smiled suddenly. "He wants to go to the United States and become a rock star."

That was just what I needed. A would-be troubadour who was an ex-Volkspolizei—a member of the organization whose job was to kill runners and Wall climbers.

"Has he got a name?"

"Erich."

"Erich what?"

"Leyden." She smiled slyly. "He was living with a cousin of Rykov's. He is reliable, Brian. He was almost accepted into the Grenzschutz." The ultimate endorsement. West Germans swore by the Grenzschutz, the border guard.

"Isn't it odd he turned up in Nuremberg?"

"He drove me to Nuremberg from Riesa. He could be in Leipzig tonight."

"That's damn convenient."

"What does that mean, 'convenient'?"

"It means I can do without a guitar player."

Annaliese looked at me. "It bothers you that I was talking to him in the hotel in Nuremberg?"

"Yes." What the hell, I thought. Why not be frank? "Up front," my daughter, Elissa, might call it.

"I only wanted him to tell the people we know, I was leaving Nuremberg." I thought her eyes showed a spark of contempt. "That I was going away for a week with a rich American."

"If that's what you think you're doing, you had better pack up. I'll buy you a train ticket to Riesa."

"You are an innocent stranger in Germany, Brian."

"And Herr Leyden?" I thought of the man in the hotel drive in Nuremberg, who might or might not have been Dean Lockwood, and his two thugs. For a moment I was tempted to sign on some muscle.

"Erich will work for low wages. And he has a pistol."

I took Annaliese by the shoulders. "No."

"But why, Brian?"

"Because," I said in my best High German, "I do not need a bodyguard who wants to be a rock star and who owns a pistol. That's final."

She really didn't seem to understand.

"I didn't know how it was here before," I said, "but the new state is going to be hard on lawbreakers. Owning weapons is illegal in this country. I suggest you call Leyden's friends and tell them to let him know it's no deal."

It surprised me, how much I sounded at the moment like the Colonel.

There was no further protest from Annaliese Rykova.

12

"Clef had no granddaughter."

IT SOUNDS RIDICULOUS to use the phrase "lover's quarrel," but that's what we got into, Annaliese Rykova and I. A silent quarrel. The worst kind. Her attempt to use me to provide employment for—possibly a lover? how was I to know?—of questionable credentials had brought my sex-addled mind down to earth with a jolt. There was nothing wrong with what she had tried to do; in similar circumstances anyone might do the same. Gainful employment of any sort was hard to come by in eastern Germany, and it was even possible that the unmet Erich Leyden or some other of Annaliese Rykova's *Ossi* associates might be an asset. But then again, an ex-Volkspolizei was not someone I wanted around me, with or without his guitar.

The truth was that I didn't really want to know anything about Annaliese's life. I didn't want to be touched or angered or jealous. Yet I *was* all three. I was ready to imagine almost anything.

So we spent a cold night in the same bed, back to back, in a posture that reminded me of my last weeks with Reeder. My sleep was restless.

Annaliese apparently slept the untroubled sleep of the young.

119

* * *

We drove out of Leipzig in the early-morning dark. I'd intended to stop in Berlin, but once on the road, I decided against it. I wanted to be done with the whole business of the Eagle Dagger. I wanted to be done with Germany.

The E51 autobahn points northeast across the Brandenburg plain toward Berlin. A dozen kilometers from the city, I switched to E55 to stay clear. I had seen enough of German opulence and angst. This country's troubles, I told myself, were not my business. I wanted only to lay the old ghosts and be gone. I had a family, an identity, a country. I needed to stop dreaming about the German woman who abandoned her child on the bank of the frozen Pegnitz. After all, what did I really owe her and all those who had disappeared with her into time?

We stopped to eat in the *Raststatte,* where we switched from the E55 autobahn to the E28, which would take us straight to the frontier and the Oder River delta. The food was ordinary rest-stop fare; the company was silent and cautious. My bad temper was unjustified, of course. I had no right to be angry with her for being half my age and a child of her times. Her offer of an ally was meant well, but it made me ask questions I didn't want answered. After all, what did I know about Annaliese Rykova? I knew the damp warmth of her most intimate part. I knew her cries as she made love, the smell of her skin in the heat of lust. In another time that would have added up to considerable intimacy. But in these last years of the twentieth century it seemed everyone knew everyone else and intimacy had been lost in promiscuity. I had been acquainted with Annaliese Rykova for three days and I had fucked her until my back ached. That was it, the sum total, I told myself.

The sergeant major, chauvinist that he was, once told me: "Never make decisions while you're pussy-whipped." I suspected he would give the same advice now.

* * *

The *Raststatte* had a variety shop. Most of what was there was junk, but the management had contrived to obtain some small bottles of French perfume. I bought a bottle of Antilope. Yes, I remembered, of course, that it was Reeder's favorite and, I think, Miriam Halprin's. In love or lust I have never been an inventive man.

As we returned to the autobahn heading north, I produced the small package and put it between Annaliese's Levi's-clad thighs. She accepted the parcel as though it were a gift from the Magi, opening it with great care, folding and saving the gaudy wrapping paper. She held the bottle against her cheek. Her eyes were bright with tears.

She moved closer to me, caught my arm hard against her breasts.

"I'm sorry I'm behaving badly about your friend," I said. "I just didn't want him along." That was as near to a confession as I could manage. Declarations of affection come hard among the Lockwoods. Even the adopted one.

We drove on through the long afternoon, crossing the flat country of the *Vorpommern* at 110 kilometers an hour, a conservative speed for a German expressway.

The E28 runs almost straight north for a hundred kilometers and then bears away to the east toward the Oder River. Here and there the open fields became marshes and wetlands. One could see limned against an overcast the color of tarnished silver an occasional undulating line of geese flying south away from the northern German winter.

The traffic was like before, mostly trucks—huge machines pulling triple trailers at crazy speeds—and private cars with old Bundesrepublik number plates.

The National Police drove Porsches and needed them. I've probably given the impression that driving on German roads scares the hell out of me. It does. Germans drive like escaping terrorists. Reunification hasn't slowed them down. It's only brought a few million more Germans into the reckless game. I hadn't yet witnessed my quota of highway mayhem but expected that I would and soon.

It was a few klicks from Radowitz, a town a kilometer or two from the border, that we ran into our first highway accident. A new Mercedes with Bavarian plates had smashed into a bridge abutment at high speed. It had disintegrated, strewing its contents all over everywhere. An ambulance was picking up the human remains, and a set of national policemen in their Porsches had narrowed the roadway with flares and pylons. The light had begun to fade from the overcast sky. It made the blood on the roadway black.

Annaliese looked on as the line of cars and trucks we had joined was guided past the congestion by policemen. There was a small bundle on the grass verge. It almost certainly was the body of a child.

Annaliese looked at the destroyed Mercedes as we passed. "What a waste," she said. "The price of one of those would keep a family of *Ossis* until the Russians come back."

In a complex of concrete block shelters beside a reedy lagoon we stopped for gasoline and to telephone for accommodations in Pomellen. There was a gasthaus in the border guidebook I had bought in Nuremberg. I wanted a base of operations on the German side of the border. Poland was terra incognita to me.

The newly capitalistic proprietor of Der Rötischer Lachs was delighted an American was coming. I could have what I liked. I reserved a double room.

As I stepped out of the telephone kiosk, I caught the clear, salty smell of the sea. It surprised me that I had not been aware of how foul the air smelled in much of the country we had been crossing. The sad fact was that the Communists never bothered with environmental concerns as they drove forward straight into the sweaty and sooty nineteenth century astride their primitive industrial technology. When advancement depends on one's ability to fulfill quotas set by apparatchiks far away, quotas of goods no one wants and no one sells, who's to worry that the factory's effluent fouls the rivers and factory smoke turns the air brown?

People aren't really idiots, just self-concerned. If a man's sausage and beer depend on a few million fish being poisoned in the Baltic, why, then, poison the fish. A man's beer and wurst are the world. Fish are only fish. That's a mainline truth. A man isn't about to let his children go hungry for the sake of the spotted owl or the snail darter.

The Baltic breeze blowing down the Oder River was suddenly like a flash of silver. I was tired and still shaky with the remnants of the fever. The highway accident had sickened me. But the smell of the sea was bracing. Annaliese seemed unmoved by what we had seen, interested in the perfume bottle I'd given her.

I wondered how I would feel if I had grown up in this country. How many of my American verities would have survived a real postwar German childhood? It made me feel like a changeling, abandoned on the Colonel's doorstep by a cold and beautiful ghost. It made everything German make me sick to my stomach.

Annaliese looked across the marshy ground to the northern horizon. There were rusted pieces of unidentifiable machinery in the marshes, probably left behind when some attempt to drain the water from the wetlands was abandoned. In the twilight we could still see scraps of paper and trash caught in the pale grasses, and the oil scum floating in the roadside pools.

"Mutti used to tell me that Germany was the most beautiful country in the world. She lied."

I got behind the wheel and started the engine. I tried to imagine Fräulein Clef trying to explain to a child what Germany once had been. I couldn't.

"Do the Von Stossens live around here?" Annaliese asked.

"Von Stossens?" I'd said nothing to her about any *von* Stossens.

"Did I say that?" She gave a short jagged laugh. "I suppose I thought *von* Stossen because Mutti used to say that after the war everyone was a *von*. It helped them get work with the Americans."

I started the car north and east again, toward the darkening horizon. "The Stossens live on the other side of the Niese."

Annaliese rested her head on the seat back. "Then they have nothing."

"War costs," I said. For some reason I thought of the Colonel rather than the Stossens. The Colonel had taken on a battle of some sort, and it had cost him. I wondered what it would now cost me.

*   *   *

We drove straight on to Pomellen, which turned out to be little more than a wide turnout on the road to Poland. There was the Red Salmon, and there were a few desolate houses with thatch roofs and barren gardens. A Trabant garage faced the gasthaus with four rusted hulks of the little car standing in the forecourt.

Annaliese looked around with distaste but said nothing.

At the gasthaus we were the only guests. A boy with lank yellow hair and a pimpled complexion carried our bags in. The host was a fat, pale man wearing workers' canvas trousers who asked for our passports and registered us.

"I am Franz Reineke," he said. "I am the host and the concierge. Please to follow me."

He took us to what he said was the best room in the Red Salmon. It was cold and smelled of mildew. The floor's single bath was at the end of the dark hallway.

"I hope you will be comfortable," Herr Reineke said.

Annaliese rushed into the bath the moment Reineke descended the stairs. She had a fetish about bathing.

I stopped at a window, which opened to the north under the eaves and caught the wind from the Baltic. For a few minutes I stood in the gathering dark, looking north along the moor toward the river and the sea; then I went downstairs to telephone Dieter Langan.

The telephone was in an alcove behind the registration desk, now abandoned after our arrival. I dialed *Die Zeit*'s office number.

Dieter answered. By this time in the evening most of the magazine's staff would be gone. "Are you alone?" he said.

"Yes."

"I have some information."

"First tell me about Dean Lockwood."

"All right. My people found out he was in Germany until last month. Since then no one has seen him."

"How has he been living? Surely your sources have mentioned that."

"These aren't things to be talking about on the telephone."

"*Is* he a dealer in objects of art?"

Langan gave a short, hard laugh. "One might say so. Until recently your uncle has had a reputation for knowing where to find things lost during the war."

"Lost?"

"Stolen."

"Keep trying to find him. He's a part of all this."

"Now, there's something else," Dieter said. I waited. I didn't like the tone of his voice. The ever-ironic Dieter Langan was suddenly someone else.

"Brian? Are you there?"

"I'm here."

"You called your sister from Leipzig."

"Yes." There was only one way he could know that. Dieter had spoken to Claire.

"You told her you were traveling with Fräulein Clef's grand-daughter."

"You called my sister?"

"No. She made the call."

"To check on me? Claire's not like that."

"She is if she's worried about you. She said you were traveling with Marianna Clef's granddaughter. Is that so?"

For a moment I felt betrayed.

"Is the girl with you now?"

"Upstairs."

"Clef is dead."

"I know that. Annaliese told me."

"Clef had no granddaughter."

Like ice water in the face. I felt cold and angry. No fool like a middle-aged Romeo.

"Brian?"

"I'm still here."

"Clef's daughter, Ursula, died in a road accident in 1950. She had no children."

"Thanks for the information, Dieter."

"I don't know whom you are with, but it is *not* Clef's grand-daughter."

I said nothing. What in hell should I say?

"I'll try to get you some information on Dean Lockwood."

"Do that."

"About the girl . . ."

"I'll handle it, Dieter."

"Carefully, please."

"I *said* I'd handle it."

"She could be Stasi, Brian."

"Good-bye, Dieter."

I sat with the telephone in my hand. I should have been grateful. I was not. I stood up and opened the door. I clamped down hard on my sense of betrayal. I found the piece of paper on which I'd written the telephone number Dieter had given me in Düsseldorf. I had to call the international operator to place the call to Stettin. In spite of the new détente with the East, the call was routed through Berlin to Bonn and from there to Warsaw and finally back to Stettin—which was no more than a dozen kilometers from where I was sitting.

A voice answered in Polish.

I said in English, "This is Lockwood."

The reply was also in English. "Where are you? We expected you yesterday."

"I am here now."

"You have something for us?"

"Yes." A thousand U.S. dollars.

"Where are you calling from?"

"Pomellen."

"It will take you ten minutes to get here. Drive back to Road Nine and the Gartz border crossing. The Grenzschutz is taken care of. Go straight on to the Polish post."

"How will I know you?"

"I will know you, Herr Lockwood. Start now. Come alone."

I hung up and went to the registration alcove. The porter had been replaced with a girl. "Go upstairs and tell the woman in my room I will be gone for an hour," I said.

"Is that all, *Kamerad*?"

What we have here, I thought angrily, is an unreconstructed *Ossi*. "That is all," I said, and put away the D-mark note I had been going to give her.

* * *

I left Pomellen and swung south to the junction with Land-strasse 2. The sky was black and overcast. In the light of the headlights I could see rusted tank traps and rolls of old concertina wire half-buried in the marshes on either side of the road. Souvenirs of Armageddon, of the war that was never fought. The Soviets fortified their border with Poland, the Poles fortified their border with the GDR, and the GDR its borders with the rest of the world. Now it was all rusted wire and great jacks abandoned by giant children. I wondered what the Colonel would have thought.

When I got to the crossing, a minor post, the Grenzschutz on duty waved me through to the river. The border was the Oder River, narrow and almost too small to bear the weight of history it has been burdened with. I crossed the narrow concrete bridge and approached the Polish post. A sign bearing the Polish coat of arms was illuminated by a floodlight. I stopped at the shabby hut, and a man opened the right-hand door and slid into the car beside me. "Drive on. I will tell you where to stop."

It was too dark to read features but the man was large, burly, and he smelled of days-old perspiration and vodka. I wished I had armed myself with more than the dagger. The darkness closed in on us. The headlights made an island of illumination in a black world.

"This is far enough. Stop here." The man's English was accented but fluent. I wondered about his background. Stasi, almost certainly. What did these chosen champions of the old ways feel now that their world had crumbled? Perhaps I made too much of it. There was a good bit of the entrepreneur in this one.

"A thousand American dollars," he said.

"The Stossens," I said.

He took a packet of papers wrapped in plastic from his coat and opened it. "Turn on the overhead light," he said.

I did. He leafed through the papers in the packet. "Addresses. Medical records. Veterans' papers. Photostats of their internal passports. Enough?"

They looked authentic. "You do business with people in Düsseldorf."

"So?"

"So these had better *be* authentic."

"They are. The money."

I handed over a parcel of ten one-hundred-dollar bills.

"*Scheiss*. Haven't you anything smaller?"

"That's what I have. Do you want it?"

He stuffed the parcel into his coat pocket. "Use this crossing. No other. You will be expected tomorrow. Now take me back and get out. Americans are trouble."

I turned the car around and drove back to the border. The entire transaction had taken fifteen minutes. Dealing with the young woman calling herself Annaliese Rykova would take considerably longer.

13

"What would a lover matter?"

I RECROSSED THE BORDER into Germany without incident, but instead of taking the road north to the Red Salmon, I turned south and drove hard and fast back along the route we had come on earlier in the day. My pulse was pounding. Now that I had the Von Stossen dossier, my control weakened and I reacted to the news Dieter Langan had delivered.

Who *was* the girl I had brought with me into the East? When I thought of her naked in my arms, it gave me the strange feeling of being suspended, weightless, over an abyss. Even as a young man in the sixties, I had never been at ease with casual sex. My experiments, barring Miriam, had been far less daring than suited the reputation of my generation. But Annaliese Rykova—what else was I supposed to call her?—had shunted me into an unknown country. Worse still, she had touched me, loved me. And that made me angry. I'd been manipulated by a *Niemand-skind*, and here I was about to attempt my self-appointed mission with a deceitful girl who had lied to me and led me here by the penis. I managed an angry smile at that. Both Reeder and Janice would sign on to that opinion of what governed my behavior the last two days and nights.

I gripped the steering wheel of the Mercedes until my hands

ached and drove fast through the flat, dark countryside. The fever of the last few days, which I'd almost recovered from, was back. Anger drained away my strength. I fumbled in my pocket, found the nitroglycerin pills and put one under my tongue. I was pretty sure the pain I felt in my chest was emotional rather than clinical, but I dosed myself anyway.

Once I reached the autobahn, I put my foot down hard on the accelerator and let the Mercedes run. The speedometer leveled off at 175 kph, about 110 miles an hour. There was little southbound traffic, and what there was I overtook with a wailing of the Mercedes's airhorn. I opened the window on the driver's side and let the cold night air roar past. It felt good. There is something mindlessly appealing about driving too fast when one is angry.

After driving as far as Joachimsthal, halfway back to Berlin, I slowed and stopped in a rest area. I parked the car and got out to lean against the warm grille in mindless, angry indecision. Did I even want to return to Pomellen? I was tempted to abandon Annaliese Rykova and her lying ways.

A white Porsche with police markings pulled off the southbound lane of the autobahn and stopped directly behind the Mercedes. The blue strobe on top of the Porsche rotated like a pulsar. I could hear the radio. The driver was reporting his stop, identifying the Mercedes as a rental, telling his controller that "the suspect was standing outside his vehicle in a suspicious manner." A policeman got out of the Porsche and, flashlight in hand, approached me.

In German I said, "What is this suspect business? What am I suspected of? Spending dollars in Germany?" I was so angry I was ready to take on anyone.

The policeman, shown to be very young by the cold halogen lights, was wearing an ankle-length leather coat and a cap with a high peak reminiscent of the coats and caps of another generation of Germans.

"Are you having trouble, *mein Herr*?"

If you only knew, I thought. I said, "I have come from Pomellen and remembered something I must return for."

He said in English, "Your driving license? And your passport?"

In spite of my fluent German, the young man had swiftly identified me as an American. That said something about the upbringing the Colonel had given me. I produced the required documents. We stood in the lights, our breaths steaming in the frigid air. It was growing steadily colder and misting over. The stars had vanished. A few errant snowflakes spiraled down to earth through the headlight beams.

The policeman returned to the Porsche, and there was a five-minute conference with his colleague and more radio chat. I had a hard time controlling my impatience. I was anxious to return.

Who in hell *was* Annaliese Rykova? Meaning, really, not who but what was she? Whom did she work for? Dean Lockwood seemed the obvious choice, and the idea made me sick. Dean had sent me the Eagle Dagger in what I had thought an act of simple malice. But it had come to be far more than that. The killings in Brooklyn, and the attack on Ershad in Carmel, had already made it all much more than a family puzzle. Dean, or someone close to him, wanted me to follow the trail laid out for me. Wanted it so much that he had planted a *Niemandskind* on me to see to it that I performed as required. It made me feel like a damn robot. A very angry one now.

Finally the policeman returned and handed me my documents. "You are returning to Pomellen now?"

"Yes."

"I suggest driving with more caution. There is fog coming south from the Baltic."

"I'll be careful."

He touched the peak of his cap, clicked his bootheels and marched back to the police car. *Why do they insist on doing that?* I asked myself.

The Porsche remained where it was until I restarted the Mercedes and drove back onto the autobahn. It was now almost three hours since I had left the Red Salmon.

Thirty kilometers from Pomellen I drove into the fog the *Polizist* warned about. It was typical of the fogs of the north German plain, thick, ground-hugging and sudden. The mother of all fogs. When the dew point is low and the temperature drops, the icy mist can form as if by malign magic. It slowed me to a crawl. Occasionally a monster truck materialized out of the brume behind me and roared by, leaving swirls and rooster tails of mist in its wake. I gripped the wheel hard and drove at a steady speed. The hundred-mile-an-hour man who had left the border three hours before was metamorphosed into a careful one by the atmospherics of northern Germany.

The fog was so thick it took me another three-quarters of an hour to drive the eight kilometers from Radowitz to Pomellen. I crawled along the autobahn, praying one of the occasional trucks wouldn't rear-end me at its customary 120 kph. To die in a traffic accident in the middle of a northern Teutonic nowhere would be the ultimate futility.

As I neared the Red Salmon, I saw lights spearing through the fog. A great many lights. And when I reached the gasthaus parking lot, I saw that most came from the half-frozen marsh behind the building. There were three police cars in the parking area. And a medical van.

I parked the Mercedes and hurried inside. The narrow hallway that served as a lobby was crowded with the pasty concierge, the girl I had spoken to before leaving for the border and two policemen, one in uniform, the other in civilian clothes worn so much like a uniform that no one could mistake his occupation.

The plainclothesman looked up from his questioning of the girl as I came in. He referred to his notebook. "This would be Herr Lockwood, yes?" Through the windows at the end of the hall I could see bright lights being moved about behind the hotel.

"I'm Lockwood," I said. "What's happened here?"

"*Bitte, mein Herr.* Allow me to ask the questions." I wondered why it was that, even being polite, German policemen scraped at my sensibilities. "You are the traveling companion of the young woman upstairs?"

"Where is she? Has something happened to her?"

"She is being interrogated. Please answer my questions." He leafed through the notes he had made earlier. "Are you acquainted with an Erich Leyden?"

I don't normally lie to policemen, but something warned me to deny even having seen Leyden before.

"No," I said.

"You are quite certain of that, Herr Lockwood?"

"I don't know any such person."

The conversation was in German, and the policeman had no hesitation about talking to me in that language. Somewhere, somehow, he had done research on me.

"I will be happy to speak with you later, *Herr Polizist*," I said, "but first I intend to speak to my traveling companion." Clearly, if he was asking me about the guitar player, someone was asking Rykova the same questions. I wanted to hear her answers.

The plainclothesman nodded his consent, which surprised me. "I will speak with you again in a few moments, Herr Lockwood," he said. The repeated use of my name suggested a familiarity I could have done without. I went past him and up the stairs, two at a time.

The door to our room was open, and the room was a shambles. My luggage had been scattered; the feather bed was off its frame; the bedclothes were thrown about; drawers had been emptied. In the midst of all this stood Annaliese, being questioned by a leather-coated *Polizist* with a bull neck, long hair and a trunk like an oak tree.

Annaliese seemed in shock. She wore my traveling robe. The hem was stained with mud. Her bare feet were clotted with it. Marsh mud. Her hair hung in tangles. Her eyes were swollen from crying. Whatever else she was feeling at this moment, whoever she was, I believed her grief was genuine. I had a heavy premonition that the guitar player was the object of all the activity in the marsh behind the gasthaus.

The large cop turned on me. "Wait outside. There is an interrogation taking place here."

You officious, overbearing bastard, I thought. He loomed over Annaliese like a collapsing building.

Annaliese whispered, "I thought you had gone." She spoke in English, which the policeman almost surely did not understand.

I said, "Be careful what you say. How did this happen?"

"He just came in. He did this. I tried to stop him." She indicated the destroyed room. By "he" I knew she meant the guitar player. But even then, genuinely upset as she seemed, I felt she was still lying. Perhaps it was for the cop's benefit. He might, after all, have *some* English.

"Is Frau Rykova being accused of anything? If so, what?" I said.

The policeman said, "Do not interfere. I am in authority here." That outraged me.

"This young woman is my employee," I said in my most German manner. "If she is not under arrest, then you are *not* in authority here. I want you out, I want to speak with her privately."

The man was red-faced. "My superior will decide. I will ask him for instructions."

"Do it downstairs," I said.

He snapped his notebook closed and strode from the room. I closed the door behind him.

Annaliese's arms were around my neck in an instant. It had been years since I had seen a woman cry like that.

Words poured out of her. *"He is dead, Brian. Someone waited for him while he was here, and when he went downstairs, they killed him out there in the marsh. . . .* I sent him away and he left and then I heard the shots. . . ." Her face was chalk white. There was the sound of a terrible loss in her voice.

"Leyden did this?" I gestured at the room. "Tell the truth or I can't help. He came here. Why?"

No answer.

"Damn it, answer me, Annaliese. You told me that Marianna Clef was your grandmother. '*Mutti*,' I think you called her so tenderly." I figured if there was ever a time when I might get the truth, it was probably now, when she was vulnerable. I didn't like myself for doing it, but if not now, when? "Now please tell me how your guitar player knew where we were, how it was that he was following us and why he trashed this place."

"He was looking for the dagger. He knew it was valuable. He should not have done that. I would not have given it to him. But they killed him for it, anyway—"

"They? Who are *they*?"

She looked up at me accusingly. "Your uncle and his men."

"Jesus Christ, Dean." But even as I said his name, I had to

doubt that he had planned this elaborate charade. The letter, yes. I could believe that he had written that malicious letter, even that he had hired Annaliese and her friend to lead me up the garden path. He might have been the go-between, but he wasn't the key player in this weird game. Dean was window dressing, I was almost sure. There was a darker side to the business, but *what* it was and *why* it should be remained a mystery. Well, the only way to solve it was to slog on.

"When did Dean first contact you, and why you?"

"In Nuremberg, Brian. We had no money, and he said he needed a girl who could play a part. So he hired me, but he wouldn't hire Erich. We were to get a hundred DM at the beginning, and then, when I had done my part of the bargain, we were to get nine hundred more. But he didn't pay when he said he would, when you and I left the city. Erich went to see him to collect the money, and when he asked for it, some damn thug threw him out in the street. Erich needed money badly. He thought he could steal your dagger and sell it—"

"God damn it, Anna, why didn't you tell me about him?"

"I tried, Brian. I tried to get you to hire him. He wanted to go to America. That's all. But he needed the dagger. 'I hid it,' I said . . ."

I closed my eyes and counted ten. "Stop *lying.* I have the dagger with me." I took her by the shoulders and shook her lightly. "We don't have time for that. Tell the truth. For some reason, Erich came here tonight to take you away."

"It isn't what you think—"

"To hell with what I think. He's been trailing us, informing the man who hired you every mile of the way. But tonight was different. Leyden came for you tonight. Why? Why tonight?"

"He was frightened, Brian. Erich isn't . . . wasn't . . . very brave. Whatever happened when he went to collect the money, terrified him. He wanted to give it up, for us to run. He looked for the dagger, yes, but that was because we have no money."

"What frightened him so badly?"

"Stasi."

"There is no Stasi any longer, Anna."

"There may not be a GDR, Brian. But there is still a Stasi."

And somehow Dean Lockwood was a part of it? "You should have told me. Damn it, you should at least have *told* me."

"He promised us money, Brian. Enough to get us away from this country. Erich hated being a Vopo. He was a musician. An artist. We were getting out, don't you see? We were not going to be *Ossis* any longer. We were going to *America*."

She began to cry, and in spite of myself, I cradled her head with my hand. "Poor girl," I said. "It's hard to lose a lover."

She pushed herself away and looked up at me out of a devastated face. The borrowed robe that reached to her ankles made her, somehow, pitiful.

In a barely audible voice she said, "A lover? What would a lover matter? It's my baby *brother* out there in the marsh."

14

"There is no East and West now."

I MOVED TO THE WINDOW and stood behind the shabby curtain to look at the fog-shrouded activity below. Two medics in high rubber boots were crouching in the brackish water of the marsh. Between them the body of Erich Leyden lay half submerged in the mud. A policeman circled the floodlighted area with a camera, strobe flashing, taking photograph after photograph.

Annaliese came to stand beside me. Her breathing was fast and shallow. "I heard the shots," she said, as if to herself. "There were so many. Erich had run into the marsh. The light was very bad, but I could see him. He fell into the water and rolled over. Then I saw a man in a dark anorak, black, I think, with the hood pulled over his head. The man had a shotgun. He shot right into Erich's chest, both barrels. It made a terrible sound." She drew in a jagged, shuddering breath. "*I should have done something.*"

"There was nothing you could have done—"

"You don't understand. I argued with him. I told him he was wrong. I sent him away."

I tried to draw her away from the window. They were working the corpse into a dark green plastic body bag.

Annaliese's voice was stretched and strained, like a wire

about to snap. "The man, the one who shot Erich, he looked up at me. Then he reloaded the gun and shot Erich again—"

"Had you ever seen the man before? Was he the man who hired you?"

"No, no, never."

All right, Lockwood, think, for God's sake. There was an answer somewhere to all this crazy violence. I had to get to Von Stossen's parents, find out what part they played in this grim scenario.

Annaliese said in that same voice, "Erich screamed for help. There were people in the Trabant garage, but they were pigs, cowards. They were afraid of the man and his gun. I ran downstairs, but all I could do was watch while he drove away."

"In which direction?"

"What?" She seemed dazed by the question. "I don't know. I was out in the marsh looking for Erich when the police came."

"How tall was he? Blond or dark? Young or old? Fat or thin?"

She tried to concentrate. "Not old. He moved too quickly and easily in the marsh. He was tall, I think, clean-shaven, wide shoulders. The hood covered his hair."

The murders in Brooklyn, the attack on Professor Ershad and now this. It didn't fit. Dean Lockwood was a liar, thief and cheat, a con man certainly. But he was also a physical coward. He might conceivably kill someone quietly, secretly, though I doubted it. He just wasn't up to killing by violence or even hiring people who could.

Then what was left? *Who* was left?

I asked, "The person who hired you. Can you describe him at all?"

She made a gesture, as though brushing cobwebs from her face. "He was old, Brian."

"What else? What *else*, Anna?"

"He was tall. I don't know. I didn't really look at him."

"How did he find you?"

In spite of her grief over her brother, Annaliese gave me a look of pity. "Erich was once a Vopo. He had records. Many of them. And I have been arrested before. Little things, but they leave records, too. The Stasi knew us."

That again. The Stasi. True enough, it had been all-powerful before reunification. Was it still? I was beginning to be a believer. I remembered Dieter had said, "The Stasi is learning free enterprise, Brian. But it is still with us."

I tried to make sense of it all. A Stasi connection didn't absolve Dean Lockwood. Far from it. If he had been the con man Stein Davis thought he was for the last few years of his activities as a so-called dealer in art objects, he would almost certainly have had Stasi connections; he couldn't very well have operated in East Germany without them.

But my doubt remained. The savage violence that had been following me was simply out of character for a man like Dean Lockwood. Crime, yes. But this, and the killings in Brooklyn, no —all wrong for the Lockwood black sheep.

I had the feeling that we were between the jaws of the beast, that they were closing on us moment by moment. There was no going back. With each move I made, the bridge just crossed was burned behind me.

"Is there actually a Rykov?" I asked.

"Yes. We lived together in Riesa. But he went back to Russia. I told you that, didn't I?"

"Yes. You told me that."

She went again to the window, fixed on the scene below. The medics were loading the body bag onto a stretcher basket. Heavy mist curled and drifted through the lights. Annaliese shuddered. Her speech was rambling, disjointed.

"They took my passport. It says my name is Rykova. We bought it in Dresden. You can always get false Bundesrepublik papers in Dresden. . . ."

We, I thought. Erich and I. Youngsters living on the ragged edge of poverty and just outside the law. Hustling. Anything for a few marks. Until along came the Lockwoods, bearers of opportunity. A bad day for the Leydens.

Below, the medics and the policeman were carrying the mud-smeared plastic bundle away from the lights. The plainclothesman and his partner would be here within minutes.

"Did you tell the police Erich is your brother?"

She gave me a look. "No, oh, no—"

"The police knew his name."

"He had a driving license. A real one. It must have been in his wallet." Her eyes, once so green, looked black and cavernous, pupils dilated with fear. "Will I be arrested, Brian? Will they put me in prison?"

"If they put in prison everyone in this country with false papers, there would be no room inside for criminals." That was an overly optimistic view of the situation, but she did not need more trouble just now. "The police will be here in a minute or two," I said. "Let me talk to them. If you must answer a question, answer it. But volunteer nothing."

Her eyes widened. "They are in the hall," she whispered.

There was an authoritative knocking at the door. I opened it. The plainclothesman stood in the doorway with the large cop behind him, filling the hall.

"Herr Lockwood. May I come in?"

I moved aside.

He produced the passport he had taken from me downstairs and inspected it before returning it to me.

"And Frau Rykova's, if you please," I said.

"Frau Rykova is a German national, Herr Lockwood." His eyes were gray, nested in fleshy hammocks of tiny lines. He looked sad and tired. I had seen cops at home who looked like that, cops who see the drive-by shootings and the crack addicts and the ghetto homicides.

"You have no reason to hold her documents," I said. "She's done nothing illegal."

The plainclothesman looked steadily at Annaliese. "Did you see the murder, Frau Rykova?"

Annaliese shook her head like an accused child. The too-large robe she clutched to her breast heightened the impression.

"Are you certain? You were in the marsh when the police arrived. The killing took place right under your window."

I said, "She was in bed."

"Is that correct, Frau Rykova?"

"Yes." Her voice was scarcely audible.

"And why were you in the marsh?"

"I heard a call. I thought someone might be lost or in trouble. A marsh can be dangerous."

"Yes. That was very brave of you. Marshes are unpleasant places."

The plainclothesman took her passport from his coat pocket, opened it and looked at the pages. "Are you East German, Frau Rykova?"

"I was born in Bonn. It says I was born in Bonn."

"Yes. I see that it does. And it also says you are married to a Soviet citizen."

The large cop said, "She's *Ossi*. You can smell it on her."

"Tell your man to watch his mouth," I said.

He told "Kroger" to keep quiet. Then to Annaliese: "You should obtain a new passport, *gnädige Frau*. There is no East and West now."

"Surely there's nothing illegal about not having brought one's papers up-to-date," I said, not that sure of my ground as I sounded.

"Not yet—"

"Then you won't mind returning Frau Rykova's passport to her. She has the German regard for her official documents. I'm sure you understand that, *Herr Polizist*." A good offense was the best defense, it seemed.

"I do, Mr. Lockwood, I do." He spoke ironically, and in English for the first time, then handed the passport back to Annaliese.

He moved closer to the window. Below, they were dismantling the floodlights. "You did not see the crime, then, Frau Rykova?"

"I did not."

"And while you were in the marsh, your room was ransacked. Is that what happened?"

"Yes. It must have happened like that."

"You muddied your feet for nothing then," the plainclothesman said.

"Is there anything more?" I asked quickly.

"For the moment, no." The policeman looked at the room. "Anything of value missing here, Herr Lockwood?"

"There was nothing of value to be taken," I said.

"Then what do you suppose the thief was seeking?"

"What do hotel thieves usually seek, *Herr Polizist*? Money, I suppose."

"The people at the Trabant garage heard the shooting."

"Then I suggest you interrogate them, *mein Herr*," I said, slipping back into his language. German is a language in which it is easy to establish hierarchy.

"Are you by any chance a lawyer, Herr Lockwood?"

"A journalist," I said.

"Ah. Well, I see." He sighed heavily and moved toward the door. "It is late."

"Good night," I said.

"We will leave you for now. But please remain available. The Grenzschutz has been notified that a serious crime has taken place. Border crossings will be difficult until the matter is clarified. If you get my meaning, Herr Lockwood?"

"Your meaning is very clear, *Herr Polizist*."

"I hope so, Herr Lockwood."

He nodded to Annaliese and turned to his subordinate. "We will go now, Kroger, but there is still work to be done here."

Annaliese closed her eyes and swayed. I put my arm about her shoulders and held her. When the door closed behind the policemen, she whispered, "They didn't believe me."

"It doesn't matter," I said. "We're leaving here tonight."

15

I want to make amends . . .

THE PLAINCLOTHESMAN AND the medics did not depart with Erich Leyden's body until after three-thirty. Annaliese and I stayed in our room until then. There was no question of sleep. We packed our belongings and waited. Annaliese was still in a state of shock, but it was no longer what an American would have called grief.

You had to have lived as Annaliese had, in a country like the German Democratic Republic, to grasp how she felt. I thought I understood. Not because of any special perceptiveness but because I was *there.* I had seen the decay, the ugliness. I had smelled it and tasted it. Annaliese and Erich were looking for any kind of ticket *out,* and they were willing to do almost anything to earn it. *But live in a Communist state—*

There was the question of his body, for example. Most Americans would probably have been very concerned about it. Annaliese was not. Her grief was genuine, but Erich, having had the bad luck to be murdered, had no further claim on her. An inmate of a Nazi death camp or the Soviet gulag would have empathized instantly. Annaliese was, above all, a *survivor.*

* * *

I heard the medic's van depart into the black, foggy morning. When one of the police Porsches followed, I told Annaliese: "I think the officer left his man here. I'm going to see what I can do with him. Be ready."

Dressed now and wearing her anorak, she huddled by the window. I was concerned about her, but there was nothing I could do. Either she would perform when the time came or she wouldn't. It just never occurred to me to give up my quest—if that was what it was—across the border into Poland. Did that make me a sort of survivor, too?

I went downstairs. The *Leiter*—the Red Salmon's manager— had surfaced, his face ruddy with sleep, his thin black hair newly combed and wet so that it resembled a nest of pinworms. He wore a threadbare robe and scuffed slippers. The farther east we traveled, the more impoverished and unattractive the people became.

"Herr Lockwood," the man said, "what terrible times we have experienced, how unpleasant it has been for us all."

I looked down the hallway at the open door to a small room near the entrance.

"Yes," he said. "They have left one of theirs here. The big one. Kroger. It does a guesthouse no good to have policemen about at all hours."

"Have you any liquor to sell?"

He opened a cabinet behind the registration counter. "I have no license to sell alcohol out of hours, Herr Lockwood. But under the circumstances . . ." He took a nearly full bottle of schnapps from the cupboard. "May I offer you . . . ?"

"Sell me the bottle," I said. I intended to use it on Kroger.

"Would thirty D-marks seem too high?"

It was damned high for an opened bottle of cheap schnapps, and he knew it. But it was what the traffic would bear. I paid him and took the bottle. "What has the policeman been doing?"

"Watching dirty Polish television from Poznan." The manager folded the bank notes carefully and put them in his pocket. "For better days to come," he said.

"Have you a couple of glasses?"

From behind the counter he produced two paper cups. I took

them and started down the hall. The manager stopped me. "Are you still planning to depart after breakfast, Herr Lockwood?"

"Perhaps it would be best if I paid my bill now," I said, understanding what he wanted.

"If you wish. Of course. Shall we say three hundred D-marks?"

"D-marks, yes, but one hundred fifty, *Herr Leiter.*"

He looked at the illegally sold bottle in my hand, smiled and said, "Yes. One hundred fifty, Herr Lockwood. Three hundred was, uh, a slip of the tongue." More smiles.

I counted the bills into his hand. "Good night, *Herr Leiter.*"

"Good morning, Herr Lockwood," he said, and shuffled down the passageway to the rear of the gasthaus.

I walked down the hall to the open door. Kroger, the ugly cop, sat in a chair in front of an ancient Russian television set. A scratchy print of a Polish porn film in black and white flickered silently across the small screen. Kroger had taken off his leather coat and shirt. In spite of the chill, there were half-moons of sweat at the armpits. He was listening to an earpiece at the end of a twisted wire. The room smelled of stale tobacco smoke. There was an ashtray on the floor by his feet and several old and tattered skin magazines on the bed.

I knocked on the doorjamb.

"What do you want?"

"I was impolite earlier. I would like to make up for it. May I buy you a drink?"

He looked at the bottle of schnapps. "I am on duty," he said.

"Only to see that we don't leave, which we have no intention of doing. Or don't you drink?"

"I drink when it suits me."

"Then what harm can a drink do now?"

"None, I suppose."

I filled a paper cup with schnapps and handed it to him, then poured one for myself.

"*Prost,*" I said.

He drained his cup.

"I shouldn't have criticized you in front of your superior officer," I said. "I was upset."

His only answer was to hold out his empty cup, which I refilled.

Kroger drank with silent relish. "This needs beer to follow," he said. "Schnapps and beer are a proper man's drink." He regarded me with a kind of official malevolence. "You should watch what you say to officers of the law."

"Yes, you're right. I should."

"Your girl is *Ossi*. I can tell."

"You're wrong, Herr Kroger. She is from Bonn."

"I know an Easterner when I see one." He drank the second paper cup of schnapps and belched. "That's why I was assigned here to the border. Because I know about *Ossis*."

I filled his cup again, and my own. "If you say so, Herr Kroger."

"I do say so. I am an authority on Reds. I was only four years from retirement when they begged me to return to field duty here." He belched again. "The Bundesrepublik made a mistake taking on this wasteland. It will all end in a shitstorm. You won't be here to see it, of course. . . ." The thought appeared to upset him. "You'll be safe in America. But it will end badly. We opened our doors and look what happened. Now Germany is overrun with kikes, Easterners and black foreigners." He drank more schnapps, sloshed it between his teeth and lips. "Big fucking deal. The Wall is down. You people are going to run out on us. You'll see . . ."

For an instant I thought he meant Annaliese and me, but Kroger was dealing with larger things. Schnapps and the availability of an American ear had broken a logjam of resentments in Polizist Kroger. Now that the Wall was down, the reunification about which Germans had dreamed for so long did not look nearly so attractive. I heard echoes of Dieter Langan's political doubts in Kroger's bigoted whining.

He lurched to his feet. "Schnapps makes me want to leak. How much is left there?"

"Plenty," I said, holding up the bottle. "Give me your cup."

Kroger did, then twisted his doughy face into a sour smile. "Don't spit in it, I'll be right back."

I watched him. He was unsteady.

When he disappeared down the hallway, I took the tiny bottle of nitroglycerin pills I carried in my pocket, put five in Herr Kroger's glass and filled it with schnapps.

My cardiologist, Gary Fry, had warned me that when I used nitro, I should be careful not to stand too still for too long. Nitrostat, he said, was an arteriodilator. Taken with booze, it could bring on fainting spells. Well, if I made this prince of pigs sick, I really didn't give a damn.

"What are you doing there?" Kroger stood in the doorway.

"Filling your cup."

He stumbled as he came into the room. He had pissed himself. There were small dark spatters on his twill uniform trousers. I handed him the paper cup.

He sank down in the chair again, stared vaguely at the television screen. On a rocky beach a pair of naked girls were fondling the genitalia of a scrawny young man with long hair and a pointed, sunburned nose.

"Look at them," Kroger muttered. "Filthy Polish cunts."

"*Prost*," I said. "Here's to Polish cunts."

Kroger drank. "Did you see the film *JFK*?" he asked. "I did. Paid twenty D-marks for a ticket in Prenzlau. You Americans are corrupt."

"Oliver Stone apparently thinks so."

"Everybody thinks so."

"More schnapps?"

"No."

I stood up. Put the bottle in his lap. "Then I'll say good morning. Enjoy the schnapps."

He slumped against the back of the chair, his eyes rolling slightly upward. Sleep well, you shit, the *Ossis* are coming to steal your pension. Kroger lurched to the bed and threw himself belly down among the porn magazines. As I went through the door, I heard the bottle hit the floor and roll. He sucked in a rattling, snoring breath.

I left the door open behind me.

Upstairs Annaliese was in exactly the same position by the window. She was staring out at the foggy marsh. I wondered what it was she saw out there in the dark. Lost dreams?

"We're going now."

"All right." Naked Jews stepping into the death pits might have said it the same way. It was as though she no longer cared what she did or with whom she did it.

I shouldered her backpack and lifted my own carryall. "Kroger is in a room near the front entrance. I think he's asleep or passed out. We'll take our chances."

She waited for me to lead the way. Her face had no color. Her lips were gray, almost white.

We went silently down the stairs, along the dark hallway. I looked in at Kroger as we passed. He still lay on the bed among the porn magazines.

The air outside was wet and cold. The snow had melted on the ground, turning the near court to mud. I led Annaliese to the car and opened the door. "Are you all right?"

"Yes. All right."

I walked around and got behind the wheel. Started the car. I thanked Providence for German precision. The Mercedes idled silently. I engaged the first gear and let the car roll, out to the road back toward Gartz. Once on the autobahn, I turned on the headlights and accelerated. Behind me, the Red Salmon vanished into the fog.

We reached the border post after a half hour, rolling through the thick mists. I'd assumed that the Grenzschutz were already corrupted with payoff for my first border crossing. I was right. There was only a momentary hitch as a border guard signaled me to hold up and show our passports. "Weren't you through this post last night?"

I said that I was. Now I was back. You need a certain *attitude* when dealing with uniformed Germans. The guards returned our passports and lifted the barrier. Five minutes more and we were across the Oder and into Poland.

16

"I never wanted to know."

THE ROAD WE WERE TRAVELING curved to the northeast away from
the river. I rolled the window down to stop the windshield from
misting. The air had a cutting edge. The headlights, angled as
low as could be managed, still turned the way ahead into fea-
tureless silver-white. Yet from time to time I could catch a
glimpse, through the upper part of the arc cleared by the windshield wiper, of a clear night sky shot with diamond-bright winter stars. The fog lay low, a shroud on the land.

I glanced at Annaliese. She sat motionless, staring straight
ahead into the mist.

"It was too easy," she said.

"What was too easy?"

"They wouldn't have left one policeman alone to watch us.
They do not do things that way."

I was a little surprised by the suddenly cold calculation in her
voice, yet one of the things that bothered me most was exactly
what she was saying: It *had* been too easy.

"The old Stasi still control the National Police?"

"Of course they do." The grieving sibling had vanished. This
was the *Ossi* survivor by my side.

She spoke from a long short lifetime of experience. Hadn't

Dieter warned me that the Stasi were desperate now? Looking for deals. Doing the odd murder. "It had to be a Stasi who killed Erich," she said in that voice without inflection. She turned to look at me for the first time since we had crossed the frontier. There was fear and hatred in her eyes.

What was she thinking? That I was the one who had brought the Stasi? In her grief Annaliese displayed a remarkably cold perception. She and her brother had apparently convinced themselves that getting what they wanted would be easy, and they had been wrong. Dead wrong. Instead, they had become victims.

"You would have been better off to leave me for the police," she said suddenly.

"I couldn't do that."

"It won't matter." She turned her face away and folded her hands in her lap. In her way, I realize now, she was trying to warn me.

The fog began to curl and break, the way it sometimes does before a storm. From time to time I could see the road and the surrounding fens more clearly. Although it was nearly dawn, the winter sky was still sable black and the stars were brilliant.

What lay around us was a land made for war. Fifty-two years earlier Hitler's panzers had rolled eastward here, slaughtering the Polish cavalrymen who offered to fight again, with lance and charger, the wars of the nineteenth century. The Polish plain became a killing ground. Military misjudgments exacted a terrible price. Poland's defeat earned it six years in the Nazi furnace, followed by five decades of glacial Marxist Leninism.

As the fog thinned and the sky grew lighter, the land around us emerged from the chill darkness. These Baltic lowlands had once been part of Prussia, then Poland, then Germany, then Communist Poland and, finally, Lech Walesa's curious socialist Polish state. It was a flatland steeped in bloody, bitter history. Here Teutonic Knights—one named Stossen?—had pretended to crusade, using ecclesiastical writ to carve out fiefdoms for themselves.

Against the starlight an occasional low hill topped by the

suggestion of ancient ruins could be seen. These were the fossils of the hill forts the German knights had built centuries ago in that forenoon of German aggression.

Thirty kilometers from the river and ten from Obryta, I stopped to study a map in the dashboard light.

The Nazis created a prisoner class known as *Gefangene der Nacht und Nebel*. Men and women spirited away in the night without warning or explanation, never to be seen again. It was said of them that they vanished into night and fog—*Nacht und Nebel*. Night on the fenlands brought macabre images to mind. In a way the inhabitants of this place were all prisoners of night and fog. Their lives had disappeared into the night of fascism and the fog of Marxism.

Behind us the Oder River meandered toward the Baltic, a short distance to the north. The very land seemed alien, brooding.

History has always threatened to overwhelm me. When I was growing up, the past always seemed nearby. One foggy morning, as I touched the great sarsens of Stonehenge, I actually felt the presence of the builders. I could almost hear the cries of the workmen tipping the huge stones into their pits. Salisbury Plain came to life in my imagination. And on a still afternoon at Canterbury Cathedral, I heard the iron rattle of chain mail and the stroke of steel on stone as Thomas à Becket died. Fantasies, yes. But aren't we always surrounded by ghosts?

Adolf Hitler's Einzatzgruppen had traveled these western Polish roads on their fanatic mission of making east Europe *Judenrein*. From here they moved east, marking their way with pits filled with bones, creating grisly monuments that made those left by Tamerlane seem small.

To me, the past always seemed eager to claw its way out of the blasted earth and assault the living. Was that the sum total of my German heritage? The knowledge that men of my blood had done such things?

Clouds, driven by storms in the north, raced across the sky, intermittently covering the stars. The land around us would suddenly vanish and as suddenly reappear, like the landscape of a dream. I remembered some lines by a British poet who

wrote that events were like the wars and winters "missing behind the windows of an opaque childhood."

These were my wars, and this was my winter.

I turned off the map light and drove on, past ruins of Polish
farms whose halfhearted Russian masters had disappeared into
the vast Eurasian plain to the east when their fantasy of a Soviet
world crumbled.

Now another half-ruined farmhouse appeared ahead,
crouched under the loom of a hillock that a broken tower stood
on.

I stopped the car again. It was getting lighter.

"Is this the place?" she asked.

"I think so."

"What will you do with the dagger?"

I wondered at her single-mindedness.

"I don't know. The dagger isn't important, not in the way you
and Erich thought it was. I may give it to the Stossens. If anyone
has a right to it, I suppose they have."

"You're a fool."

"Could be."

"Why do it? Why even come here? We could go back now."

"Why do you care? Until you met Dean Lockwood, you'd
never heard of the Stossens."

"My brother died for that dagger," she said coldly.

"We don't know that."

"*I* know it."

Did I really intend to give the Stossens their Nazi son's Eagle
Dagger? Would that free me from whatever it was that was
driving us on? All I knew was that the run-down farmhouse set
in the barren fenland looked like an evil, haunted house.

I was an adult, an American. I wasn't a child abandoned in
the snow by a German river. But my fear was genuine, like that
child's.

Annaliese was watching me closely.

"Tell me what you were told to do," I said.

"What is there to tell you?"

"Your instructions. Exactly."

"I was given a key to Marianna Clef's house and a list of things to memorize. About you. About the house where you lived as a child. That sort of thing. I was told you would come. I was to stay with you and guide you where you wanted to go."

"You knew where I would want to go."

"Your uncle told me."

"If it was my uncle."

She shrugged. "I followed my orders."

How German, I thought. I said, "In bed and out."

"You Americans make sex too important."

"Did the man who killed Erich have a name?"

"Erich called him Eugen. No last name. He kept saying that we had to get away before Eugen found us."

She drew an agitated breath, as though she felt a trap closing. "He followed. Erich was careless when he was frightened. . . ."

"And what frightened him?"

"Eugen beat him up when he went to get the money the old man owed us."

"So Erich came to you to try and find the dagger?"

"He knew it was valuable." She sounded almost exasperated over my lack of understanding of these matters. "He thought we could sell it and go to the United States. I didn't lie about that, Brian."

"And Erich knew where to find you because you were keeping him informed about where we were. What you told me about Erich needing a job was another lie. He already had one. He transmitted your messages. To Eugen?"

"I never wanted to know. Leave me alone."

"Poor old Fräulein Clef. Mutti, no less. What a cozy touch."

"I was ordered to speak of her to you that way."

"What else were you told about her and the war?"

"That she was raped by the Russians and that Ursula was the result. I was the right age to be Ursula's daughter, if she'd had a daughter. The old man said not to worry if I made a mistake, just to laugh and say you must have forgotten what happened. After all, you were very small when you left. The rest wasn't difficult."

"To fool me? I shouldn't think so."

"You wanted to be fooled."

Another thought struck me, chilled me. How very convenient that Fräulein Clef should suddenly die. Cyndi Genovese and the Brooklyn messenger, Erich Leyden—and Marianna Clef, too? Was it *possible?*

The eastern sky was swiftly growing light. The stars disappeared. A flight of birds flew like darts of darkness away from the sea. If there had once been productive, cultivated ground surrounding the farmhouse, there was no evidence of it now. These old sometime-Prussian holdings were severe in design and cold in intent—like parade grounds. But once they had been working country estates. The Prussian chill was evident everywhere, but it was more than grim austerity. The house was surrounded by hectares of deliberate neglect.

"What a terrible place," Annaliese said. "Prussians live here. Germans hate Prussians."

Between wars they do, I thought.

The sky was slowly turning blue-white; it looked like skimmed milk. The wind drove the low, chalky clouds from north to south. A higher level of black cumulus lay in the horizon. The air was cold and smelled of brackish water. I stopped the car in front of the house. There was a door, but it was blocked by dead potted plants and a pile of old lumber. I got out of the Mercedes and walked slowly around the curve of the dirt road toward a cottage grafted long ago to the main structure. Light gleamed behind a grimy window.

Annaliese was alongside me when I rapped on the door. There was movement inside. The door was opened a few inches. Behind the crack was a face that seemed made from fine parchment.

"Frau Stossen?" I stood in the shadow of the overhanging eaves.

The woman behind the door said, "Stand out of the shadow so I can see you." Her speech was the local dialect—an *alter Hochdeutsch,* the old High German that had been used here for centuries. It was much too imperious, too regal for these dreary surroundings.

I said again, and with less patience, "Frau Stossen, I've come from the United States to talk to you. I have something that belonged to your son."

"Move back. Away from the door." There was command in the voice. The door opened.

A tiny, ancient woman stood at the threshold. Behind her, a bulky man appeared. Perhaps in his mid-sixties, he was dressed in the corduroy and leather of a gamekeeper. He carried an old Mannlicher 6.5 millimeter mountain carbine, and it was pointed at my chest.

"Dolger! Stop it, you fool. Can't you see who it is? Don't hurt my grandson!"

17

"He did his duty as a soldier."

IT WAS LIKE A KNIFE in my chest. With that single phrase the old woman made real a nightmare.

Now I had a clear look at her. She was no more than an inch over five feet but straight as a sword blade. Her hair was the color of spun steel, like a helmet on her narrow head. She wore an old black dress. There were heavy farm shoes on her tiny feet. Her eyes were the color of an Arctic sea.

Don't hurt my grandson! My God, had she really said it?

She reached out with a hand—not to caress but to command. She said in a thin, tightly reined voice: "Have you the token?" She used the German word *"zeichen,"* which has a strong secondary meaning of "memorial." But before I could answer, she spoke again. "Dolger, go wake up the baron and bring him here."

The room was large, low-ceilinged, cold and dark. It was furnished with an astonishing range of pieces: a harp, a grand piano (closed and populated with dozens of framed photographs); there were chairs and armoires, chests and hutches of polished wood, inlaid antiques. The furnishings of a far grander place.

A massive oblong table stood in a clear space near the ancient

156

wood-burning stove. Frau von Stossen was by one of the heavy wooden chairs. The man she called "Dolger" glowered at me over his weapon.

"*Verdammte,* Dolger, do as I tell you," Frau Stossen commanded.

The man left the room.

The dagger in my coat pocket seemed suddenly very heavy. *die zeichen,* the old woman called it. I took it out and dropped it on the table. At that moment there was no object in all the world I loathed as much as Sieg Stossen's *Adler Dolch.*

It was obvious that to Frau Stossen the Eagle Dagger was the most important object, animate or otherwise, in the strange room. But in spite of her obvious longing to touch it, she stood like a soldier at attention, hands at her sides.

"Do you know who I am, *Enkel?*" Again. *Grandson.* I had the same disoriented feeling I remembered from my bout with the drugs in the Stanford hospital. It was as though part of my mind belonged to some stranger I had been afraid of and hated all my life.

"I am Baroness Freya von Stossen." She waited, expecting a comment. I made none. I had only glanced at the Stasi dossier; the packet was on the floor of the Mercedes outside the farmhouse.

"You brought the token. How can you not know us?" Freya von Stossen demanded.

"The dagger was sent to me," I told her. Now I was sure that Dean had only been a means to an end. But what did Dean Lockwood have to do with these people?

"You will want to know what your responsibilities are. Good. Let me educate you. Come." She moved away from the table across the room to the grand piano. "You, girl," she said, "there is coffee on the stove and cups in the cupboard. There will be three." I expected Annaliese to resent the old woman's tone, but she didn't. The baroness's manner had apparently taken over. Even with someone of Annaliese's rebellious generation. I had seen this happen before with Europeans. Often the most rebellious could be cowed by a word from the owner of a title—any title.

"Frau von Stossen," I said, "Fräulein Leyden is not a servant. Her brother was killed last night—"

"A matter of no importance."

"Of much importance."

The baroness favored me with a wintry smile. "How American you are, *Enkel*. Very well, girl. Do nothing. It won't matter to the baron." She selected a framed picture from among the many on the piano and held it out to me. "See," she commanded.

I studied the photograph. A man and a very young woman stood together in a stiff, formal pose. The man wore the dress uniform of a Luftwaffe officer, but it was the girl who caught my attention. She was slender, blond, no more than seventeen or eighteen and dressed in a bridal gown. Her features were sunlit, yet they somehow conveyed a sadness of almost unbearable poignancy.

It was a face I had seen uncounted times when I dreamed of the icebound Pegnitz. Even more startling was the similarity between that face and the one I saw each morning in the mirror. The woman was beautiful and I *certainly* was not, but the resemblance in other ways was striking. I was looking at a photograph of my mother on her wedding day. A day that should have given her joy had not. The young face showed only sadness. Because she really loved someone else? At her age it was certainly possible. Sieg Stossen (it could be no one else) was looking at his bride like a hunter who had just brought down a quarry. His dark brows were drawn tight together above his deep-set, narrow eyes.

I looked at the photograph a long time. What I saw was sadness for what? Freedom lost? Youth ended? A Prussian dynastic marriage, even in those Nazi times, was not likely to have been a love match. The beauty in the photograph had faded and the sadness deepened until the face became that of the woman in my dream.

And eventually her fate came to claim her in a forest by a small, bitter river far from home.

Yet somehow, in a way I'd yet to discover, she had met American Brian Lockwood—and loved him. Then what? Had he just abandoned her? Gone home without making some provision for her? I couldn't believe it. He had reached out across the ocean and claimed me. To me, that meant he must have loved her. Enough, after all, to adopt her child. And now I had to face what I most dreaded—myself, the child fathered by the man in the photograph.

I studied Stossen more carefully. My God, I thought, I've *seen* this man. Or someone like him. This was, I thought, a younger version of a face I had seen from my window in Nuremberg. The one I'd first thought was Uncle Dean. I was almost sure of it. *A man who was supposed to have died in the Battle of Berlin forty-six years ago.*

It was as though my own murky past were slowly forming in front of me. Everything I feared and could never bring myself to believe, everything I had taught myself to loathe. Images of cruelties beyond reason, arrogance beyond endurance. If the photograph in my hand did not lie, I was the son of a Nazi war criminal, and somehow Dean Lockwood had discovered it and brought me to this place. Why?

I thought about Claire. Had she any idea where I really came from? It was something she had a right to know. It would also explain a lot about the reserved, austere man who was her father.

"There is very little of my son in you, Enkel," the baroness said. "And everything of *her*."

"Who was she?"

"She was one of us. This land was Prussian then." The eyes glittered with an ancient hostility. "The damned American loved her, for whatever little *that* is worth. But in the end even he couldn't save her from the Russians."

"Tell me about her. . . ."

"Her name was Kristina Erika Obryta. Her family once owned the land on which we stand. A border family, understand? They had Polish blood. Royal, some said. I doubt that. But they owned ten thousand hectares. The Stossen land marched with theirs. It is gone now, most of it. Stolen by the Communists. But she was an heiress then. And she *was* beautiful. The pictures do not do her justice. My son worshiped her."

I remembered a six-meter sloop on San Francisco Bay. The *Erika.* So the austere Brian Lockwood had been sentimental enough to name his boat after a lost love.

And I remembered, too, the talks with Claire when we speculated about what powers he had offended to be sent home so abruptly from Germany to take up what amounted to a permanently damaged career. "Even he could not save her from the Russians," the baroness had said. But he tried, surely. And for that they shipped him home. . . . And then, when he had gone, the Russians came for her. But how had she so offended them? Of course. To begin with, by being Sieg Stossen's wife.

I looked at the other photographs ranged across the top of the piano. There were rows of them. Men with hunting trophies. Women sidesaddle on tall hunters. There were several sepia prints of men wearing leather flying clothes and standing in front of airplanes of the Great War, World War I. And more photographs of the wedding party. One in particular caught my attention. A throng of people—half a hundred or more—stood in ranks before a stone church. In a beautiful old-fashioned copperplate script, someone had written across the bottom of the print: "Obryta, 20 Juli 1944."

The identity of one of the guests, a very large man in an ornate white uniform, was unmistakable.

"You entertained some interesting guests that day," I said.

"The *Reichsmarschall*," the baroness said, nodding. "He fancied himself a Teutonic Knight, but he was only a Bavarian petit bourgeois." Her tone was contemptuous. "I could never understand what Sieg saw in him. A morphine addict. Gross in his habits and manners." She might have been discussing the breeding and gaits of a saddle horse. "The Nazis were scum, but they rewarded distinguished service."

"At Sachsenhausen?" I said.

She looked at me closely. "You disapprove?"

"Of course I disapprove."

"How like a naïve American you are, grandson."

"Frau Baroness," I said, "I remind you that the war ended with Berlin in rubble, not Washington."

"With an Austrian corporal as supreme commander, how else could it possibly have ended?"

"Your son"—I could not bring myself to say "my father"— "your son was a physician."

"He was a genius. A pioneer in aviation medicine. He was

graduated from the faculty of medicine at Marburg at the age of twenty-one."

"What else did he do for Göering?"

"He did his duty as a soldier."

I looked across the room at the dagger, which lay on the table. "He tortured prisoners for *that?*"

"What a fool you are." She stared at me. "Thank God, my son never knew you," she said. "But then perhaps he could have given you some sense of blood and tradition. You obviously have none."

She took a tarnished silver frame from the piano top. It held a very old picture, a daguerreotype so faded by time that the figures were nearly lost. But I could make out a middle-aged man in uniform standing between an old man and a boy in formal civilian dress.

The baroness said, "This was taken at my father-in-law's wedding at Schloss Stossen in 1882. The man with Baron Alfried von Stossen is Richard Wagner. This photograph was taken a year before the old gentleman died. The boy is his son, Siegfried. The boy loved and admired my father-in-law. The families were very close. The Stossens had many important connections."

Dolger reappeared then. He was pushing an ancient wheelchair. In it sat a desiccated old man. Helmuth von Stossen was the color of dust. Thin gray hair, gray skin, gray eyes. He wore a gray uniform jacket. At his throat hung a silver and black cross —the Knight's Cross of the Iron Cross, Hitler Germany's highest award for valor. It could not possibly have been his. He was too old to have seen active service in the Second World War, except perhaps at the very last, in the Volkssturm—a force of old men and children. There had been no medals for the Volkssturm. The cross must have belonged to his son, Sieg. Another trophy of his loyal service to the Third Reich.

The eyes in the raddled gray face were blank. Baron von Stossen, I guessed, had suffered a stroke, perhaps a series of them. It was impossible to know how much of what went on around him he was aware of.

In the photograph of the group before the church in Obryta stood this Baron Helmuth von Stossen as he had once been: tall, erect, soldierly in World War I army dress gray. But even then he must have been in his late forties. He was in his mid-nineties now and fragile as a bird.

The baron was a husk of a man. Of what possible interest could his son's Eagle Dagger be to such a relic? When Dolger wheeled Von Stossen into the room, I felt gravity shift between reality and fantasy.

Frau Stossen quickly gave Dolger specific orders about where the old man should be placed. The location of the chair at the head of the oblong table was overseen with a Prussian precision and sense of hierarchy. It took Dolger several minutes to adjust Von Stossen's chair precisely as the baroness desired. And all the while the old man stared at empty air as a bubble of spittle formed at the corner of his mouth. Dolger wiped it away with a cloth. An act of kindness, performed with hatred in Dolger's eyes. How long had Dolger been relegated to acting the male nurse and cleaning up spittle and worse for the baron? And where had he come from?

Sieg Stossen's *Adler Dolch* lay on the table like an officer's sword at a British court-martial. I could not guess what came next. I was held by the oppressiveness of the room, the house, of the ancestral lands my mother had brought as dowry to Sieg Stossen. My stomach cramped with the weight of unwanted knowledge. I was deeply regretting that I had come to this place.

I felt a hand on my arm. It was Annaliese, whom I had nearly forgotten during my exchange with the baroness. "Are you all right, Brian?" she whispered.

I managed a half-smile. "Ever since I met you, you have been asking me that question."

"But are you?"

"Yes. These people were not what I expected, but they are not *more* than I expected."

She glanced at the baroness, still giving detailed instructions to Dolger while her husband stared into nowhere.

"Don't be afraid," I said.

She shook her head. "I was at first. But not now."

What, I wondered, did Annaliese Rykova, Leyden, whoever she was, see? A very old aristocrat whose personal world had ended many years ago and who now lived like a dirt-poor peasant remembering past glories?

Baroness von Stossen could not be an object of fear, I thought. More one of pity. I looked at Annaliese's eyes. They were cold and steady. The young of the new Germany were not greatly known for pitying the old.

18

"It is the von Stossen legacy."

At FREYA VON STOSSEN'S COMMAND we all gathered around the table. I studied Helmuth von Stossen, who sat immobile at the head of the table. At closer range his face was essentially a crumpled paper mask stretched over a skull. How old was he? I wondered. He had served in the First World War as a lieutenant of artillery. Young, but Prussians married young. Sieg von Stossen had been born in 1916. Helmuth von Stossen had to be in his nineties.

Then why was the baroness subjecting him to this curious ritual over Sieg Stossen's dagger?

"Sit, all of you," the baroness commanded. "You may sit, too, girl. But be silent."

Annaliese gave the old woman a cold stare. She had lived all her life steeped in the politics of class envy, and Freya von Stossen was the embodiment of the ancient class enemy. I caught a glimpse now of the Annaliese I had first encountered a week ago in Marianna Clef's house. I told myself that if she saw Frau von Stossen as the enemy, that designation might soon extend to me, too.

"You, *Enkel*," Freya von Stossen said, "sit here at my side. Yes,

I know, but you *are* my grandson. That is a fact of life that cannot be avoided. Do as I say."

She looked at Dolger, then back to me. "Dolger was my son's aide-de-camp for the last year of the war. He was not the sort of man one would have made a German officer before Hitler, but he has the virtue of loyalty." When she looked at the man, there was contempt in her expression, yet both she and her husband must have depended on him for almost everything.

It was as though the baroness had read my thoughts. "The Nazis were a revolting lot, with habits learned in the Bavarian gutters. But Sieg believed in them. 'They are loyal,' he said. In that, he was right. Even about this one. Sieg gave him to us." She spoke to me as though Dolger did not exist.

I looked across the table at the man, heavy, sloping shoulders, eyes sunk deep in pillows of fat. How many insults, how many humiliations had he taken from these arrogant old people?

We sat for a moment, a strange tableau gathered around the *Adler Dolch.* The baroness seemed strangely animated, as though this scene were somehow the culmination of a long-held dream. When she spoke, it was directly to me.

"You asked if my son had performed experiments for the reward of that dagger. The task that Sieg undertook was unpleasant work. But it was his duty and he performed it as a Prussian officer. German airmen were dying of exposure after parachuting into the English Channel. The medical department of the Luftwaffe needed information that could be obtained in no other way than by using human subjects."

"Do you actually believe that?"

The old face closed. I had challenged her and the integrity of her son.

"My son did his duty as a soldier . . . *always,*" she said. "No matter how distasteful."

"Is that what it was, Frau Baroness? *Distasteful?*"

Dolger was scowling at me across the table. The baron still stared at nothing, the medal on his gray breast glittering in the dim light filtering in through the grimy windows.

"The Eagle Dagger was given Sieg by Reichsmarschall Göering for a secret task only the most trusted of his aides could carry out." She laughed harshly. "Sieg said it was like a blessing from God in the midst of hell. He knew that he held in his possession the way, the only way, to save the family."

"Göering fancied himself a connoisseur of art. Of course, he was nothing of the sort. But he had advice, a great deal of advice, and some of it was excellent. He collected things, beautiful things. When the British and American terror bombings began in earnest, he ordered Sieg to find places where some of the best pieces could be safeguarded until the war ended. In 1945 Sieg crossed the frontier into Switzerland and found the Swiss accommodating. As they usually are when one brings things of value into their absurd country. Sieg found safe havens for every one of the articles that had been entrusted to him. When he returned to Germany, he told me that the value of the treasure was eight hundred and fifty million marks. Think of that, *Enkel.* What would such a trove be worth today, do you think?"

I looked at her, marveling. So the most trusted aide of the *Reichsmarschall* had double-crossed his mentor and stolen the booty he had carried off to Switzerland. I glanced at the squalid surroundings. They had waited here all these years in these conditions, and if I was right, their beloved son was living in luxury not five hundred miles away. It was hard to believe that anyone could be that cold-bloodedly inhuman. The sheer cruelty of it . . . But it did all fit the pattern at last forming in my mind.

The woman's icy old eyes fixed me. "That includes you, *Enkel*, no matter how American you think you are. Oh, I know more about you than you believe. Dolger, bring me the dagger. . . ."

Dolger lifted the dagger as though it were a holy relic. As he moved around the table, I caught a glimpse of the bronze buckle of the black leather belt he wore. It was decorated with the stylized lightning bolts of the SS. Sieg Stossen, a Luftwaffe doctor, must have had great influence to rate a Schutzstaffel aide.

Watching Freya von Stossen accept the dagger, I recalled what she had said when she identified me as Kristina Obyrta's son: *"Habst du die Zeichen?"*

Now she held *die Zeichen* in her hands, the ceremonial weapon that I had carried from California to this Polish marshland. So, that was what I had been transporting—the key, the token, *die Zeichen,* to Göering's stash? With the Stasi, or what was left of it, dogging my footsteps, killing when it seemed expedient, and watching, always watching?

"You look disapproving, grandson. How can you possibly judge us? Look at the baron. He was once a man to be feared and respected. He had his first stroke the night the RAF burned Dresden. He has not spoken since." The old woman's eyes filled suddenly. "They say the old cry easily. Don't believe it. There are not enough tears to mourn what I have lost. The lands are gone, stolen, sold, confiscated by a government of *Untermenschen*. Schloss Stossen is a bombed-out ruin; American fighters saw to that. The town houses were burned or blown to bits or torn down by people I would not hire to clean my stables."

She turned the dagger over in her hands. "Sieg showed this to me a week after he was given it by Göering. He was proud of it, it signified all the beautiful things he had saved." She brushed away her tears with a fierce gesture. "That was on a January evening in 1945. We were at the villa in Brandenburg. The Americans had been flying over us to and from Berlin all day. Thousands of them. Their condensation trails made the sky white. Then it grew dark, and the RAF began. We could look east and see Berlin burning. Sieg said to me, 'Mama, the war is lost. The Allies are across the Rhine and the Russians are across the Niese. I want you to take Father and get to Switzerland. I will tell you where. And then, if I cannot bring it myself, I will send you a token. I will give you the key to all the beautiful things the fat man stole—' " She managed a bleak smile. "You see, grandson, my son had finally come to his senses about Göering. Hitler, too. And when I asked why he could not leave Germany with us, he told me that although Von Stauffenberg and the others had failed at Wolf's Lair on July 20, there would soon be another attempt on Hitler's life. 'I will send Kristina to you,' he said. 'She will have a token—the Eagle Dagger Göering gave me. It will be our secret; Kristina won't know what it contains. After the war it will buy back our lands and titles. One day Germany will recover, and the family will be there to see it.'

"But we never were able to cross the frontier, and Kristina never came. Instead, she went to Nuremberg and betrayed us. But the Russians knew where the famous Sieg Stossen's wife had run, and they found her. They found her and took her east, and in one of those camps where the nights are twenty-four hours long, they killed her."

And I remembered a dream of a child abandoned, no, *hidden*, on the banks of the frozen Pegnitz. They shot her, then took her north to the black winter and killed her there.

What I said was: "Frau Baroness, if that weapon is what you believe it to be, think carefully before you go on. You call me 'grandson.' I refuse to accept that. I am not German. I am an American, the adopted son of an American soldier. I know what I came to learn here. The answers you have given me are not the answers I hoped for, but so be it. I think I pity you, Baroness, but that's all I feel. My hunt ends here."

She shook her head. "It is difficult to believe my son fathered you. But you are who and what you are, regardless of whether or not it suits your American priggishness." Her voice took on a peculiar emphasis. "Sieg was loyal to the things that truly matter. To Germany. To the family." She handed me the dagger. "Remove the pommel. If it is too difficult for your hands, give it to Dolger, but I would prefer that you do it." A smile brushed her thin lips. "You brought *die Zeichen* to us; you should know what it contains."

I took the dagger and strained to unscrew the eagle and cabochon pommel from the tang. The metal inside was corroded. This was, I thought, what I should have done long ago in Carmel the morning the dagger arrived.

The eagle's head came free in my hand. The baron looked at space, and the baroness looked at me. Dolger and Annaliese watched intently.

"Now remove the grip."

I worked the wire-bound ivory handle loose from the tang. As I withdrew it, a paper rolled around the tang was exposed.

The old woman's voice was trembling. "Now give it to me."

She took the paper with a shaky hand. She did not immediately unroll it. "The Ministry of Propaganda said that Sieg died in Berlin defending the corporal's bunker. That is not true. The Gestapo murdered Sieg when the last plot on Hitler's life was uncovered. They killed him the way they killed the Von Stauffenberg heroes. Hanged him from a butcher's hook with a piano-wire noose." Tears streaked her cheeks again. "After the surrender the filthy Stasi showed me the films the SS took. Motion pictures of my son and the others in the plot dying naked in a slaughterhouse with hoods over their heads. Do you know what the Stasi told me? That Sieg von Stossen was an enemy of the German people. They told that to me, his mother." She looked hard at me. "I lied to you." She made an angry gesture in the old man's direction. "It was not Dresden that did this to the baron. Dresden stole his manhood and made him afraid. The Gestapo destroyed his love for Germany. But it was the visits from the Stasi that turned him into what you see."

She believed what she said. But was it true about Von Stossen's dying on a meat hook in a Gestapo prison in 1945? The men she said she saw in the film had hoods over their heads. Surely her sad story seemed to be contradicted by the resemblance between the man in the wedding photographs and the man I had seen only a day ago in Nuremberg? The man I had foolishly thought to be Dean Lockwood?

For years I had heard rumors of a second attempt by members of the officer corps to kill Hitler. There was never any evidence to support the stories, and I had never believed them. I did not believe them now.

The baroness unrolled the paper carefully and spread it on the table in front of me. It had a list of numbers. "There," she said. "Our gift from Sieg. Box numbers. Identification numbers."

Dolger spoke now, and when he did, I realized that I had not heard him make a sound, even when I appeared so unexpectedly at the farmhouse door. *"It is all true,"* he said in a voice that sounded rusty, as though it had been unused for years. *"He promised there would be wealth."*

He. Sieg Stossen. He had promised Dolger. How long ago?

Annaliese said, "Is there a reward for recovery?" I turned to look at her. The girl was what she was.

The baroness closed her eyes. "It is hectares of land, houses, an island in the Baltic, a summer manor in Brandenburg. It is the Von Stossen legacy. *Your* legacy, grandson, as much as it is ours."

19

"Brian, I think he's dead."

FREYA VON STOSSEN'S STATEMENT hung in the air.

Outside the farmhouse the wind was rising. Growls of thunder rolled across the Polish plain. The morning, never bright, darkened.

I sat there in a state of semishock. These were my grandparents, this paper-and-bone pair of bitter, impoverished aristocrats, whose son's callous behavior had left them to wither away in grief and squalor, thinking he died a hero's death for the fatherland. Their son was my *father*, a war criminal never brought to book, a man who had left a bloody trail wherever he had gone for more than fifty years. And now I was being told that I must make myself accomplice to the crimes my father committed. Reclaim his treasure. It was absurd, and I'd be damned if I'd do it. I'd been raised by an honorable man to honorable standards. I would not agree to this pact, which stank of age and corruption.

"I'll have no part of this—"

"Grandson," she said, "you *must*. You are all we have left. God has brought you to us."

Senility and long isolation were in that statement.

Annaliese spoke up. "She is a crazy old woman, Brian."

170

Freya von Stossen looked sharply at Annaliese. "Don't try to understand what you are not capable of grasping, girl." To me, she said, "By the time your father decided to save what he could for the family, the Russians were pouring across the frontier, befouling the fatherland. Sieg knew what would come of it. The Brownshirts were supposed to protect us. Instead, they persecuted us for being of better blood than the bourgeois corporal. Even as Germany fell to pieces around us, the Nazis could not forgive us for being their betters. As I told you, Sieg finally understood them. He prepared for the family's survival. Even from the grave Sieg Stossen defeated them. He defeated the Reds, too—"

I was suddenly overwhelmingly tired of paranoia and Prussian fantasy. "Baroness," I said, "the Nazis are back on their street corners. The Russians have gone home. The war ended fifty years ago. It is *over.*"

Dolger was glaring at me. "What's your connection, Herr Dolger. Everyone has one. What's yours?"

Annaliese whispered, "He is *Stasi.* Can't you tell? My God, Brian, don't you see it?"

Freya von Stossen seemed lost in her world of ancient hatreds. Her voice was freighted with bitterness. It was as though I had not even spoken. As though the dam of years had finally broken, all her bitterness came plunging through the breach. "They promised us that we would be protected," she said. "They marched about in uniforms they had no right to wear. They put on pageants, strutting about, imitating their betters. They were so very grand and brave when it was only Jews and Gypsies they wished to rob and murder. But when the time came for battle, to protect the fatherland from the Red horde, they failed us." She looked at Dolger. "You people made so many promises, and you kept none of them, none at all. The Russians came looting and raping, and it was we women who suffered." She looked across the table at her husband. "Helmuth? Can you hear me?" She raised her voice to shout in her husband's face. *"Damn you. Damn you all. You didn't protect us. . . ."*

How long, I wondered, had she suppressed this furious indictment? A whole half century? German men had failed her, and at the table with her were the two German men with whom she had spent many bitter years. "Only Sieg understood what it would be like. Only Sieg tried to save us." She looked at her husband and Dolger. *"You—all of you—German men—"* Her breath caught in her throat as though it would strangle her. *"You watched and kept silent while they looted and raped. . . ."*

Baron von Stossen, the near vegetable, suddenly reacted to his wife's tirade. His ancient hands, gnarled and nearly useless, clutched at the arms of his wheelchair. He struggled to speak. He was glaring at the items on the table with furious eyes. The baroness had brought a corpse to life. It was an awful thing to see. With an enormous effort, he reached out one hand for the roll of paper I had taken from the Eagle Dagger.

Dolger reacted first. For years he had lived with the Stossens, performing degrading tasks for the old couple, and had learned to hate them as much as Freya von Stossen despised him. When the old baron reached for the list of bank numbers, Dolger's reaction was reflexive, driven by years of hate. He struck the old man in the face with his fist, spilling him out of his wheelchair like a sack of potatoes. The gray head hit the flagstones with a dull, breaking sound. Blood showed at his nostrils. He began to convulse.

Frau von Stossen's reaction was remarkable. Instead of going to her husband's aid, she gave out a furious cry, snatched up the Eagle Dagger and lunged at Dolger with it.

She hadn't the power to drive the blade into Dolger's leather-clad chest, but her intent to kill was plain enough. At the moment the point of the dagger touched the man's chest, a pistol appeared in his fist. It was an old Luger P-38. Not all weapons look lethal. This one did. There was a roar as the pistol discharged. I felt the sting of burning powder on my face. My ears rang.

Like a rag doll, Freya von Stossen was flung back a dozen feet by the impact of the bullet striking her narrow breast. And I heard Annaliese scream out, *"Stasi . . . Stasi pig . . ."*

Allan Cobb, among other things, had taught me unarmed combat. It's a skill you don't forget. With my left hand I seized Dolger's wrist and smashed his hand against the edge of the table. A second shot discharged from the Luger. I felt it tear my shirt, burning the skin. My heart seemed crushed within steel bands. I am going to die, I thought. If this murdering bastard doesn't kill me, my heart will.

I brought my right hand up and smashed Dolger's nose with the heel of the hand. It can be a killing blow, driving the bone splinters of a broken nose through the upper sinus cavities and into the brain. Dolger spasmed, arms and legs splaying. The Luger struck the floor and discharged again from the impact.

I got to my feet, trying to get some wind into my chest, trying to stop the pain there. I fumbled in my pocket and found my vial of nitroglycerin pills, shoved one under my tongue and felt the familiar burning sensation.

I looked at the baroness, a stick figure, broken and blood-stained. The baron had stopped convulsing and lay still. Annaliese knelt over him, looked at me and said, "Brian, I think he's dead."

Still not able to move, I looked down at what I had done to Dolger. His face was a red-streaked mask. His eyes were open and filled with blood.

Annaliese got to her feet and began to tug at my arm. "We have to get away from this place, Brian. We have to go *now.*"

I shook my head. I might have just committed a homicide. Dolger had committed two. My law-abiding American instincts shouted at me to go to the local authorities and call the nearest United States consulate.

The Lockwoods' seeming attraction for tragedy and violence was a kaleidoscope of fractured images: my adoptive father, dead on a mortuary slab in Mexico City . . . Professor Ershad, beaten . . . two innocents, dead in Brooklyn . . . Erich Leyden, dead in the marsh at Pomellen. Now this . . .

Annaliese was shouting at me, "Brian, *let's go.*"

Still sucking air into my lungs, I let her lead me across that cluttered room and out the door. The winter daylight had changed to a stormy dusk. The wind buffeted and swirled about the littered farmyard. A bolt of lightning flashed through the clouds overhead.

"Give me the keys," she said, then shoved and pulled me into the right-hand front seat of the Mercedes.

It occurred to me now that it would be crazy to try to explain all this to a bunch of unsympathetic Polish police. . . . The son of Sieg Stossen, war criminal, looking for understanding from Poles? I had to be as crazy as the poor dead woman we had left inside the farmhouse.

Annaliese accelerated the car onto the main road and turned back toward the frontier, not toward the Gartz crossing but north toward Altdamm and the Oder River estuary. I remembered that this part of Germany and Poland was familiar territory for her.

"Are you all right now?" Annaliese asked.

She seemed to be in motion, like a willow in the wind. I made myself hold her image steady. "That again," I said. "Yes, goddamn it, I am all right."

"Sit back. Breathe slow."

"The dagger," I said. "We have to go back for the dagger."

"No, we don't." She held it up. She even had the grip and the eagle pommel. "This, too," she said. Her small fist opened to show the paper with the bank account numbers. "We will have to talk about this, Brian. I have an interest now," she said.

20

"Summer for the living. Winter for the dead."

ANNALIESE DROVE with a skill that made me wonder where and how she had learned. Had Rykov taught her? KGB? Stasi?

The highway, which hardly deserved the name, stretched ahead, empty and rutted, no doubt once heavily used and never repaired, now neglected, perhaps even abandoned. The nations of the Warsaw Pact had laid down the burdens of coping. Post-Gorbachev Poland had much in common with the new unified Germany: the same shock of surprise at the onslaught of freedom, and the same stupefied confusion when the costs began to be examined and felt. The former satellites seemed to be saying to the West: "For fifty years the Soviets took our freedom and our dignity and gave us subsistence. Now it is your turn. Or not. You choose. But *if* not, we shall just fall farther and farther behind you, planting the seeds of future war. See what winning the Cold War has brought you? A bunch of welfare nations."

The storm sweeping down from the Baltic buffeted the car as we sped toward the border. In the darkening morning I could make out the rusty-looking polluted water of a large lagoon that showed on the road map as Jezioro Miedwie. A marginal note stated that the "lake" was a "valuable source of water for the industry of western Poland." From where I sat, it was difficult to see any sign of "industry." The landscape was flat, littered with trash and spotted with marshes and brackish ponds. Dieter had mentioned that this part of the Baltic plain was a district of resorts and vacation sites. That seemed improbable, in spite of the occasional hutlike dacha standing like an abandoned sentry in the marshland.

As we angled north, the dead water of Miedwie Lake separated us from the road to Altdamm and the frontier.

"Do you know where you're going?"

"Yes. We have to go to Stargard before we can make for the border at Stettin. We can cross there. Erich and Rykov were friendly with the Grenzschutz commander. He will remember me. I crossed there many times."

The full dimensions of Annaliese Rykova were emerging now. She had grown up, God knew how, on the streets of East Germany. She had decided to better her condition and her brother's any way she could, and that had made her into—what? A smuggler, no doubt. There were things in the West that the *Ossis* would pay a great deal to possess. Walkmans, tapes, records, blue jeans—the list was endless, and Annaliese was the right age to know every item. Be grateful, I told myself. For the moment I was in Annaliese's hands, and given the circumstances, I could think of none better.

"The Polish police will be getting to the farmhouse soon. They can't have been far behind us," I said.

Annaliese was angry. "We were supposed to stay at the farmhouse. It all went wrong when that Stasi pig hit the old man."

"Why were we supposed to stay there?"

"All I know is what Eugen told Erich. It doesn't matter; now they will just kill us—"

"Who, Anna?"

"Eugen, for one."

"The man who hired you. Tell me more about him. Did he ever give his name? Did he have a mustache and short beard? Where did you meet him—at his home or in an office?"

She shrugged. "In an office. Very shabby, with no name on the door. The two of them sat behind the open door in the inner office while we stayed out in the reception area. I was handed a list of names and dates and asked to read them out loud, as if I knew them. The old man did have a beard. I only saw him once, when he looked out at me to be sure I looked all right. He nodded to the other man and closed the door. I was taken out into the hall, and Erich made the arrangements with Eugen."

"So you did recognize Eugen." She started to protest, but I interrupted. "Never mind. Just tell me how long ago you were hired."

"He never really spoke with us. Eugen did."

"How long ago?"

She gave me an exasperated look. "What does it *matter*? After what happened at the farmhouse, we are dead if they find us."

"How long ago, Annaliese?"

"Three weeks. Maybe a day or two less." She swerved to miss a deep rut in the road. The Mercedes skidded, righted itself and raced on.

Three weeks. It was easily possible, then, that the man I saw on the berm in Carmel could have been the shadowy Eugen. The man who attacked Professor Ershad would have been some thug hired to watch the cottage. And the gunmen in Brooklyn? That killing had had the look of a bungled professional job. If Eugen had hired the gunmen, he had not hired the best.

I thought about that old couple lying dead on the floor of their grimy farmhouse. And of Dolger, the old Nazi who lay with them. Was that all he had been? It made a properly Teutonic, if deceptive, picture of loyalty. What did the SS take for its motto? *Meine Ehre ist Treue.* My honor is loyalty. But was that all for Dolger? The baroness had said that during the war Dolger had been an aide to Sieg von Stossen. "Sieg gave him to us," she said. Was it as simple as that? Would such a man stick for almost fifty years? Fifty years of slights and ancient arrogance? For the sake of a dead commander? It didn't seem likely. But for a *living* one, a man like Dolger might do it. For a strong enough living commander, a Dolger *would* do it.

It meant Sieg von Stossen was *alive.* My *father.*

He was the man I glimpsed in Nuremberg, the man who had looked up at me with what struck me as hatred. There was no other answer. Whatever else about this affair remained murky, the emergence of a living Sieg Stossen seemed undeniable.

I carefully unrolled the brittle paper we had taken from the dagger. Only a list of numbers. Nothing more. But they spoke larceny and betrayal on a vast scale, on a political and personal scale.

I thought about the old couple. What sort of people waited for years in the conviction that the theft was committed for them and would bring them out of poverty into some aristocratic reincarnation that could never be? *My* grandparents? I battled a dull nausea as the Mercedes sped north toward Stargard.

Annaliese spoke up suddenly. "You were brave at the farm-house, Brian. Also very stupid. If that fool hadn't hated the old woman so, he might have killed you instead."

"Why are you so sure he was a Stasi?"

"Because he *was*. He had the stink of cellars about him. The same with Eugen."

It was certainly possible. East Bloc intelligence, as well as police services in many countries, recruited former Nazis, sought them out as prizes after the war. Former SS people were getting old now, but the recruitment policy was as old as the Iron Curtain.

Then what about Sieg Stossen? How had he survived all these years? The answer seemed frighteningly clear, if you accepted its plausibility. He survived just as his subordinate had done. Much better than his subordinate had done. Sieg Stossen had hidden himself away inside the new state. And he had kept Dolger with his ancient parents to protect the secret he had once shared with them.

My God, it was so simple, and ugly. He was brilliant, arro-gant, amoral, ambitious. And merciless . . . What price would such a man pay to win a place with the new Stalinist masters of East Germany?

Would he sell his wife? My mother?

Of course he would.

"Stop the car."

"We shouldn't—"

"God damn it, stop the car."

Annaliese did, pulling over onto a muddy roadside. Rain had begun to slash at the windshield.

I made it only a few feet through the heavy rain before I was racked by a spasm in my stomach and gave up its bile.

"What?" she asked when I had climbed back into the car.

"Nothing. Let's go."

Once we were on the road again, she said, "It isn't what you did to the Stasi, is it?"

I shook my head.

"I'm glad. He deserved what he got."

As we drove on through the wind and rain, I asked myself what Stossen's plan had been. To take me at the farmhouse? And then what? What purpose was there in it? To recover the dagger?

Annaliese must have been thinking along similar lines. "Why did you have to come here?" she asked suddenly. "Was it so important?" She meant, was it so important that Erich had to die for it?

"I'm sorry about your brother, Anna," I said. "But he didn't die on account of me. He died . . . well, I'm sorry, but he died because he thought the answers were easy. . . ." Would she have any idea what I was saying? He died looking for money to travel, to buy Reebok shoes, Levi's, disco tapes, boom boxes and electronic guitars. For an image of himself being adored at rock concerts. He may even have died, God forgive us Americans, for believing that America's streets were paved with gold.

"That's a rotten thing to say, Brian. He wanted to help you."

"No, sorry, what he wanted was this." I held the dagger in my fist. "When Eugen got ugly, he wanted to grab it and run. But he didn't run far enough or fast enough." I realized it was a cruel thing to say, but if Annaliese was going to survive, she had to stop indulging fantasies about her brother.

She slammed her foot down hard on the accelerator and the Mercedes leaped forward. "You bastard, Brian. You *Schwein- scheiss*. You know nothing about Erich and me. Nothing."

"I know some things, Anna. And I am truly sorry you've lost Erich. But you have it in you to survive, even if he didn't."

She looked at me evenly. "Have you never in your life loved anyone, Brian? Or have you been too tangled up in this mystery?"

Too perceptive, this girl. I had replies. But no answers. Not yet. We'd not finished this bizarre journey. Stossen was out there

somewhere, maneuvering us toward an end only he could
know.

Spatters of rain struck the windshield and froze there. We
passed ancient Russian-built trucks heavily loaded and laboring
across the Baltic plain wreathed in funereal diesel smoke.

I looked behind us. I had the strong feeling that we were
being followed, although there was no one in sight.

"What is it," she asked. "Is someone back there?"

"No. Just keep driving." I thought of something I had once
read in a Sharyn McCrumb thriller, "The Rule for the Solstice
Alignment of Standing Stones: *Summer for the living. Winter for
the dead."* Being stalked across this bleak landscape seemed an
inevitability. After all, the winter solstice was nearly upon us,
and it is always winter for the dead.

We passed through the grimy outskirts of Stargard, weaving
our way through shoals of bicycles being ridden through the
steadily falling sleet and rain by people wrapped in every sort of
rainwear imaginable. Here and there among the drab ranks
could be seen a Day-Glo orange or fluorescing green anorak—
sure signs of a visit to the West. The clouds had lowered until
their underbellies rested on the roofs and chimney pots of Stargard.

As Annaliese followed the signs to the Altdamm road, we
threaded our way through a chicane of three police cars. I was
sure we would be stopped and questioned, but the policemen
were too miserably cold and wet to leave the relative shelter of
their Pobeda sedans. One *militza* rolled down his window and
appeared about to signal us, but Annaliese made a waving gesture and drove the Mercedes past him in a flurry of spray. I
thought: The gods are looking out for us. How many Mercedes'
with German rental plates could there be at this moment on this
part of the Baltic plain?

Once on the open road again, Annaliese increased our speed
as we crossed the marshy top of Jezioro Miedwie. We were only
twenty-seven kilometers from the border.

"That was a near thing back there," I said. "Were you so sure
they wouldn't stop us?"

"No."

"What about the border crossing?" I asked. "There is a better than even chance they will have a description of us and this car."

"I'm not so sure," she said. "Maybe they want us back in Germany."

"They? The Stasi again?"

Annaliese stared hard at me for a moment. "Erich was right about you," she said. "You don't believe in danger, Brian Lockwood. You have grown up American, and you think all Americans have charmed lives."

"Is that why you want so much to get to America?"

"Erich wanted that. I'll stay in Europe."

I marveled at the way she was now calmly making plans. Based on what, it was hard to say.

Once she'd started on Americans, she had no inclination to stop. "I used to think that what they taught us in school was all propaganda, but it isn't. You Americans believe that nothing will ever go wrong for you because someone, God maybe, will pick you up, kiss it and make it well. Vietnam should have taught you a lesson, but since the war in the Gulf you have grown even worse." She clenched a fist and smacked the leather-bound steering wheel. "You make a mess of things and then God smiles at you and everything is well. It won't always be like that, you know. One day it will be the Americans dead in the marsh."

"Aren't you forgetting something?"

"What?"

"That I am German."

She made a derisive sound. "Don't believe it for a minute. You are pure Ami. And since the Marxists turned over and died, you've all become the fucking lords of creation."

She had a point, this old young teenager. Hadn't I been thinking almost the same sort of thing earlier this morning as I considered the trail of disaster I had left behind me?

I looked at the instrument panel clock. Not yet noon, and the storm brooded over us. We were far to the north of my usual haunts, where the November days, even in fair weather, were short. I thought again about McCrumb's rule: Winter for the dead.

I looked at Annaliese's pretty, set, immature face. Be wrong about us, girl. I thought. For your sake and mine, be wrong.

21

"You? Or you and me?"

ALTDAMM TURNED OUT to be a rest stop and a few decaying buildings on the extension of what used to be the Polish end of an East German autobahn, the same route E28 we had used coming north about a hundred years ago.

A dozen klicks to the east, the freeway ended abruptly at an almost abandoned airport. Annaliese didn't even slow down in Altdamm; she turned southwest to cross the Oder River and a bit of the Stettiner Haff at Sydowsaue. I realized she was making straight for the crossing point at Stettin-Sud, which was the largest damned Grenzschutz post along the entire northern border.

I was in Anna's hands completely. She knew the country, and I didn't. I also suspected that, if knowing the angles could help us get back into Germany without being turned over to the Polish police, Annaliese could be depended on. Once we recrossed the Oder River, we would be about 180 kilometers from the outskirts of Berlin, and once back inside Germany, I would be among people I could call on for help. Begin to try to sort out my life—even as the son of Sieg Stossen.

I was facing a nightmare come true, trying to face my reality without collapsing into self-pity. Not so easy. My heart kept

183

thumping like a damn jungle drum, mocking me with my own
infirmities. You need a strong heart and a strong stomach to deal
with the discovery that your father was a world-class criminal.

"We are coming into South Stettin now," Annaliese said. "I
am taking us straight to the border post. If we are lucky, the
Poles won't try to stop us, but if they do, and they separate us,
you tell them you are an American journalist. But not for a *Wessi*
magazine. For some important American paper . . . so tell
them you work for the *New York Times* or that newspaper in
Washington. If they ask about me, tell them I am your whore.
They will accept that. Poles do."

"The police will be watching the border by now."

"They are not Grenzschutz. They are only Poles," she said
with a flash of German arrogance.

"*Sehr hochmütig*," I murmured. "Very haughty."

"It's the truth. If you lived here, you would know."

There were still few private cars in the district, and none we saw
was nearly so grand as our rented Mercedes. Passersby in labor-
ers' clothes looked at it with *Osthunger*. We emerged from the
paved street into a cobbled square. I remembered reading somewhere that the East Bloc countries had tried to rid themselves of
cobblestones because they are easily dislodged by rioters and
used as missiles. I looked around the square. In the West it
would have been crowded with illegally parked vehicles. Here
there were only a few Trabants and a Yugo or two. There were
two concrete pedestals that had once supported statues. Lenin?
Jaruzelski? Whoever the local Heroes of Socialism had been,
they were gone now, their broken bronze waiting in some junk-
yard to be collected for melting down. Only the pedestals remained, sprouting a few twisted remnants of armature like the
protruding bones of a compound fracture.

"The Polish post is just down that street," Annaliese said. The
alley she indicated was relatively free of walkers, and there were
no vehicles. Stettin-Sud on a cold and wet December day was
not a popular crossing point. In the East people had learned
long before not to cross frontiers where the police presence was
heavy. All that was supposed to be changed, but in Stettin-Sud,

at least, the people were few and the signs of regulation many. And then there was the unpleasant fact that the German Stettin-Sud post supported the largest border guard garrison in the region.

Annaliese let the car roll slowly across the square. The tires rumbled on the cobbles, and the windshield wipers made a wet, whooshing noise as they swept the rain and grime from the glass. "I have a connection with the Grenzschutz district commandant on the other side of the border," she said. The girl was full of surprises. She might have managed it in any number of ways. She might be a part-time police informer. Or she might have established her "connection" while on her back.

She read my expression. "I do what I have to do," she said. "All right?"

"It is, if you say so. But your story changes every twenty minutes."

Her eyes flashed. "So I slept with the Grenzschutz colonel from time to time. What is that to you?"

"Not a thing," I said. "I just hope you were good."

"You should know, Brian. Now just do your part, and we will be in Germany in fifteen minutes."

"I'm sorry," I said quickly. "I had no right to speak to you that way. I don't know why I did."

"You Americans don't like to believe women you have slept with sometimes sell sex because that's all they have to sell." She hesitated. "But I didn't sell it to you. I want you to know that."

Of course, I knew nothing of the sort, but she wanted me to believe her. "It's all right, Anna. It really is."

"Where will we go when we cross back into Germany?"

"Berlin, then to Bern."

"You? Or you and me?"

Damn the girl, I thought. When I least expected it, she turned waif. "You and me."

"Will you give me to the police?"

"No," I said, and smiled. "What good would it do? You have friends in high places."

She was in no mood to smile back. "I believe you, Brian. Remember that. I believe you." Her green eyes looked huge and

shining. I remembered the nights we'd had together, and it
didn't seem like whoring to me.

Rain hammered on the metal roof of the car as Annaliese drove
toward the Polish guardpost. The buildings crowded the street
here, forming a wall on both sides. Windows had been bricked
up or cemented. It was like moving down a storm drain. Ahead
lay a cleared area where the surrounding buildings had been
razed. I could see two sandbagged emplacements that could
only be gun positions, and rolls of razor wire lining the street.
Beyond all that was a glassed-in shelter with a bank of search-
lights on the roof. From where we were, we could see three
Polish guardsmen wearing rain-soaked capes and steel Warsaw
Pact helmets.

It would have been daunting, but the concertina wire had
been pushed to the side of the street, where it lay in coils rusting
in the rain, and the sandbagged positions had no ordnance. First
perestroika, Polish style, then Lech Walesa and his followers, and
finally the emergence, in the Eastern political fog, of the Commonwealth of Independent States had made the crossing point
at Stettin-Sud less menacing than it once had been. Still . . .

As we approached the last barrier, a border guard raised the
painted bars and signaled us through with a flashlight. I held
my breath as we crossed the open space that had been cleared
long ago to provide a field of fire. We rolled to a stop at the main
post.

Another guard in dripping cape and helmet waited for Annaliese to lower the window. *"Papieren, bitte?"* His German was
softened with the liquid consonants of his native Polish.

Annaliese handed him the West German passport that said
she had been born in Bonn. He held out his hand for mine.
When he had it, he looked at me and tried a friendly smile.
"Amer-i-can citizen? From Califor-ni-a? I have cousin in Chi-
cago, United States. You wait, no?"

"I'll wait, yes."

He vanished into the glass-fronted hut with our passports.
Annaliese said nothing. She was staring straight ahead into Germany.

Presently the young guardsman reappeared and returned our stamped passports. I began to breathe again. "Goo-d-bye, mister," he said, touching the rim of his wok-shaped helmet.

"*Do widzenia*," I said, exhausting my Polish.

Annaliese rolled up the window and started the car toward the far more elaborate post on the German side of the border.

There were nearly a dozen Grenzschutze in view as we pulled up to the German barrier. A red, black and gold flag snapped wetly in the wind. The ground surrounding the post building was manicured and planted with shrubs. In the spring the area around the German post would be a blaze of flowers.

I couldn't help remembering all that I had read or seen of the extermination camps. They grew flowers in those places, too, and greeted the incoming cattle cars of new arrivals with Mozart and Haydn played by prisoner chamber orchestras.

There were no threadbare army capes here. The garrison of the post was immaculately turned out in gray-green ankle-length leather coats. Only the newness of the silver braid on some of the peaked caps gave any hint that this was a mixed garrison of newly enlisted *Ossis* and long-service *Wessis*.

A guardsman appeared at the open driver's window and asked for our travel documents. He looked no more than eighteen, but the Schmeisser machine pistol hanging from his shoulder somehow made him seem much older.

"Have you Polish currency to declare?"

"No," I said. "We were only in Poland a day."

"Wait, please." He marched off, our papers in hand.

Another Grenzschutz with new cap and uniform sauntered by, looking at the car covetously.

Annaliese sat rigidly behind the wheel.

I tried to remember whether or not Annaliese had given the posted guardsman any sort of private note or correspondence. If she had, I hadn't seen her do it.

Looking through the curtain of rain at the windows of the concrete hut, I could see uniformed figures, many of them, moving about inside. My throat felt very dry.

After a long while a Grenzschutz sergeant appeared at Annaliese's window. "Frau Rykova? Would you come with me, please?"

I started to protest as I had some hours ago to the policeman at the Red Salmon, but Annaliese squeezed my hand in warning and got out of the car.

They vanished into the concrete block hut.

I waited.

Ten minutes after Annaliese disappeared, a single Grenzschutz emerged from the blockhouse and walked slowly around the car. He paused, noted the number plate, returned to the shelter of the building.

My eyes felt grainy with lack of sleep. I felt like a man sitting underwater. I thought about the sad, beautiful face of my mother in the wedding picture. I could not even imagine a tragedy as profound as the life she had led. First Stossen, then the war. For a brief moment a reprieve with Brian Lockwood. Then the fall of the steel curtain. To think of her dead in the gulag filled me with anger. Great anger.

For twenty-five minutes more I waited. Then Annaliese reappeared, unescorted this time and wrapped in her own plastic raincoat. She had our papers clutched against her chest. Without a word she got behind the wheel, started the car and accelerated away from the border post.

I was shaky with relief, and then I began to ask myself questions.

Had I been taken in again by a complicated scheme that used some nonexistent Stasi threat to bring me to heel? After all, I had a list of bank numbers of potentially great value. Was that what all this was about?

I looked at Annaliese's face. It was drawn, the skin stretched across the delicate bones. She looked terrified.

"What happened back there?" I asked. "Did you see your friend?"

"Oberst Müller is in the district headquarters in Prenzlau. He spoke to me on the telephone."

It took me a moment to make a connection. The police who had interrogated us at the Red Salmon had returned to Prenzlau.

"They know about the police dossier you bought. They don't

know yet about the farm and what happened there. But they will. The German authorities have notified Warsaw about your interest in the Von Stossens," Annaliese said. "My friend gave orders not to detain us. He told me to lose myself as fast as possible." She managed a shaky smile. "He says we have enemies. Isn't that a surprise?"

I wondered if it might have been wiser to turn ourselves in. But what security would that offer? The district commandant of the Grenzschutz had warned us to get lost. Fast. Annaliese took his warning seriously. She was hammering down the autobahn toward Berlin at 140 kilometers per hour.

"What's the nearest airport?" I asked. "Someplace with European airlines. Lots of them."

"Tempelhof," Annaliese said.

In South Berlin. An hour and a half away, at least, given the weather. "Make for it," I said. "But find a telephone first. We're going to need help."

"Your friend Dieter Langan?"

"There's no one else."

"Is he trustworthy?"

Was he? I had no choice but to believe it. "Of course," I said.

She asked, "Did anyone come near the car while I was inside the border post?"

"Yes. A guard looked it over rather carefully."

"There may be an electronic tracer on the car," she said.

"Stop and I'll look for it."

"No. Leave it alone. They will get suspicious if we get rid of it. They will get suspicious if we even look for it. Let them trace us to Tempelhof. Oberst Müller told me to vanish. I don't think they will interfere. I think we are an embarrassment to them."

I only hoped she was right.

THREE

30 November
to
3 December
1991

22

"Welcome to Switzerland."

THE SWISSAIR AIRBUS from Tempelhof to Bern was a night commuter, crowded and noisy. The flight originated in Bremen in
the late afternoon and ended up in Bern after midnight, first
touching down at Hamburg and Berlin. At this time of year the
passengers were nearly all foreign workers and Swiss businessmen. We were lucky to get space.

At about five in the afternoon I had called Dieter from Lanke,
a wide spot in the autobahn between the Polish border and
Tempelhof. He had news for me. He had been talking to Claire
again, and she had told him to tell me that, along with Stein
Davis, she was leaving for Germany in an hour. That could
mean only one thing. She had found something in the boxes of
the Colonel's things that was important, so important it would
not wait until my return to California.

"Will you meet them, Dieter?" I asked.

"Of course, my friend. But where will you be?"

"In Bern."

"Bern? I thought you were returning here."

"In a day or so. But first, I need a name, Dieter. Someone with
some influence in the Swiss Ministry of Finance."

"You have found something."

193

"I think so. I've left a mess behind me, too. Have you heard anything?"

He said he hadn't, but I wondered about that. Dieter was well informed and not what one might call a slave to the truth. It was, he said, his most journalistic characteristic.

"The Stossens are dead," I said.

"Jesus . . ."

"Don't panic, I didn't kill them. But Annaliese Rykova and I are material witnesses. We saw what happened, and we didn't report it to the Polish police."

"The girl is still with you? What are you thinking of, Brian?"

"I'll explain it when I see you. I'm leaving my rental car at Tempelhof." I didn't tell him I thought the Mercedes was bugged. If the German police were letting us run, there was no immediate need for Dieter Langan to know. "Can you have it picked up? And I'll need some money. Wire three thousand dollars in Swiss francs to . . ." I leafed through a Swiss touring guide and found what I wanted. The address of the Bernerhof, a small hotel I remembered from a previous trip. I gave him the street address and the telephone number.

"Brian, my friend—"

"Damn it, Dieter, will you do it, please?"

"Yes. Yes, of course. The man you'll want to see in the Ministry of Finance is Joachim Prinz. He is in Banking Security. His office is in the Municipal Building. I will call him personally. Tonight."

"Thanks." I left it at that. He didn't report any progress tracing Dean Lockwood yet. Well, no one had said that would be easy. I had the list of bank numbers, and I still had the Eagle Dagger. Dean had to have known what the dagger's hilt concealed. It would have amused him to think that possession of the list might incriminate me in that ancient theft. Surely he never would have parted with the list if the treasure were still intact. I sighed and sat upright in the uncomfortable seat. I seemed to recognize all the players on my program. I just couldn't keep them straight. They danced on and offstage, apparently at will. I suspected that they were laughing at me behind the curtain. I dreaded the outcome, but I had to keep along after them.

Whatever, the son of a bitch owed me. For the trail of havoc I had left behind me and for his part in what his ex-Stasi hood had done to Annaliese and Erich Leyden and those people in Brooklyn. He might be a Lockwood, but I intended to see that he paid what he owed.

The Airbus flew over moonlit peaks and glaciers. The rain and sleet that covered most of western Europe stopped at the northern edge of the Alps. Below lay weather the ski resort operators relished. Very cold, clear and windless. Many years ago Reeder and I had lived for sixteen months in Switzerland. It was while I was trying to write a novel and while Reeder still thought I might just do it for fame and fortune. The country was good to us, but the novel was never finished, and Reeder was very disappointed. I guess she hoped the ex-German waif would cop a Nobel Prize.

I looked at Annaliese, sleeping beside me. A very different female from Reeder. Unique. My tired mind was hopping from one subject to another, scattering unresolved thoughts like chaff from a bomber.

The cavernous interior of the airplane was still dark. Swiss cabin attendants let passengers sleep until just before landings. It was easier on staff and supplies aboard these red-eye commuter flights.

I longed for sleep, but my thoughts swerved and jittered. I had not been out of my clothes since leaving the Red Salmon many hours ago.

Why, I wondered again, had Claire suddenly decided to round up the Lockwood family's lawyer and take off for Germany? What had she discovered that wouldn't keep?

Annaliese twisted restlessly. Put her head on my shoulder, murmuring in her sleep. Only a day and a night ago she had seen her brother murdered. And since then she had witnessed more death. No wonder she slept restlessly. What were her dreams? I wondered. Were they as chilling as mine?

The aircraft encountered some turbulence. Far below us, moonlight traveled, glinting, on the dark surface of some mountain lake. I closed my eyes. Consciousness slipped away, and I fell into darkness. My last waking thought was a prayer for dreamlessness.

I could not have slept more than a half hour, but I came alert quickly as a cabin attendant touched my shoulder.

"*Signor*. We are landing in Bern. Please sit up." She was a dark-eyed Italian Swiss, no older than Annaliese. Around us people were preparing for arrival. Sections of lights came on in the cabin, and the tone of the jet engines lowered. The voice of a crewman came over the speaker system.

"Ladies and gentlemen, we are commencing our descent into Bern International Airport. The local time is twelve-seventeen; the temperature is minus four degrees Celsius; the weather is clear with unlimited visibility. We shall be landing in eight minutes. Please fasten your seat belts. Swissair hopes you have had a pleasant flight." The announcement was repeated in French and German.

Ten years ago, I thought, the French would have come first, the English last. It made me think of Freya von Stossen, who somehow had managed to convey a deep hatred for my adopted country. Greater, even, I thought, than what she had felt for the Soviets.

"Brian"—I felt Annaliese's hand on my arm—"did you sleep?"

"Yes."

"How do you feel? Are you all right?"

"Never better."

She sat up and ran fingers through her hair. "I must look terrible."

I raised my seat back and looked around. The cabin was crowded, and the passengers were milling about, fetching parcels and hand luggage from overhead storages. The admonitions from the public-address system were, of course, ignored.

I leaned across Annaliese to look at the landscape below. Lake Neuchâtel glinted in the moonlight. The undercarriage lowered with a grinding noise, locked into place. I fastened my seat belt.

The sound of the jets became a sigh, and the Airbus settled toward the airport. Lights raced by below. I could see headlights and cars on the roads. Annaliese slipped her hand into mine. The airplane settled, settled again. Tires squealed on the concrete, and the pilots reversed thrusters and advanced the throttles so that the engines roared.

A cabin attendant said on the public-address system: "Welcome to Switzerland. Customs and passport control will be found open at the south end of the terminal building. Please remain seated until the aircraft has come to a complete stop at the deplaning dock. We wish to thank you for flying Swissair."

Everyone stood up. I found our baggage in the overhead bin. The other compartments were filled with people preparing to deplane.

The Airbus rolled to a stop, then began to taxi toward the terminal. The cabin was filled with a babble of mixed German, Italian and French.

"How about you?" I asked Annaliese.

"I slept, a little." She flashed a sad, innocent smile at me.

"We'll do something about your brother," I told her.

"Yes, we must do that. Someone should pay. . . ."

"A promise, Anna."

The Airbus was at the dock. The cabin attendants opened the doors. Passengers streamed toward the exits.

We passed the cabin attendants, entered the deplaning trunk and walked with the crowd into the terminal.

Standing behind the barriers near a column was a tall, burly blond man. He stepped forward toward the rope, and our eyes met. He smiled, or smirked, at me and raised his hand. His index finger pointed at me as if it were a gun, in that universal gesture used by children playing good guys against the bad guys. It was the man I'd seen on the berm in Carmel. I turned to Annaliese to confirm that the man on the berm, the man who killed her brother, and the mysterious Eugen were one and the same.

By the time I caught her attention, he was gone.

There was only the Eagle Dagger in our luggage to interest the Swiss customs people. Annaliese sighed with relief when her not-quite-genuine passport was returned without comment.

"What is this, m'sieu?"

"A ceremonial dagger. A replica. I bought it in Berlin."

The man handled the dagger as though it were hot. He seemed undecided about what he should do with it and was clearly wondering what kind of man bought such a Nazi souvenir. But he returned it to the bag in which I had placed it after leaving Stettin-Sud. "I will pass it along, m'sieu," he said, frowning, "but I am surprised they allowed it on the aircraft." He should not have been. Internal European flights were dispatched with the most minimal security since hijacking had fallen out of style.

At the currency control window the clerk asked, through pursed lips, where we would be staying in Bern. I told him the Bernerhof, all the while searching the crowd of people in the terminal for the blond man. I didn't see him.

"You say the Bernerhof, m'sieu?"

I forced my attention back to the currency control clerk. He looked like a young Heinrich Himmler, with small eyes behind thin steel-rimmed glasses.

"Yes," I said impatiently. I kept searching the faces of the people in the terminal bay. Had I been mistaken? No, I had not been. The man I had seen in Carmel was here, in Bern. Watching me.

"In Brückfeld, yes?" A broad smile transformed the pale face. "A fine little hotel, m'sieu. It is owned by a second cousin of mine. You will be very comfortable." Ah, the Swiss, I thought. Did every man in the Helvetic Confederacy have a second cousin who ran a hotel?

The hotelier's second cousin handed our passports across a compartment to another clerk, who stamped them and returned them to me.

"Have a pleasant stay in Bern, Herr Lockwood."

Outside, small banks of snow lined the roadways around the airport. I looked up and down the street. The stars were brilliant, and a late moon cast everything in a cold light. It was nearly one in the morning, but the traffic around the terminal was heavy. And orderly. Swiss policemen wearing reflective gauntlets directed the stream of taxicabs and private cars that had gathered to meet the incoming flight from Germany.

I said to Annaliese, "Have you seen him?"

"What? Who? I saw no one." She held on to my arm. "Please. You're frightening me, Brian."

"The man I saw outside my house, God damn it. The man on the berm in Carmel. He's here."

She clung to me. She seemed near to tears. *"Brian, please,* let's just *go."*

There was nothing else I could do.

On the taxi ride into Bern and across the Kirchenfeldbrücke, my heart was beating as though I'd been running a sprint.

Annaliese said, "You could have been mistaken, Brian. It would be understandable, after all we've been through."

"It's no mistake, damn it." I was tired of the cat-and-mouse game. I wanted a confrontation, a showdown.

Annaliese said, "You sounded like my father just now, Brian. I hate it when you do that."

That snapped me out of it. What man wants to hear such a statement from a young girl he's been sleeping with?

"Does that shock you?" she asked. "Didn't you think I had a father?"

We were crossing the Lorrainebrücke, back to the north side of the floodlit Aare River, which roared far below at the bottom of the five-hundred-foot-deep ravine that contains it like an artery in the heart of Bern.

Annaliese went: "I had one, Brian. He was a noncommissioned officer of the army. Loyal. So loyal. All the time the state was rotting and falling to pieces around him, he was never wrong, never mistaken. When he came back from Angola with an American bullet in his lungs, he never doubted it was right to go to Africa to fight for socialism. When he died, he died praising Honecker. To the last day of his miserable life, my father talked about the triumph of the masses. Can you believe it? The Leninization of Valhalla, he once said. I don't know what else. I stopped listening to him when I was thirteen. Sometimes I hate men—" She turned from me to stare at the storefronts and business buildings of Bern as we left the river and crossed the sleeping city toward the Brückfeld district. "You know, Brian, you terrify me with your angers and your private battles. You break things. You break *lives."*

It was so very much like what Freya von Stossen had said at that mad hatter's meeting in the farmhouse near Obryta. I had still another flash of my mother's melancholy face in the wedding photograph. Had she felt the same? Lord knew she had seen her world shattered and dismembered by men. . . .

With more confidence than I really felt, I said, "It will be over soon, Annaliese."

She rounded on me like a small angry cat. "Oh, *will* it? You guarantee that, do you? When, Brian? *Lieber Gott*, the games men play. My brother . . ." She stopped, as though the words jammed in her throat and gagged her. She was remembering Leyden lying in the marsh mud. The dark green body bag.

I put my arm around her. She buried her face in my jacket and began to cry.

The Bernerhof had changed since my last visit. It was appreciably more glitzy than it had been. Some rooms had been remodeled and others added—at the cost of some fine views of the medieval city on the peninsula between meanders of the Aare and the rising mountains of the Bernese Oberland to the south.

I had taken two connecting rooms. I told Annaliese it was to keep the Swiss from asking questions. It was, up to a point. When I had the porter unlock the connecting door, he favored me with a very un-Swiss leer.

From the second story I had a clear view of the street below and, at some distance, of the floodlighted spire of the Matthias Ensinger Cathedral. A fine example, the concierge told me with pride, of Late Gothic architecture, completed in 1421.

I was not interested in the architecture of Swiss churches. I was more absorbed in the city map he had given me, searching out the quickest (and most hidden) route between the Bernerhof and the Town Hall (what Dieter had referred to as the Municipal Building), where I would find Herr Joachim Prinz of the Ministry of Finance.

It had been impossible to know if we had been followed from the airport. An experienced cop or private investigator might have known, but I was neither of those things. And I was still badly in need of sleep.

While I was in the bathroom, Annaliese closed her eyes on the bed in my room. I found her, still fully dressed except for her boots, face buried in the bolster. I undressed her as gently as I could and put her under the covers, then double-locked the hall doors, virtuously climbed into the bed in her room, turned out the lights, and, finally, went to sleep.

23

"These are old bones rattling."

I WAS AWAKENED at eight-thirty by the telephone ringing in the other room. I got out of bed and answered. It was the concierge informing me that I had received a postal draft for three thousand dollars from Dieter Langan in Düsseldorf, together with a telegram that was being delivered to my door.

Annaliese was in the bathroom. I sat and listened to the sounds she made. It was remarkable how accustomed I had become to her presence since I'd met her in Nuremberg.

A porter tapped at the door and delivered Dieter's telegram and a draft on the Crédit Suisse. The concierge had also included a bank teller's card with the draft. His nephew? Uncle? Brother-in-law? Switzerland is a nation run on nepotism. And run very well, no question. The bank was on Laupenstrasse, near the railway station. "Two kilometers from the hotel, Herr Lockwood, not more," the porter assured me.

I asked him for the location of some women's shops.

"A long block east. On Tiefenaustrasse. There are some nice shops for ladies there."

When he left, I closed the door and tore open Dieter's telegram. It raised more questions than it resolved. He had sent it last night, about the time Annaliese and I boarded the airplane at Tempelhof. "FRAU WARNER'S FLIGHT DELAYED. SHALL FLY HER AND PARTY TO BERN PERSONALLY. HAVE RESERVED ACCOMMODATIONS AT YOUR HOTEL. MUCH TO DISCUSS. ARRIVE BERN APPROXIMATELY 1900 DECEMBER 2. PRINZ EXPECTING YOU 1000. DIETER LANGAN."

Much to discuss, indeed, I thought. What would conspiracy-loving Dieter Langan think of the reappearance of the berm man half a world from California? Would he believe it? Something was stirring his juices for Dieter to order up *Die Zeit*'s Lear business jet. I wondered if his underworld connections had come up with something about Dean Lockwood. Of all the Lockwoods, Dean was clearly the one Dieter thought most worthy of *Die Zeit*'s attention.

I picked up the telephone and dialed Dieter's private number in Düsseldorf. There were five rings before a female voice answered with: "*Herr Langan's Büro.*"

"This is Brian Lockwood. Is he available?"

"Herr Lockwood, this is Hilda Lindley, Herr Langan's secretary. I regret. He has gone to Frankfurt suddenly. I believe to meet Frau Warner and her friends. They were unable to get proper connections to Düsseldorf."

"Can I reach him in Frankfurt?"

"He left no number, Herr Lockwood. You could have him paged at Flughafen Frankfurt/Main, but he said he would call me before departing for Bern. I can give him a message."

"Thank you, no, Fräulein Lindley. I'll speak to him when he gets here. Good-bye."

Annaliese stepped through the door of the bath. She wore her shabby miniskirt and nothing else. The swift changes in her mood still disconcerted me. The grieving sister and feminist fury of last night had vanished again, leaving the provocative street girl. Sleeping in separate rooms had apparently unsettled her, and this was her answer.

I said, "I have to go out for a while. You're going shopping." Her eyes lighted up. *Osthunger.*

"I have no money; are you going to buy me something?"

"I am going to give you some money, and you are going to buy something for yourself. An outfit. Dress. A skirt and sweater. Blouse. Whatever you can get for five hundred dollars."

Anticipation was replaced by fear.

"What's the matter? I thought you'd be pleased."

"You said you wouldn't leave me. You *promised.*" She threw herself, half naked, into my arms and pulled me toward the bed. How many benefactors had paid her off with a few trinkets and vanished before she settled on this ploy? I wondered, feeling ashamed of myself for the thought, no matter how justified.

I said, "No one is leaving you. My sister is coming to Bern, and I want you to buy some clothes for yourself. I have to go to the bank and then to the Ministry of Finance. I should be back here sometime after one o'clock. Wait for me. I'll come with you when you buy the clothes. I don't want you going out of the hotel by yourself."

"Take me to bed first."

"Damn it, Anna, get dressed and have some breakfast. I have something important I've got to do."

"Yes, Brian." I had never heard her so meek. She let me go and began to pull her blouse over her bare breasts.

She went down to the lobby to see me off. I'd given her five hundred dollars' worth of Swiss francs in traveler's checks, and we'd gotten instructions from the concierge on how to find the women's shops on Tiefenaustrasse.

"I'll meet you here at one or a little after," I told her. The *Osthunger* I'd been counting on had apparently faded, leaving her merely downcast. "And if I'm going to be late, I'll telephone you here at the hotel. But you are *not* to go out unless I am with you."

"Yes," she said dutifully, and, clutching her purse in both hands, watched as I got into my taxi. As we drove away, I looked back. She was standing on the sidewalk, still watching.

I walked from the Bernerhof to the Crédit Suisse, cashed the postal draft Dieter had sent and then took a taxicab to the Town Hall, where the clock bells in the tower struck the hour as I walked into the echoing Gothic structure.

A security officer telephoned into the bowels of the building when I told him I had an appointment with Deputy Minister Prinz. Dieter had done his work well. I was expected. The security man escorted me to the steel-cage elevator and turned me over to a burly young man in a dark gray suit who somehow had the unmistakable aura of a policeman—which isn't very different in Bern from Monterey, California.

We went up to the fourth floor and then down an echoing marble-floored hallway. It was not exactly like being under arrest, but it had that flavor.

At the end of the hall was an office grand enough to rate a brass plaque on the door. All it said was: "Herr Joachim Prinz." In a society in which titles are as important as food and drink, Prinz's importance in the Ministry of Finance required no title on the door. That impressed me, as it was meant to.

Prinz himself was a short, slender man in solemnly conservative British tailoring. I estimated him to be my age or a few years younger. His hair was dark and thinning, but his eyes were gray and bright as new coins.

"Herr Lockwood," he said. "Please. May I offer you something? Some coffee. Have you breakfasted?"

"Coffee, thanks. The slope-shouldered downstairs security man did not excuse himself. Instead he silently stationed himself near the door.

I couldn't help wondering if the man at the door was meant to protect Prinz from me or to protect me from anyone who might be following me. A single plainclothes constable seemed unlikely to be much of an obstacle to an adversary determined to finish me off on the spot, even here in the heart of Swiss bureaucracy.

Prinz poured *caffè filtro* from a sterling silver urn. It steamed and smelled delicious. His cups were porcelain.

"Please, Herr Lockwood. Do sit down." He indicated a deeply padded leather armchair facing his meticulously empty desk. I wondered if this splendidly furnished office was no more than an interview room, a place where those of interest to the security arm of the Ministry of Finance were interrogated. There was certainly nothing in sight that suggested it belonged to a *person*. "A handsome office, Herr Prinz," I said.

A smile touched the Swiss's lips. "My secret is discovered. I do not work in this room, Herr Lockwood."

Prinz spoke to the security guard in Italian. "I think you can go, Benno."

"*Prego*, Deputy Minister."

When the door closed soundlessly behind the man, Prinz regarded me speculatively. "When Herr Langan telephoned me last night, I was surprised at the mention of your name. The name Lockwood has recently come up in the course of a very old investigation."

I took the list of bank numbers from my wallet and laid it on the desk. "Regarding these, perhaps, Herr Prinz?"

The gray eyes glanced at the list. "You are a journalist, Herr Lockwood?"

"Yes."

"Are you employed by Herr Langan?"

"No. I am a free-lance writer."

A hint of disapproval drifted over Prinz's face. It was a reaction with which I was very familiar, particularly from bankers. Free-lancers have no company retirement plans, no benefits, no insurance. It's a rare banker who isn't put off by such improvidence.

"This list is a compilation of Swiss bank account numbers dating back to 1945, Herr Prinz."

He turned the list with well-manicured fingers and glanced at it. "Yes. I believe that is so, Herr Lockwood. This series of numbers has not been used for many years. May I ask how you came by this list?"

"It was sent to me. From Germany."

"Ah? And the sender, Herr Lockwood?"

"The sender preferred to remain anonymous. But I think it was sent by an estranged relative. Dean Lockwood. My father's younger brother." I took the Eagle Dagger from my coat pocket and laid it on the desk beside the brittle old paper. "Actually the list was hidden in the hilt of this dagger."

A flash of interest showed in his eyes.

"I've reason to believe," I said, "that the former owner of this weapon obtained the listed vaults sometime in 1945."

"Are you investigating this for personal reasons or as a journalist intending to write about it in Herr Langan's sensational magazine?"

I had never heard *Die Zeit* referred to in quite that way. I suspected Dieter would be offended. He had pretensions to loftier journalism than what Prinz referred to as "sensational," which, in turn, conjured images of supermarket checkout lines.

"You don't seem interested, Herr Prinz. Perhaps I made a mistake coming here."

"Not at all, Herr Lockwood. The matter of the bank vaults interests me very much. Switzerland has very strict banking laws, as I am sure you know."

I was in no mood for games. "I asked Dieter Langan to call you with the hope that you can investigate the boxes listed on that paper. I have good reason to believe they contain stolen items of great value. Can we discuss that now?"

Prinz steepled his fingers and regarded me like a schoolmaster.

"Those boxes were examined some time ago, Herr Lockwood. All were empty, and had been for varying amounts of time. From as long as twenty years to two months. All, however, were visited by a client with the proper identification codes. That client, by the way, has been identified as a Mr. Lockwood." He waited for me to comment. I sat mute. I was, as the techies of Silicon Valley say, behind the learning curve on this affair.

After a while I said, "May I ask how you came by your set of numbers, Herr Prinz?"

He steepled his fingers again. "It was sold to us by a former high-ranking officer of the East German Stasi. The name given was ex-General Gerhard Ober, but then names mean so little these days. The banking records we were able to dig out of the old files confirmed that the bank vaults in question were, in fact, leased in 1945."

"That list is evidence of massive looting," I said.

"We have come to the conclusion that the so-called General Ober has bilked us," the deputy minister said. "We Swiss are a serious people. We should like very much to find the general and question him, but we are limited in the resources we can devote to the matter. These are old bones rattling, Herr Lockwood. Empty bank boxes are no proof of anything illegal. Therefore, higher authority has decided to close the case."

"That's absurd—"

"Is it? Are you a policeman by avocation, Herr Lockwood? Or perhaps an expert on international law? Are you offering a professional opinion?"

"None of the above," I shot back, "but those boxes were leased and filled by a German Nazi named Sieg Stossen. The contents were valuables stolen by Hermann Göering during the war."

"Valuables such as these?" Prinz opened a drawer, extracted a sheaf of papers and slid them across the table to me. It was a list of works of art, some famous, some less so, but all priceless, that had been stolen by the Germans during the war.

Listed were miniatures by Holbein, two Rembrandts, several gold and silver pieces of sculpture by Cellini, almost a dozen Fabergé eggs and figurines. The list ran on for a dozen pages. There were several drawings by Albrecht Dürer, a Raphael triptych and an item listed only as twenty amber panels from the Catherine Palace.

I looked up at the Swiss. "Amber?"

"Yes. I find that one of the most interesting items. The original panels were made for the Prussian King Frederick I between 1701 and 1709. Apparently master artisans chose pieces of amber from the king's vast collection, polished them, heated them to change the colors, cut them into interlocking pieces to form a mosaic. The patterns were glued to wooden panels and mounted on a wall. Each panel included a Prussian crowned eagle. The room must have been a breathtaking sight. But Frederick William I, who hated his father's taste for display, gave the panels to Peter the Great, who ignored them and left them in boxes while he went about his business of making Russia into a modern European state. It was Peter's daughter who unearthed the panels and created the Amber Room of the Catherine Palace. Then during the war, so it is said, the Nazis stole the panels." Prinz shrugged. "None has ever been recovered. Nor has any of the items on that list, Herr Lockwood. Conservatively, on today's illegal market, what is listed there is almost a billion dollars' worth of art. All, quite likely, sold to private collectors and beyond recovery. The wealth of the person or persons disposing of those items must be enormous. Such wealth commands great power, Herr Lockwood."

* * *

The specter of the Obryta farmhouse rose again. The pitiful dreams of that arrogant old couple.

"Herr Lockwood," Prinz said suddenly, "when was the last time you were in Paris?"

The veering change of subject seemed without any purpose, but a man like Prinz did nothing without a reason. "I haven't been in Paris for years."

A door opened, and two uniformed cantonal policemen appeared and stationed themselves against the wall.

"Have you your passport, Herr Lockwood?"

Frowning, I handed it over. Prinz examined it carefully. If he was looking for French customs stamps, he would be disappointed.

He looked at the pages again. "Japan two years ago. The Philippines. Australia. Suriname. But not Europe."

"Not recently," I said again. "Is that so strange?"

He returned the passport to me. The policemen stayed in the room. "You know Paris, of course."

"Not of course, Herr Prinz. I've been there only twice in my life."

"The first visit was a honeymoon trip?"

How the hell did he know that? More to the point, *why* did he know it?

"If Herr Langan had not called me last night, we might have sought you on our own." He tapped the paper on the desk with a polished fingernail. "General Ober's list informed us that East German investigators discovered that an 'asset' of their security service was suspected of dealing in stolen art that was legally the property of the German Democratic Republic. We were supplied with a list of code names—all worthless—and no usable description or fingerprints. It was clear that the Stasi did not want their man arrested. All they wanted was to lay a foundation for a claim that the East German government had notified the law enforcement community of the man's illegal activities—*if* he should ever be arrested by Western authorities. It's a common trick used by the East Bloc secret services, a blank check ready to be used to exculpate the illegal's service. It was the technique used to fog the guilt of the Bulgarians when Pope John Paul was shot, you may remember."

Prinz stood and walked to a window. "When we purchased further information from General Ober, we considered the possibility that the Lockwood he named was you, Herr Lockwood." He turned and regarded me steadily. "But you are too young. The records show that the boxes were visited by the *other* Lockwood as long ago as the mid-1950s. You were a schoolboy then, as was I. Then we investigated the movements of your adoptive father, Colonel Brian Lockwood. But his movements did not match the dates of withdrawals from the boxes." He shrugged, returned to the table and sat down across from me. "When did you last see your uncle, Herr Lockwood?"

"Years ago. While I was in school. We heard he had surfaced in Europe a few years ago, but there was no contact between Dean and the Lockwood family. There are hard feelings."

"Do you dislike your uncle?"

"It's mutual."

"You say you received the Eagle Dagger anonymously. Please explain that."

"Well, anonymously isn't exactly the word. It was common knowledge that when Dean Lockwood last saw the family, he left with a number of items that didn't belong to him, and the dagger was one of them. When it arrived in California again after all that time, there was a note." I opened my wallet and took out the sheet of paper. "This note," I said, handing it to Prinz.

He studied it carefully. "There is no question in your mind that the dagger was sent by your uncle?"

"None."

Prinz picked up the dagger and ran his finger along the inscription. "Stossen."

I said, "Sieg Stossen was supposed to have been killed by the Russians in the battle for Berlin."

"Supposed to have been killed. Not killed?"

"I think not killed."

"And?"

"He may well be your fictitious General Ober."

"An interesting hypothesis."

"I saw a man at the airport. Not Stossen. A young man. I'm certain I saw him only days ago in California. And I am almost certain he works for Stossen—Ober—whatever he's calling himself now."

"When exactly did the Eagle Dagger arrive at your home, Herr Lockwood?"

"Ten—no, eleven days ago. November twentieth."

"You are certain of the date?"

"Yes, it was the day before I was to go on a trip to Germany. To see Dieter Langan, in fact. I postponed the trip so that I could do some research in Colorado Springs."

"From where did you fly to Germany?"

"New York. There's no direct flight from Colorado Springs. Two people were killed in an incident in Brooklyn. . . . I think it was a botched attempt to kill me."

"A moment, Herr Lockwood," Prinz said. He stood and walked across the room to one of the policemen still standing behind me. A whispered conversation took place, and the policeman left the room.

Prinz returned to the elegant table serving as a desk. He did not sit behind it; he leaned against it so that I was forced to look up at him. At this point he was a policeman interrogating a suspect, or so I felt.

"I have done some research on you since Dieter Langan called me last night. You wrote extensively on the Green Party's activities in Germany some years ago, didn't you?"

"Yes." When policemen with fancy titles like Deputy Minister begin to ask a writer about his work, it's best for that writer to become laconic. The only thing more threatening than such a policeman is a critic who doesn't share the writer's politics. Political correctness and police interrogating methods have much in common.

"And you also wrote extensively about East Germany's intelligence activities in California. I obtained excerpts of those pieces by computer from *Pacific Currents*. Remarkably knowledgeable. Did you have sources inside the Stasi?"

"We did what we did, Herr Prinz. I prevailed on my publisher to buy material from stranded Stasi agents willing to sell. I can't give you more detail than that."

"Ah, yes. The American journalistic devotion to protecting sources."

"You, Herr Prinz, had even better sources. The Stasi were in your debt for the information that the safe-deposit boxes had been looted."

"Point taken, Herr Lockwood." He regarded me speculatively. "You were a soldier, I believe."

"For a short time. I was discharged from the Army for medical reasons."

"From the Special Forces, I think."

That really surprised me. Not even the members of my family knew I had volunteered for Special Forces and had been accepted when the meningitis leveled me.

There was a knock at the door, and the policeman opened it. Prinz looked up expectantly, nodded, then said, "Please give me a few moments with my staff, Herr Lockwood. Help yourself to the coffee. It is still hot."

When Prinz left the room, the policeman closed the door and stationed himself in front of it. I didn't need his words to tell me that I was not free to leave.

Deputy Minister Prinz's "few moments" stretched to two hours. When he returned, he carried a thick file folder.

"Forgive me for keeping you waiting, Herr Lockwood. I had to go far afield for these records. Would you please come with me and examine this material?" Prinz went to a side table and spread the contents of the file. On some of the papers I was surprised to see the stamp of the Sûreté Nationale, the secret police intelligence service of France.

There were eight-by-ten photographs facedown on the table. "These are ugly, Herr Lockwood. You are forewarned." One after another he turned the prints over.

He was right. They were very ugly. On a mortuary slab lay the partially decomposed body of a man. Maybe an expert could have made more of it, estimated his age, race, other things. Not I. The face seemed to have melted into a blackened mask. There was gray hair on the chest, but the head was thick with black oil.

The hands lay clawed, like hooks clutching at nothing. The genitalia were shrunken, almost childlike.

Comparing this corpse with others I had seen in South Asian and African wars, I guessed the man had been dead for at least a week. The cause of his death might have been apparent to a pathologist. It wasn't to me.

Reading from a flimsy sheet, Prinz said, "This man was found floating in the Seine on November twenty-second. He did not drown. He was killed by a blow that ruptured the carotid artery. Such a blow as a man skilled in unarmed combat might strike. He had a police record, Herr Lockwood. His name is—or was—Dean Lockwood."

If he had meant to shock me, he succeeded. I looked again at the gruesome photographs. Uncle Dean? The Colonel's black-sheep younger brother? Lockwoods died in war and accidents; they didn't get murdered and dropped into the Seine.

Then the significance of the date hammered me, hard. If Uncle Dean had been dead in the Seine on the twenty-second, then it had to be Stossen who had hired Annaliese and Erich Leyden. And it was Stossen who had sent me the dagger after he'd persuaded Dean to write that note. It made the link between them certain.

I had detested Dean Lockwood for good reasons. He had made the Colonel's life hell and upset the rest of the family. But how had he come to this?

Prinz said, "I think we shall discover that this man, your uncle, fell in with the East Bloc police long ago, Herr Lockwood. I believe they made him one of their assets. They did that sort of thing very well, you know. But when the boxes were finally emptied, he was no longer needed. And he ended like this."

I closed my eyes for a sick moment. How long ago had Dean become a Stasi asset? Years, perhaps. He had almost certainly stolen the Eagle Dagger at Stossen's command.

But how had the Colonel come by it? I now remembered clearly old Freya von Stossen's story. Sieg von Stossen told her he would send the dagger—*die Zeichen*—to them with Kristina Erika. But Stossen had never told her the dagger's secret, if Frau von Stossen was to be believed. Instead of following Stossen's orders, my mother had taken it with her when she escaped to

the American lines. Pregnant? With *his* child? Finally to be free
of the man she hated and feared?

"Yes," Prinz said. "I was developing a hypothesis, Herr Lockwood. It involved your uncle and your father, the Colonel."

I stared at the man. "That's absolute bullshit," I said.

"I found it so when I learned that Colonel Lockwood died in
Mexico City. Killed by a mysterious hit-and-run driver." Prinz
shrugged. "I apologize, Herr Lockwood. My suspicions were
unwarranted. The Mexican authorities have yet to close the case
on your father's accident."

"I didn't know that."

"There was no reason you should. It is a police matter, not a
matter for personal revenge."

I kept silent.

Prinz watched me. "I did not hear you agree with me, Herr
Lockwood."

"No, you didn't."

"You are justified in feeling some anger, Herr Lockwood. But
try to see this from my point of view. There is a mystery here."

"There must be records of payment for the boxes on that list,"
I said.

"The boxes were acquired during the war under a special
agreement between the German authorities and the then minister of finance. Payment was made in gold bullion to reserve the
use of the boxes until the year 2000. There were no names.
German efficiency at its most baffling, Herr Lockwood."

Swiss efficiency as well, I thought. It explained a great deal.

I stared at the brittle paper taken from the Eagle Dagger. It
had been secreted in the dagger, given for safekeeping to Kristina Erika Obryta von Stossen, who fled to the Americans and
eventually, in Nuremberg, gave the dagger to her lover, the
American colonel, Brian Lockwood.

But it hadn't ended there. The Russians had been gung ho to
catch Stossen as a war criminal. But they had been almost
equally determined to trap the man who had smuggled part of
Göering's hoard out of Germany. Particularly the amber of the
Catherine Palace? Yes, very likely. The Bolsheviks had enormous pretensions concerning the ideology of art. So they had
contrived to get Colonel Lockwood, the troublesome American,

sent home. Once he was gone, they could close in on his lover, Kristina Erika. But the dagger had gone. With the colonel.

And how had they known she had the dagger? Why, from Stossen, of course, who shopped her to the NKVD in exchange for his faked death and a place inside the East German apparat. It was an affair of such sickening cynicism that it made me ill to think about it.

"I am sorry to have held you in suspicion even for a moment, Herr Lockwood," Prinz said, "but these old, muddled cases are fascinating, and when Herr Langan called, I actually imagined myself solving a mystery." He shrugged. "For a moment."

"I've made the mystery worse." And then I told him what had happened at the Red Salmon in Pomellen and in the farmhouse in Obryta.

He listened without any show of emotion to an account of things that had happened far from this stately room of gilded cornices and elegant antiques. When I finished, he said, "So it is far from over. You claim three German citizens have been killed. If that is true, I must notify Interpol. I shall speak to the Germans and the Polish National Police Authority to see if there are charges against you. I also assume that the man you call Dolger was a Stasi or KGB agent in place. Those services have always been profligate with their human resources."

Profligate, I thought. A nice euphemism.

"Herr Lockwood," Prinz said, "is there more you should tell me?"

"No."

"I will have you driven back to the Bernerhof." He turned the dagger and list with a manicured index finger. "Don't forget these, Herr Lockwood. They appear to be your property now."

24

"Is that you?"

AT THE BERNERHOF I stopped at the concierge's desk for my key and was told that there had been a telephone call. It must be Dieter, arriving a little early, I thought.

"No, Herr Lockwood," the concierge answered in response to my question. "It was a gentleman who called, but he left no name. He only said he would call again."

Was it Dieter? As I walked away toward the elevator, the concierge called after me.

"Sorry, Herr Lockwood. I forgot to tell you that Frau Rykova left a message that she would be back at the hotel in time for lunch."

I was furious. Goddamn her anyway. She had to know that she could be in danger. I'd damn well warned her. I took a deep breath, ordered coffee and went upstairs. The rooms been cleaned. Nothing was out of place. The beds were tautly made. It all made the rooms look . . . empty. I went to the window and opened it, looking down into the street. Traffic went by in an ordinary way, tires hissing in the remains of the last snowfall. The sky was no longer clear. It had turned to a muddy gray—a Swiss winter-afternoon sort of sky. The mountains of the Bernese Oberland are majestic, but they were hidden in the lowering overcast. It was so dark there were already some lights on in the buildings along the street.

At two the coffee came. By two-fifteen I'd drunk it all and was pacing, ready to call Prinz at the Ministry of Finance for help. I didn't because he had made it clear that he wanted as little to do with me and my story as possible. Herr Joachim Prinz was, after all, a bureaucrat. I had told him about the sighting in Bern of the man on the berm in Carmel, and he had all but ignored it. Perhaps he thought Americans were subject to fits of imagination. I was beginning to feel like a character in a Franz Kafka novel. Nothing was what it seemed to be.

I paced around the room. Had Annaliese maybe gone to tell Eugen or Stossen where we were? Gone back to the enemy? I couldn't believe that she would contact either of them, especially after the way her brother had been killed. But then, I hadn't thought that Lockwoods ended their lives floating in the Seine. I'd been out of my league with everyone I'd met since that damned dagger arrived on my doorstep.

The telephone rang.

It was not a call from Dieter. Not a call from Annaliese either. I heard a man's thin, harsh voice. He spoke in German, a hard-edged Prussian dialect, a dialect I had heard not so very long ago in the farmhouse near Obryta. And I could detect just the suggestion of a Russian inflection, as though the speaker no longer used his native tongue as his primary language. "Is it Brian Lockwood to whom I speak?"

"Yes. Who is this?"

The question was ignored. The thin knife-edge of a voice went on. "We have business, you and I. Unfinished business. But first . . . pay attention . . . listen carefully."

There was a sound of a handset being passed from hand to hand, other noises, then a woman's terrified voice.

"Brian? Brian, is that you? Can you hear me?"

The thin voice returned. "Did you recognize her voice?"

"Leave her *alone*," I said. "There's no need for this. I'll give you what you want." A day ago I would have been sure that Sieg Stossen's list of box numbers was the prize. Not now. The list was worthless, and it had served its purpose. But it was all I had that anyone could want.

"I asked you question." Only Slavic-language speakers habitually drop articles that way.

"Yes, damn you, tell me what you want and I'll do it. Don't hurt the girl—"

"I am touched by such devotion to vulgar little whore." The speaker used the German word *billig*, meaning not only "vulgar" but "worthless, ordinary." The arrogance of it broke through my numb anxiety for Anna. My God, I thought, *I am talking to Sieg Stossen*. I couldn't bring myself to make the mental adjustment to admit I was speaking to my *father*.

"At this moment an envelope is being delivered to your concierge. When this conversation ends, collect it and follow instructions exactly. Call no one. If you involve the Swiss authorities, the girl will be killed. You are being watched."

"I'll do whatever you say, just let the girl go."

"*Verdammter baurischer Amerikanski.*" The epithets, the unique mix of ethnic colloquialisms came through loud and clear.

I lost my cool and shouted into the telephone: "Stossen? *Damn you, Sieg von Stossen, is that you?*"

"Follow instructions," the voice said, and the line went dead.

I walked down to the lobby because I could not wait for the slow-moving elevator. I was shaking inside. *Stossen.* Had he simply surrendered to the Russians in Berlin in 1945? Surrendered and made an arrangement? Why not? We had hired Nazis when we thought we needed them. The Russians had collected twice as many as we had. In Stossen's case there was no need for mysterious organizations like ODESSA, the underground railway that spirited Nazi war criminals out of the collapsing ruins of the Thousand-Year Reich. Sieg Stossen would have needed no such assistance. My father—I forced myself to acknowledge it— was a man of ingenuity and enterprise. The way in which he had, as an ex-general of the Stasi, cheated the Swiss was proof enough of that.

I visualized the man I saw from the window in Nuremberg. I had *expected* to see my uncle Dean, so that was whom I had seen. But it had been, as I had come to suspect, Sieg Stossen, in his seventies, undamaged by his crimes, enriched by the life he had made for himself in the Stasi. It had to be the Stasi, or even the KGB. Sieg Stossen would have been a golden find for the KGB.

The concierge was busy with arriving guests, and I had to wait while he dispatched them to their rooms with a porter pulling their luggage on a cart.

"A letter," I said. "A letter for me, hand-delivered."

"Moments ago, Herr Lockwood." He explored his mail slots while I suppressed my urge to yell at him. After what seemed an eternity of fumbling about, he produced the letter, a large manila envelope with my name written on it.

I tore it open. Inside was a marked map of Bern and a note instructing me to cross the Aare River on the Lorrainebrücke, follow the Nord Ring to Scheibenstrasse and then past the Waffenfabrik—the famous weapons works of Bern—then under the overhead roadbed of the N1 autobahn to the edge of the Aare in the wooded parkland of the Wylerholz. And then *wait*. The command was written in English and underlined twice.

"The man who left this envelope for me, concierge, can you describe him to me? Was he an older man?"

"No, Herr Lockwood. He was tall. In his thirties, I would guess. As fair as yourself. I concluded he was Russian."

"He spoke to you?"

"Yes, *mein Herr*. He spoke Schweizerdeutsch with an accent."

I turned and searched the lobby and foyer of the hotel. There was only the hotel staff—a passing maid, a porter, the clerk at the registration desk. Prinz was showing his lack of interest in me. There was no one in sight, no surveillance.

The hatred I'd heard in Stossen's rasping, old man's voice had sounded *personal*. "Give me some paper and an envelope." I stood at the desk and wrote a note to Dieter Langan: "Stossen is alive and in Bern. He has Annaliese Rykova, and I am going after him."

I folded it with the map and put it in an envelope. I wrote Dieter Langan's name on it, sealed it and handed it to the concierge.

"A Herr Langan and some other friends of mine will be arriving this afternoon. Please deliver this personally to him."

I wrote a second note: "Claire—Let Dieter explain. I have to do it."

It went in a second envelope with Claire's name on it. "This is for Frau Warner."

I tipped the man extravagantly. I wanted him to remember details. Then I left the building and hailed a cab from the rank waiting near the hotel courtyard. The sky was much darker, and it had begun to snow. I gave the driver instructions and settled back in the rear seat, wondering if, as bad as this was, my life had at last found some resolution. The driver turned on his headlights and windshield wipers.

I gripped the hilt of the Eagle Dagger in my raincoat pocket.

The wipers stroked squeakily back and forth over the oily glass. Strange requiem, I thought, for a man setting out prepared to kill his own father.

25

Where do you hide, Father?

IT WASN'T A LONG RIDE, but it was like a journey to the end of the world. All the subtle feelings of persecution and fear that had haunted me since leaving California suddenly had a sharp focus. Sharp, though the person or thing at the very center was still blurred and indistinct. Lack of focus creates monsters. . . . Suddenly the man I had seen from the window of my hotel room in Nuremberg was ageless, robust, stronger than I. And driven by emotions and a purpose I could hardly imagine.

It was understandable that he would hate me. . . . I was the son stolen away by the wife who had, by his lights, betrayed him. What I was doing, I realized, was something very American. The American weakness, which I shared, was not the arrogance our European associates always attributed to us. It was something very different. In fact, an American, faced with evil, almost invariably told himself, "There, but for the grace of God, go I." The American weakness was compassion—guilty compassion. Remember, I thought, a surfeit of compassion can kill you.

* * *

221

As my driver turned onto Neubrückestrasse toward the Lorrainebrücke, I looked back. An Opel was behind us. It had the unmistakable look of a government car. Not too large or too opulent. Dull color. Two men alone in the front seats.

A hand seemed to close on my throat. If I was mistaken, and Prinz had been interested enough to put a tail on me, then Annaliese was in real danger. But I had been warned not to involve the authorities. I couldn't take a chance.

I leaned forward and said to the taxi driver, "I'm having difficulties with my wife. She thinks I'm having an affair, and she's hired two men to follow me. They're behind us in an Opel. Can you get away from them?"

The man, a young Swiss in leather jacket and blue jeans, turned to look at me.

"For an extra hundred francs?"

"Sit back," he said.

The cab was an Alfa Romeo, and he drove it like a race driver. A swift move through some narrow streets south of Neubrückestrasse didn't divert the trailing Opel.

The driver grinned. "They are following, all right. Now let us see."

We were back on the Neubrückestrasse, a divided expressway. He skillfully wove through the traffic until we reached a place where the eastbound and westbound pavements divided. The eastbound roadway passed under a railway bridge; the westbound connected with the Lorrainebrücke over the Aare.

At the last moment the driver cut across several lines of traffic, causing a ferocious hooting of horns, and onto the ramp leading up to the Lorrainebrücke. The Opel was jammed between two lines of bumper-to-bumper traffic that had screeched to a stop to avoid colliding with us.

Without a pause, my driver took the Alfa straight over the bridge and onto the Nord Ring. The first outlet was marked "Victoriarain." We took it, descended to ground level and turned sharply under the elevated Ring. We moved quickly through the narrow, cobbled streets of the Lorraine district. Then, as we passed through Wyler and turned toward the Aare and under the elevated train tracks on Haldenstrasse, the driver slowed. He turned and grinned at me. "Like Herr Popeye in *The French Connection*."

"Exactly," I said. "Well done."

"There is the Waffenfabrik," the driver said, pointing at a low gray building under the elevated roadbed of the N1. "The Wylerholz is beyond. Where do you wish to go?"

"Take me as near the river as you can."

I was early. Good, I needed to look at this place that had been chosen to be so isolated in the heart of a great city. And isolated it was. I could see traffic moving on the elevated N1, but at river level the scene was empty. In this climate and at this time of year the Wylerholz was almost ghostly in its solitude.

I studied my surroundings. If it *was* Sieg Stossen who waited for me at the end of this blind quest, I had better look to myself and a little to Annaliese Rykova. Sieg Stossen, the war criminal, was like a page of yellowed newsprint, his crimes almost reabsorbed into the compost of history. But Sieg von Stossen, the *man,* was another matter. What sort of human being could nurse a hatred for almost half a century, sacrificing his parents to it, feeding it carefully over the years—to what purpose?

It sickened me that I was thinking of my *biological* father—a man whose blood and heritage I shared. Never mind his political crimes, Sieg Stossen was responsible—to my certain knowledge—for the deaths of two innocent people in Brooklyn, of Erich Leyden, of his own parents, aged and demented with the promises he had made them long ago, before abandoning them to the watch and care of Dolger and whatever other Stasi hoods had spied on them over the years. He was even guilty of Dolger's death, although I was the one who finally killed him. Stossen had ordered Dean Lockwood killed, too. He used him to empty the vaults and killed him when he could only be a liability and a witness.

And there was the Colonel. Stossen, with his Stasi or KGB connections, had, I now believed, been behind his death. It was beyond proof now, but both Sergeant Major Cobb and I had always suspected the Colonel's death had been no accident. With Sieg von Stossen alive, I was certain of it. I even wondered about Marianna Clef. Had she died a natural death? The timing was suspicious.

And finally there was Kristina Erika. My beautiful dream parent, killed by Russian soldiers. How had he managed it? Captured by the Russians, then what? Interrogation by the NKVD, of course. What had he told them? What did he offer? Not just Kristina, but the Eagle Dagger that he had given her and that she, in turn, had entrusted to her American lover. I remembered the look on Stossen's face in his wedding photograph. Kristina's "betrayal" must have been worse than the interrogations by the NKVD. I had a feeling that the price was still being exacted.

All right, Sieg Stossen, I thought. Let's play it out to the end.

My stomach ached with undefined hunger. It was like carrying a stone under my heart. I had not eaten since early yesterday, yet the thought of food was nauseating.

I looked out of the car window at the late-afternoon traffic on the elevated highway. It formed a golden chain as Berners drove through the winter murk and snowfall with headlamps on. Behind us, Bern's lights shone mistily through the wet air as snowflakes spun down out of the indeterminate sky to be pushed aside by the oscillations of the windshield wipers. It was only three, but it seemed that it would be night soon. I could feel the loom of the mountains of the Bernese Oberland, gigantic Nibelungen, lost in the winter mist.

I leaned against the seat and closed my eyes. I was not thinking straight. It was as though I were edging up on the hallucinations I had experienced in the hospital. But something *was* incomplete.

A single, thin shaft of sunlight penetrated the overcast and struck the windows of the buildings of the Rossfeld district across the river. For an instant, reflected light flared under the clouds and through the gently falling snow.

Suddenly I knew what was bothering me. It was the *way* the killings around me had been done. The plot to bring me inexorably to Sieg Stossen was complex and subtle, even elegant in a cruel and ruthless sort of way. But the *killings* were another matter. Even as long ago as the Colonel in Mexico City, every stroke had been thuggish, stupidly done without regard for consequences. They lacked Von Stossen's touch of controlled malevolence. It was as though two minds were at work, two agendas were being completed.

We passed the Hallenbad—a natatorium, the Sportplatz— closed for the season. Against the dark woods of the Thormannboden Forest across the river, I could glimpse the pale, frothing green of the Aare, swollen with ice melt. The river plunged and quarreled its way through the city in great swings of its deep, millennial channel.

I had a feeling that I was finally exactly where Von Stossen wanted me to be. Had he learned about my nightmares from Fräulein Clef? I felt a chill. . . . I was back in Nuremberg with Annaliese, by the river with its black willows. Circles within circles within circles. The scheme was precise, and each step brought me closer to this moment, one which Stossen had been willing to wait for all these years, patiently contriving and manipulating.

And suddenly I no longer cared. I mean, yes, I was afraid of what was coming, but more of what I might learn than of what I might experience. Sometimes death is not the *only* possibility. A man with a father like Sieg Stossen inevitably learned the truth of that ugly proposition.

The taxicab stopped under the elevated roadbed of the N1, and the driver turned to me uncertainly. "This satisfactory, sir?"

I understood his question. In summertime the citizens of Bern used the Wylerholz as a parkland, but in December, with the snow softly falling out of a dark sky, the expanse of greenery was foreboding. The cab had stopped a hundred meters from the narrow roadway that followed the abutted banks of the Aare. The sound of the rushing water dominated what was otherwise an *emptiness*. I looked to the west and to the northeast. We were alone in the Wylerholz.

This was the way Sieg von Stossen would have it—solitude almost in the heart of the city. I said to the driver, "This is the place."

He regarded me dubiously. Not many tourists or visitors ever showed much interest in this part of Bern in winter. There was nothing here to draw them.

"Is there a public telephone nearby?" I asked.

"Yes. Back there past the Waffenfabrik. At the Sportplatz. A post kiosk. Almost a kilometer, mein Herr."

"Thank you," I said, and paid him. With the promised extra one hundred francs.

"Are you certain you want to be left here, mein Herr?"

"I want to walk by the river. I will telephone for a taxi when I want to leave."

As I walked slowly toward the river, I remembered a phrase I'd read somewhere long ago: "riparian solitude." I thought about the icebound Pegnitz. The Aare was a very different thing: a mountain river fed by springs and glaciers high in the Alps, plunging downward precipitously, seeking the distant sea. The water raced through the watercourse that the Swiss buttressed yearly to offset the hungry river devouring the foundations of Bern itself. White water. White and milky green. But the solitude seemed oddly enhanced by the plunging tumult.

I looked around me at all of the Wylerholz I could see. The cab was gone, and I was alone. Was I being watched? I looked up at the N1. There should have been heavy traffic on the road. There was none. Snowflakes fell, spinning and gliding through the heavy air. Some of the snow clung to the sere grass underfoot. A thin carpet of white was forming.

Stossen, I thought. Where are you? Where do you hide, Father? I gripped the hilt of the Eagle Dagger in my raincoat pocket and thought ironically: What do you plan to do with that now? I took my hand out of the pocket and raised the collar of my raincoat. The cold was intense.

Far overhead, at the distant base of the overcast, a traffic helicopter flew. An insect against the misty clouds. I was numb with the cold and with an overpowering sense of inevitability. But it wasn't fate, but Stossen, that had brought me here.

I reached the bank of the river. Here the air was wet with spray and the smell of mud and ancient ice. I stood looking at the tumult of white water, recalling the child I once was by another river.

Through the curtain of falling snow I saw a movement on the road beyond the N1. A long black car rolled silently to a stop. A bareheaded man emerged. He was as blond as I. He looked in my direction.

It was the man on the berm, the man in the air terminal. It was Eugen. Even at this distance, I could see the way he was looking at me.

Of course, I thought. The second agenda.

He opened the rear door, and an old man stepped out and gestured for me to approach.

26

Blut und Ehre.

I MOVED SLOWLY. The dry, frozen grass crackled beneath my feet. The snow fell gently, melting in my hair and on my face.

Where was Annaliese? The rear door of the black limousine was open, but I could not see inside. Sieg Stossen stood erect as a statue, snowflakes falling about him like the white grains in a child's crystal globe.

He removed the black homburg he wore and lifted his raddled, old man's face to the light. His hair had once been fair; it was white now, thin over a brown and mottled scalp. As I came nearer, I could see that his eyes were surprisingly blue, the color of Delft porcelain. This was the man I had glimpsed in Nuremberg and mistaken for my uncle Dean. And all the while Dean Lockwood floated in the Seine.

With my back to the river I approached the car. A dozen paces from Stossen, I stopped. "Where is the girl? I'm here. Let her go."

He was a large man, erect even though he was in his midseventies. There was still something imposing about him, but cold as the river, cold as the snow. He stood like a soldier, like a Prussian. Freya von Stossen would have been pleased with him.

"The girl," I said again. "Where is she?"

"How concerned you are for the welfare of whores," he said. "But then, you come by it naturally. It is in your blood."

I glanced at the large man standing at the open front door of the car. He was taller than I was with sloping, powerful shoulders, and thick blond hair. His mouth was thin and set in a hard line. "Eugen," I said.

"Yes," Stossen said, "Yevgeny, in his own language. He is the son I was left to raise when my whore of a wife robbed me."

I stared at the man. My God, I thought, was this my half brother? He was dressed in a black anorak and black trousers. He returned my stare without blinking. His eyes were that same shade of Delft blue as Stossen's. He was at least ten years younger than I was, ten pounds heavier and surely more fit.

Stossen said, "You should know each other. You are the son of a Prussian whore, and he is the son of a Russian one."

I was aware of the sound of the river, of the falling snow, of the bone-chilling cold. It was as though I stood by the Pegnitz again.

"Come closer," Stossen said. There was a reedy quality in his voice, a breathlessness that suggested something more than simply age.

My shoes crushed the frozen grass. Far off I could hear the sound of the distant traffic helicopter, and from farther still, the whisper of the winter-bound city.

"Show me the girl," I said.

"Yevgeny," Stossen said, "do what he says."

There was a sound from inside the car. Eugen pulled Annaliese from the car. She stumbled. She had been beaten. Her eyes were swollen almost closed; her cheeks were bruised. There was a strip of tape over her mouth.

"You rotten bastard—"

"Did my Polish bitch teach you insolence, boy? It was always what she knew best. Insolence and disloyalty." He looked to Eugen. "Take that off her mouth. Let the whore speak if she wants."

Eugen tore the tape from Annaliese with one ripping motion. She uttered a cry of pain and fell to her knees. The sight of what they had done to her enraged me.

I approached Sieg von Stossen and took the dagger from my

pocket. I snapped the scabbard away with a flick of the wrist and put the point at Stossen's throat. "It doesn't always go your way, old man."

Eugen reached into the car and came up with an Uzi assault rifle. He levered a round into the chamber and raised the weapon into firing position. Annaliese gathered herself and shouldered his knee so that he staggered. He struck her with the Uzi, and she fell with her face in the snow.

I lifted the old man's chin with the point of the dagger and said to Eugen, "Touch her again, and I'll cut his throat."

The thought I had had on the way here was confirmed. There *were* two agendas at work here. Eugen was the thug who had killed Erich Leyden, who had beaten Professor Ershad, who had hired the gunmen in Brooklyn. He was also probably the one who had put Dean Lockwood into the Seine and paid the driver who killed the Colonel in Mexico City. In his way Eugen was as dedicated to the destruction of the Lockwoods as was Sieg von Stossen.

Stossen made no effort to move away from contact with the dagger. His breathing was quick and shallow, but not from fear.

"You call yourself Lockwood," he said.

"I am a Lockwood," I said.

Eugen didn't move his eyes from my face.

Stossen said, "He wants to kill you."

"I can see that."

"Do you know why?"

"I can guess."

I lowered the dagger until it rested lightly on the old man's chest. I could hear his breathing, a wheezing, soughing sound of bad lungs and a maybe worse heart. Would I inherit all that in time? I had a sudden impulse to break into a crazy laugh. What sort of man worried about bad health in a situation like this? Sieg Stossen's son, I thought, who else?

I looked again at Annaliese. Stossen said, "She kept us informed, boy. It's as well you learn something about betrayal, too. After all, it is in the blood."

"She told me," I said.

"And you forgave her. How weak."

If Stossen was not afraid of the dagger at his chest, and if he and Eugen both figured I wouldn't kill him out of hand, then my options and Anna's were being rapidly reduced. I had to rebalance the scales.

I said, "Prinz knows about you, Herr General Ober."

"There is no Joachim Prinz, you know. There is only a name Swiss counterintelligence uses. They like to play these stupid games." The old eyes lighted with the pleasure of superior knowledge. "One learns in the gulag, boy. One learns not to believe what you see."

"You were in the gulag?"

"For more years than you can imagine. I knew Wolf, but that did not shorten my sentence." He spoke with cold precision. I realized he meant Markus Wolf, the man who had organized the East German intelligence and police units that became the Stasi.

"Seven years. For my work at Sachsenhausen. There were Russian prisoners there. The Ivans did not forgive lightly. I gave them Kristina Erika. I thought she had kept the dagger. The Soviets wanted what Göering had stolen. Most particularly the Russian things. They are such a cultured people." His voice was full of contempt. "But Kristina gave the dagger to her lover. The interrogators at Novaya Zemlya told me, and I spent seven years in the Arctic because of it."

My hand ached on the dagger. God help me, I wanted to use it.

"Does that offend you?" he said.

"Offend me? Everything about you offends me."

"What a fool you are, boy. All things in life must eventually be set right. Lockwood and the whore dishonored me. I do what must be done. *Blut und Ehre,* boy. Blood and honor."

"Don't talk to me about honor—"

"Honor always contains a measure of expediency."

Jesus, the son of a bitch was laughing at me. "What did you do with Göering's loot?"

"Your Lockwood uncle got into trouble with the police in the GDR. The man was a common thief, you know. No honor there. But an immense measure of expediency. I offered him prison or employment. He chose employment. He stole the dagger. Long ago. For pay, boy. Americans will do anything for pay. Over the years he was my agent. But when he emptied the last vault and sold the contents, I had no further use for him. I was ready to collect *you*. Kristina's son. The last dishonor."

"But you must have had a life—it's been *years* . . ."

"What does time matter? Method. System. Those things matter. Still, I might have waited longer except that the GDR collapsed and then the USSR. Even then—but no, it had to be finished at last. You, boy. Kristina's get."

"Your parents—"

"They were difficult. My mother hated the Communists and never missed an opportunity to say so. They raped her, you see, long ago. My parents could not be allowed to know I was an officer of the Stasi. But they were taken care of. Well enough."

"Taken care of," I muttered, remembering that pitiful pair in the farmhouse.

Stossen, I realized numbly, was still trying to kill Kristina Erika Obryta, who had betrayed him. He needed her "get," me, to complete the revenge.

My stomach churned. "And what about Dolger?" I said.

"Dolger?"

"Damn you, Dolger. Your man. Did you just put him in that farmhouse and forget them all?"

"Dolger was a watchdog. A dumb animal."

Who served you to the death.

"And him?" I said, looking toward Eugen.

The old man grimaced. "In exchange for Kristina, one of my privileges in the camp of Novaya Zemlya was a woman. Yevgeny is her brat. When I left the camp, she stayed. I took him back to Germany with me. I had some use for him."

What the old man was actually saying was that he had raised his prison-bred son to be a killer. It made a kind of terrible sense. Sieg Stossen was a killer in his own right, far worse than a Dolger or an Eugen could ever be. But he was old and this son was young. Old killers *need* the young. . . .

I looked into Stossen's strange eyes and tried to know him, discover something, or I would die by this cold river and so would Annaliese Rykova.

"Anna," I said quietly, "stand up."

She looked at me dully.

"Get *up*," I said.

Eugen leveled the Uzi. I looked directly into the heart of that "second agenda." Eugen wanted to kill me, *yearned* to do it. His expression, his bearing all made that clear. He was a man consumed with jealousy. So much so, apparently, that he had been willing to risk the old man's displeasure by striking clumsily and angrily at me in Brooklyn. At this moment he was barely in control, doubly dangerous.

I pressed the blade of the Eagle Dagger against von Stossen's chest. "Move that gun and he dies," I said to Eugen. I spoke as calmly as I could manage. Now it was life and death that both men believed me.

"He doesn't understand English," Stossen said.

I repeated what I said in German. Eugen stared at me. The air seemed darker, more oppressive. The snow still fell with nightmare slowness, softly coating the field around us. There was an electric violet flash somewhere above the clouds. Over the rushing sound of the Aare I heard a clap of distant thunder. Every sight, every sound seemed distinct. Yet the impression was one of total silence while snowflakes fell spiraling gently to earth.

"Stand up, Anna," I said. "Do it."

She got to her feet unsteadily. Bless you, girl, I thought. Do it for me. Do it for your dead brother. For yourself.

She looked at me out of swollen, battered eyes.

"There is a telephone by the Sportplatz," I said. "Can you walk that far?"

She nodded.

"Good. Have you any money?"

She thrust her hand into a pocket, felt for coins, nodded again. She was shivering, trembling as the cold knifed through her thin blouse. I wanted to give her my coat, but I couldn't risk the movement. "Go, then. Call for help from the Sportplatz. I will stay here."

Stossen shook his head. "She is near to being in shock." I had forgotten he was a medical doctor.

"Do it, Anna," I said.

"You are a fool, boy," Stossen said. "Do you think I have any fear of dying?"

"Let's find out, old man."

"Go, Anna," I said, and pressed the blade harder against Stossen's chest.

She began to walk, unsteadily at first, leaving tracks in the new snow. The sound of the river seemed louder. And then she began to run.

Stossen called out, "*Yevgeny. Kill her!*"

Eugen looked at me, seemed undecided. He obviously preferred to kill me. Shooting Anna would give me a moment to act when the Uzi wasn't on me.

The old man said in English, "He really hates you, boy. He thinks you are my son."

It was as though I had touched an electric wire. "*What did you say?*"

Stossen began to laugh, sucking air. "Didn't you know where you came from? Didn't the honorable American ever tell you that you were *his* bastard?"

Obsessions can be blind. I had considered every possibility except that one.

At that same moment Eugen's lifetime of discipline and loyalty to Stossen reached its climax. He wanted to kill me, but instead he jerked the Uzi into firing position, aiming at Anna. I pushed Stossen aside and threw myself at Eugen, blade foremost. The Uzi exploded into automatic fire, tearing up the ground at our feet.

I felt a wash of hot wetness on my hand. The *Adler Dolch* had slipped easily into the left side of Eugen Stossen's chest. He was as good as dead when his knees struck the snow.

I heard a single sharp crack, a pistol shot. A searing pain creased my head and sent me sprawling. Stossen stood over me, pointing a Soviet Makarov pistol at me for a second shot.

"*Look at me, boy. Look at me, Kristina's bastard.*"

I willed myself to look straight into those ice blue eyes. If I was going to die, at least I would die as the Colonel's son and damn Sieg Stossen to hell.

Then the thunder came again, but a different sort of thunder. I wiped blood from my eyes. Sieg Stossen seemed to have leaned backward across the limousine's fender. Something smeared the shining wet lacquer. The old man stared, astonished, at the sky, then slid slowly from the car and rolled facedown into the snow.

Far off and above us, on the edge of the roadbed of the N1, there were men at the barrier, looking down. One was a sharp-shooter with a scoped sniper's rifle. He seemed to be preparing for a second shot if one was needed. It was not. The helicopter I had seen earlier rested on the elevated roadbed, its rotors still spooling. It resembled a resting insect poised for flight.

The man known as Joachim Prinz stared down at me and the two dead men in the snow.

And Annaliese Rykova, filled with a single-minded resolu-tion, still ran across the snowy meadow of the Wylerholz toward the Sportplatz and the telephone that was no longer needed.

27

"But to the point. He did not kill you."

I WAS CONSCIOUS AGAIN. There was an aftertaste of barbiturates in my throat. Not the stuff they gave me at the Stanford hospital, thank God. Nembutal had let me sleep, but it wasn't much as a pain-killer. The bullet crease in my forehead ached and throbbed under the bandage.

I lay in the semidark, listening to the morning sounds of Bern coming through the slightly open window: the noise of tires on wet pavement, the short, shrill hoots of the electric railway cars and the sighing, whispering voice of any large city at dawn.

Above my bed the EKG monitor chirped softly to itself. Someone, Claire, probably, had alerted the doctors to the fact that I had "recently" had a heart attack and an angioplasty.

She had come in briefly late last night with Stein Davis and Dieter Langan. Through the narrow window I could make out the start of early-morning twilight. The snow still fell, just as it had yesterday, but there was a difference. Now, in this dark winter morning, I was no longer the "little Adolf" Uncle Dean had addressed so scornfully all those years ago. I wasn't a *Lebensborn* child scooped up by an American soldier's whim. I *was* a Lockwood, the Colonel's son, not a Nazi war criminal's. It is near to impossible to convey what that meant to me.

The surgeon who patched the groove in my skull had been fascinated by the challenge. "We get almost no gunshot wounds, Herr Lockwood," he said. "In fact, I have seen only one other in three years. A hunting accident."

He was a short, solidly made man with a bald head and soft brown eyes. His name was Raymond, a common name among the French Swiss. In any case, the hands, small with tapered fingers like the hands of a flute player or clarinetist, were steady as he put eight sutures into my forehead. "The scar will be small. Barely noticeable, Herr Lockwood." And I thought, That is my name. Not a name I have borrowed. *Mine.* And then: Why couldn't you have told me, Colonel? Actually I thought I knew the answer, but it would take Claire to confirm it.

Dr. Raymond was careful, conservative. He wanted to keep me in the hospital for a day or two, but I was having none of that. I wanted to get out, out of the country, out of Europe and back to California. The thought that I might have to appear in Stettin as a material witness in the deaths at the Obryta farm-house made me restless.

Rescue had come from an unlikely source. The mysterious Joachim Prinz. The man who, according to Sieg von Stossen, did not exist. "Without wishing to endanger your health or be inhospitable, Herr Lockwood," Prinz had said, "I want you gone from Switzerland by tomorrow evening at the latest. If the Poles want you, they can contact you in California."

He had added, "I will have permission to explain tomorrow morning, Herr Lockwood."

Now I waited for daylight.

I lay thinking that it was only Stossen's Prussian taste for kitsch and melodrama that had brought his plot to this point. A saner man would have killed me in New York or even in California. The son of a bitch came close enough to killing me, I thought. There by the Aare, where glacier melt plunged and spumed its way through Bern, old Sieg von Stossen had reached for one last effect, one proper *Götterdämmerung.* Well, damn him to hell, it had cost him his life. I was far from sorry. Perhaps I should have been grateful for his scornful disclosure that I was the son of his wife . . . the woman in my dream . . . and Brian Lockwood. In a sense, I was. But the knowledge that I had been instrumental in the death of the man who shopped my mother to the Russians, and had my father and uncle killed, filled me with a sort of feral pride. The one living person who might understand was the Colonel's sergeant major, Allan Cobb. But then I recalled the hot, sticky feel of the big Russian's blood on my fingers—and felt sick again. Killing is still killing, not something to get righteous about.

The lights went on in the corridor. The nursing staff was moving about. The clock on the wall facing my bed stood at six-ten. It was growing light outside.

I sat up and swung my legs off the edge of the bed. I rested there, head throbbing and feeling as though it might fall off my shoulders and smash on the floor. The connections to the EKG monitor pulled at my chest. The tone of the device behind me grew petulant. The floor nurses were hearing it on the repeater at the nurses' station down the corridor from my room.

My clothes, I thought, as though I would have to escape. Where had they put them? I was resolved to be ready to leave the hospital the moment Claire arrived to collect me, as she had promised. The memory of my nightmares in the cardiac unit at Stanford wouldn't leave me. But there had been no such dreams here. Only carefully reconstructed bits of memory. The sad Kristina Erika of the wedding picture. The dream mother on the bank of the Pegnitz.

Would it ever be ended? Or would I remember it all, hour by hour, year by year, whenever there was a silence in my life?

A nursing sister appeared.

"You should not be out of bed, Herr Lockwood. Not until Dr. Raymond permits it. And we are not ready to remove the heart monitor leads. Please lie down."

I sat, grimacing against the pounding in my head.

A tag on the starched uniform said the nurse's name was Sister Severa. It suited her. She produced a paper cup and presented it.

"What is it?" I remembered my adventures with triazolam.

"Aspirin, Herr Lockwood. For the headache."

She filled a glass from the thermos pitcher. I took the tablets and drank the water.

"You are going to have a visitor," Sister Severa said.

"So early?"

"The very question I asked, Herr Lockwood. But it is the man from the Ministry of Finance."

"I see."

"I do not. But he is at reception. He will be up directly." She busied herself seeing that all my connections to the EKG monitor were intact. Sister Severa was one of those nurses, rare now, who took complete possession of their patients. "I am instructed to see that you are not disturbed until the Herr Dr. Prinz departs."

Dr. Prinz. How impressive. Doctor of what? I wondered what his real name might be. According to Stossen, who would know, Prinz was a Swiss intelligence agent. Who had saved my life, if it came to that.

"Has Mrs. Warner telephoned?"

"Twice last night and again ten minutes ago. She has spoken with Dr. Raymond. She will be here to collect you at nine."

"And Frau Rykova?" I asked.

"She will recover, Herr Lockwood." A pause, and then: "What monster did that to her?"

A dead one, I thought. But I only shook my head.

"Frau Rykova asks that you visit her before you leave the hospital."

"Please tell her that I will."

"Good. Now get back into bed until the visitor arrives."

Sister Severa stood by my bed and arranged the EKG leads, the sheet and counterpane with military precision.

"You did not eat well last night, Herr Lockwood. Herr Dr. Raymond insists you eat breakfast before leaving the hospital."

"I would settle for an espresso," I said.

She frowned. "I will bring you *caffè filtro.*"

Score one for Swiss medical care. Stanford Medical Center, that temple of the healing arts, did not serve *filtro* or anything else resembling coffee.

When Sister Severa had gone, I closed my eyes and thought about Annaliese. What a strange relationship we had developed. It had been no more than days, yet I felt as though I had known her all my life. She was a survivor. Come to think of it, we both were. Perhaps that explained it.

I had offered to pay for her hospitalization. I was told it was taken care of. At first I thought it was Dieter who had offered to pay. But no. All expenses, Anna's and mine, were being paid by the Swiss Ministry of Finance. Or Swiss counterintelligence.

Why?

There was a rap on the doorframe. Joachim Prinz stood outlined against the light in the hallway.

"Herr Lockwood?"

"Come in," I said.

He closed the door after himself. "May I sit down?"

I nodded at a chair. Somehow his politeness grated on my nerves.

"You are owed an explanation, Herr Lockwood," he said.

"Yes."

"What can I tell you?"

"Begin with Dean Lockwood. Did you know he was Stossen's agent?"

"Yes. And no." You first, Herr Prinz.

Prinz said, "Your uncle sold things. Things which were not not always his. We were aware of that. He also sold information." He cleared his throat and looked down at his hands. "There can be no harm in telling you that your uncle, Dean Lockwood, worked with us from time to time. It was not strictly a matter of money. Usually it was one of quid pro quo." He paused and studied me calmly. "All this does not seem to trouble you."

"Why should it? Dean Lockwood was not my favorite uncle."

"Yes, but what a pity he did not see fit to trust us more. He might still have been alive." He paused and then said: "Your uncle was a man of interest to many European police organizations. It is hardly surprising that he would have eventually encountered our, ah, General Ober."

The man was fishing. There was no reason why I should enlighten him about any ancient connection between Sieg Stossen and the Lockwoods. If he knew it, let him keep it to himself. I didn't want policemen and investigators digging around in

memories of an American soldier and a radiant, golden girl—
both now dead.

I pushed myself erect in the bed. "You knew Stossen was in
Switzerland."

"Yes, true. We did not know where he was, but you provided
us with that information."

Bloodless son of a bitch, I thought. Anna and I both came
close to getting killed. But what did that matter?

"You feel used, Herr Lockwood."

"Damned right I do."

"It was your choice, I remind you."

"And if Frau Rykova or I had been killed?"

Prinz shrugged. "We would not have permitted that to happen."

"Of course not. Bad for banking. Bad for the ski season."

Prinz ignored it. "Let me speak for a moment about Stossen,
Herr Lockwood. A very long time ago, before either you or I
were born, as a matter of fact, Stossen crossed the border into
this country with a convoy of secret property. He was searching
for places to protect that property for a very long time. We had
such places. Many of them."

"You also had laws against assisting war criminals."

"Actually, Herr Lockwood, we did not. Such laws came into
being only after the Nuremberg trials. But no matter. Stossen
had high connections here. Very high."

"Not Stossen," I said. "His principal. A fat man who went
into prison at Nuremberg with a poison pill secreted in his anus.
A *Reichsmarschall* of the Third Reich."

"We do not believe that Swiss politicians and bankers entered
into any illegal arrangements with German personages," Prinz
said primly.

I felt myself flush with anger. "Jesus Christ. German *personages*?"

"Even today, Herr Lockwood, it could embarrass the federal
government of Switzerland."

"How old were you then?" I asked.

Prinz seemed surprised I should ask. "I was born in 1949,
Herr Lockwood. Does that matter?"

"Probably not. But you and I are members of the same generation. That bothers me. . . ."

The nurse scratched at the door. Prinz opened it, took the tray of coffee, put it on the dresser and dismissed her.

"May I pour for you?" he said.

"No."

"Shall I continue?"

"Go on."

He poured coffee for himself, sat down again. "First there is the matter of Dean Lockwood to dispose of. Forgive me, that is an insensitive way to put it." He began again. "Herr Lockwood came to Europe in the late 1950s. According to an interview with Swiss customs at Geneva, he brought this with him." He took the Eagle Dagger from his pocket. It had been cleaned, burnished. "Can you enlighten me about how he came by it?"

"He stole it," I said. "And the cantonal police never bothered to examine it, did they?" I felt myself smiling as I said it. The so thorough, exacting Swiss had the *Adler Dolch* list in their hands while it still meant something, and they never knew it.

Prinz spread his hands. "Alas, no."

"You might have recovered the Cellinis, the Holbein miniatures, even the Russian amber."

"So we might have, Herr Lockwood. But we did not." He laid the *Adler Dolch* on the bedside stand. "Since Herr Stossen has no surviving kin, I suppose this trinket is now your property."

I closed my fingers over it. The metal felt oddly warm to the touch.

"It has no magical properties, Herr Lockwood."

Hasn't it?

Prinz acted as though this were a social occasion. What bullshit, I thought, and threw the dagger onto the bedside table.

"It would be best, Herr Lockwood, if we did not fall into conflict over this affair," Prinz said, prim and wordy as a schoolmaster. "Can you reassure me concerning your journalistic intentions?"

The last thing I intended to do was to write some sensational kiss-and-tell book or magazine piece about the Colonel and Kristina Erika. But I was damned if I was going to give Prinz the satisfaction. "No, Herr Prinz, I cannot reassure you."

"I am sorry for that. I had hoped for cooperation. You see, Herr Lockwood, Swiss neutrality is a world commodity. Without it, half the world's international accommodations would cease to be. Herr Stossen, with your uncle's assistance, compromised the Swiss banking laws, and did very well at his illegal activities until the art treasures were disposed of. Did you know that Herr Stossen even engineered a quarrel between the Stasi and the KGB about the ownership of the articles 'should they ever be recovered'? The Jews would call that *chutzpah*. We must rely on the German word *Arroganz*. Either serves well in this case. And of course, you and I know that Herr von Stossen had another, more personal agenda to complete here."

"The point is now moot, Herr Prinz."

"Quite so, it is." He finished his coffee, looked with detached interest into the dregs in the cup. "Gypsies can tell fortunes by looking into cups. We Swiss have no such talent." He looked directly at me once again. "We use diligence instead. In the matter of Herr Stossen—or General Ober, as the case may be— we shall learn to live with our embarrassment. My kind of work is conducted with great patience. It is the only way. A fascinating man, Stossen. Did you know that he first served the KGB— the NKVD it was called then—and then moved back to Germany—and became a general in the Stasi. He used the name Adler, by the way. He was fascinated by eagles, apparently. In the 1960s, while he had Dean Lockwood methodically emptying the vaults and selling off the contents, he stirred up quite a fiery dispute about the ownership of the vanished art. It was quite a tour de force. It might have gone on for years, except that your President Reagan finally frightened the Soviets out of the Cold War with his Star Wars antimissile missile schemes. And when that happened, the East Bloc began to unravel and everyone's secrets became commodities, for sale to the highest bidders." He shrugged. "We purchased what we could afford. We knew that one day Stossen would come back to Switzerland or some place as convenient. We could then close his account." The eyebrows climbed his high forehead. "Yesterday, thanks to you, Herr Lockwood, we did just that."

"You let him come to me in the Wylerholz. And then you shot

him." I stared at the well-barbered bureaucrat's face. "But he killed eight people before stepping into your trap."

"He killed many more than that, Herr Lockwood." He stood. "But to the point. *He did not kill you.*"

From the door Prinz said, "It would be regarded as suitable, Herr Lockwood, for you not to return to Switzerland for several years. Five, perhaps. Or even better, ten."

28

I have not been a courageous man.

I HAD FINISHED DRESSING and found myself sitting shakily on the edge of the bed when Annaliese came through the door. I was surprised but pleased to see her. Surprised, because I could not have guessed that she was the sort of woman . . . yes, *woman* . . . who could ignore her battered appearance. And it was battered. Stossen's brutish son had broken her nose and cut her lips. A front tooth was chipped and gaping. She looked like a fighter who had just lost the last round.

She shrugged her narrow shoulders in the less-than-stylish hospital robe and said with obvious pain, "I was afraid you would not come before you left."

I stood and put my arms about her as gently as I could manage. "I wouldn't go without seeing you."

She tried a smile. It hurt her. She sat on the edge of a chair. "I am sorry, Brian. I couldn't wait to get the new clothes. I wanted to surprise you when you came back to the hotel, so you would see how pretty I could look for your sister. I didn't want you to be ashamed of me." She looked down at the floor, and her voice was very soft. "I did many wrong things."

"You're not alone there," I told her.

She shook her head, and her swollen eyes glittered with sud-

245

den tears. "We hated it so, Erich and I. We would have done anything to get away. You have to understand that. I was ashamed, but I did it. I probably would do it again. And you saved my life. Now I owe you everything."

"You owe me friendship, Anna. Nothing more."

She drew a deep breath. "I really would like that, Brian. I would like that very much."

We sat together for a while longer, but it was as though we had done and said all that we had to do with and say to each other. We had been closest companions in sweaty beds and fellow passengers on a journey to hell and back. In a third of a month we had lived a lifetime together.

"Herr Langan has promised me work so I can earn enough to live in the West," she said. "Will he keep his word?"

"He usually does," I said. In the West, I thought. How long would the divisions last? Years. The Wall was gone, but there were still the frontiers in the mind.

She stood up. "I will go back to my room now."

I was about to mention Claire's coming, and then I realized that I still had a great deal to learn about women. The last thing on earth Annaliese would want was to be seen as she was by my sister.

She stood there for a moment in the doorway, just looking at me.

"We'll keep in touch, Anna," I said. But it was good-bye, and we both knew it.

She managed another somewhat twisted smile and raised a hand to say good-bye. Then she said: "Brian. When we left Nuremberg, you did say you would pay me for being your guide." She just stood there, waiting. I didn't know whether to laugh or kiss her. So I did neither.

Instead, I said, "Do you still have the francs I gave you yesterday?"

"Oh, yes. I had no chance to spend them." Eugen had been waiting right outside the hotel.

"I will ask Dieter to give you the thousand D-marks we talked about. All right?" We had never discussed anything like that amount, and we both knew it. But all things considered, she was entitled to at least that much. After all, she and Erich had been cheated out of the thousand D-marks in blood money that Stossen had promised them.

She was smiling—with difficulty—but smiling when she left.

Ten minutes later Claire came through the door with Dieter and Stein Davis. Dieter looked wary, and well he should have been. There were explanations due, I thought. Dieter had numberless contacts, and I had used many of them. But there was more to my old acquaintance than that. Dieter Langan was a resource of Swiss intelligence, I was sure of it now. The man who currently used the name Joachim Prinz knew far too much about me to have learned it from impersonal sources.

Stein Davis, a dour little man who had handled the Lockwood family's legal affairs ever since I could remember, was bundled against the winter weather but smiling as I had never seen him smile before.

Dieter studied me. "Are you all right, Brian? Really all right?"

Hugging my sister, I said over her shoulder, "I'll want to talk to you later, Dieter."

"I thought you might. I will keep myself available."

How did he manage? I wondered. Once he ran with the urban guerrillas in Germany. Well, not *with*. That was not Dieter Langan's style. Close behind, perhaps. Then came his return to the church and respectability. Old Klaus, his father, would have been pleased. Not at Dieter's principles but his adaptability. Yes, he was almost certainly one of Swiss intelligence's resources. It was a perfect occupation for Dieter in a not-so-perfect new Germany.

"I want to see Frau Rykova for a moment," he said, and left.

Claire looked at me with a strange expression. "I have something for you, Bri. It's why I'm here. It wouldn't keep."

She opened the large shoulder bag she carried and handed me a packet of letters. I looked through them. They were in English, posted in Nuremberg in 1947, addressed to Colonel Brian Lockwood in a beautiful European script. I knew at once who had written them.

"Kristina," I said.

My mother's letters to her lover. For a moment I felt as though it would be an intrusion to open them. But Claire said, "Neither Stein nor I knew about these letters. Read them, Bri. They are beautiful."

I sat down and opened the first letter. . . .

A quarter of an hour later I looked up at my sister.

She gave me a small smile. "You're younger than you thought you were, Bri. Almost two whole years. No wonder you were so scrawny when I first saw you."

She took another envelope from her bag and handed it to me. This one merely contained my life.

"My Dear Son," the Colonel had written, "forgive me. I did your mother and my wife a terrible wrong. . . ."

Brian Lockwood was the sort of man who could write a thing like that and mean it.

With this letter, I state that you are my son and that I love you with all the fatherly affection I am capable of feeling. Your mother and I were lovers. I do not know if you can understand what that means to a man like me. Please try to believe it when I say that that love was warmth and light and life to me.

When I was sent home, the excuse the Army used was that I was "fraternizing with the enemy." That was a hollow sound now, but at the time, with the full story of Nazi atrocities becoming clear, it constituted the worst kind of behavior.

For many reasons I was slow in arranging passage for you and for her. The incredible confusion at the time was one reason. I had to find someone powerful enough to break through the barrier I met up with every time I mentioned her husband's name, and that was not easy. My personal problems in facing up to the consequences of my behavior made me hesitate as well.

And the best information I could obtain told me that Sieg von Stossen had died in Berlin, when the Russians arrived. You see, I thought she was finally safe and the time it was taking me to get the two of you out of Germany was time well spent if her name could be cleared.

But events were too fast, for Kristina's own husband, back from the grave, betrayed her to the Soviets when I left her unguarded. My own betrayal was even greater, and I will live with the pain and regret until I die.

I admit the wrong I did Janice, even though I told myself it was for her sake I would not acknowledge you. She threatened to kill herself if I let it be known you are my son. Considering her state of mind, I could not bring myself to risk it, God forgive me.

I was a soldier, Brian, but in some matters I have not been a courageous man.

Forgive me. I love you.

There was a document with the letter. It was in German, dated Nuremberg, June 1947. To Kristina Erika Obryta, born a son: Brian. Father: *Amerikanischer Soldat.*

And a photograph taken in the ruins of the National Socialist pavilion in Nuremberg. Visible was the massive peristyle at the end. Rubble atop the stones. Who did not remember the dramatic newsreel pictures of the carved stone eagle, wreath and swastika being blown to fragments by an engineer team of the victorious allies?

But this was background. In the foreground stood a smiling young woman in skirt and blouse, fair hair blowing in an unseen breeze. I had seen a photograph of the same woman not so long ago. Kristina Erika Obryta. Only here she was like a Madonna holding a child in her arms.

Claire's hand closed over mine. "There you are," she said.

I looked at Stein Davis. "The certificate is authentic," he said. "I checked it with the embassy in Washington."

I could only ask: "Is it true? About Janice?"

"I think so. Remember how she was always going away to *rest.* It must have been hell for Father. She held him that way."

I said, "When I was little she scared me." I had never, until now, put into words that childhood fear. "I was afraid she would send me back to Germany. She used to tell me that someday she would."

Stein Davis said quietly, "Janice was in therapy for years, Brian. Until she passed away, in fact. She slashed her wrists once and took at least two overdoses of sleeping pills. She had the Colonel in a vise.

"All those years from the time you left school until Father died," Claire said, "I always hoped you could learn to talk to each other. But it never happened. Janice was watching. . . ."

"I thought he was just a cold man," I said. "I remember when we sailed on the *Erika*, he hardly spoke to me except to give me an order. I looked up to him, Claire, but I always thought he disliked me, that he felt he had made a mistake by picking me up off the streets of Nuremberg."

"It wasn't a good solution," Claire said. "But it was all the Colonel felt he could do. Now you understand why."

"Does Allan know all this?"

"I don't know, and I am not going to ask him. Are you?"

I thought about it. There was no need to test the sergeant major's loyalty that way. I shook my head.

"Father would be grateful," she said. And then quietly: "Poor Janice. He may have kept silent, Bri, but he loved you for being the son Kristina gave him. At least he had that."

Suddenly I yearned for California. I wanted to hold my beautiful daughter in my arms and tell her about Kristina Erika, about how she loved and lived and died. I wanted to sit in front of a log fire with my son and talk to him about his grandfather, a man we hardly knew.

"Let's go home, Claire," I said.

"Let's do," she said.

But even as I said it, I knew I would return to that blasted empty land that gave birth to Kristina Erika Obryta. I still needed to search her out, reconstruct her memories, flesh out her image so that one day I could take her home with me on the journey she dreamed of but never made with the man she loved.